I0676601

Cast Iron

A Novel

By

Cameron Cowan

All rights reserved under the Pan-american and International Copyright Conventions. This book may not be reproduced in whole or in part in any form or by any means electronic or mechanical including photocopying recording to by any information storage and retrieval system, including the internet, now known or hereinafter invented without written permission from the publisher.

Copyright © Widgery Omnimedia and Cameron Cowan 2020
Seattle, Washington

cameronjournal.com
Printed in America

ISBN: 978-0-578-61984-2

Acknowledgements

Nana
Mom and Dad
The man responsible for this story (you know who you are)
Davyn Tatum (cover model)

Trigger Warnings

Sexual abuse (child/adult)
Prison
Homosexuality
Violence
Emotional abuse
Psychological abuse
Alcoholism
Drug abuse
Human trafficking
Trauma

Part 1

Chapter 1

"Randy, don't touch those!" Eileen reached up and lowered his teenage hand. "They are very expensive." Eileen folded her hands over her pearlescent satin dress. She looked at the bouquet to make sure it was still perfect. The flowers lent a fresh, earthy fragrance to the chapel.

"I know, I just wanted to see what they felt like."

The Missouri sun streamed into the chapel. The air conditioning hummed in the background, pouring cold air into the room to fight the summer heat and humidity. The pews sat empty as Eileen over saw the final touches on her perfect wedding day.

Eileen smiled at her son. "Maybe later, after the ceremony. Where's your sister?"

"Around." Randy shrugged his shoulders. "Kelly?" Randy sat down on the pristine chairs. A 12-year-old girl in a crinoline dress bounded out of a corner.

"What?"

"It's time to go put out programs!" Eileen said, touching her shoulder and leading her to the rear of the large hotel ballroom. "Randy, why don't you go find David?"

Randy looked around. Mom had never had a nice wedding. She talked about it a lot while she was planning this ceremony. She talked about how she got married at seven months pregnant at a courthouse. "The judge just looked at me," she seemed to add. Now, his father had gone out for cigarettes. That was five years ago. Randy hadn't seen his father since and he was still wondering where he had gone and why he had left. Secretly, at night, Randy often wondered if it was his fault. Somewhere along the way, Randy knew that they had gotten divorced. His Mom cried a lot and she carried that thick stack of official looking documents around with her until it was all over.

Eileen had met David last year, around winter break at school. Randy crossed his arms as he stood up to go find David. It was always David, never dad. He crossed his arms the same way when his mother completed her divorce. Randy still didn't like something about David but he never knew why. He just didn't like him.

"I wish dad was back,"" Randy said to himself. "I'd rather be with him than here." Randy pushed at the faux brass doors and crossed the hallway and down to the elevators where he pushed the button for the 8th floor.

1

His flat shoes made a crunching sound. The car whisked him up and when he stepped off the elevator, Randy took out his key from the breast pocket of his loose-fitting suit and opened the door to room #839. The door released with a click. David slipped the heavy polyester tunic over his compact 5' 8" frame. Randy sat on the bed and watched him adjust his chest full of hardware.

"Randy," David said.

"Hi."

"What do you think?"

"What? Nothing."

David pointed at his chest. "I worked my ass off for this uniform."

"It's cool, I guess."

David smiled and pulled on the sword and placed the white hat on his close-shaven head. Randy stood up and looked in the mirror, adjusting his suit over his thin body.

"You might want this someday."

"What?"

"Military. Serve your country."

Randy shrugged his shoulders. "I'm not really into shooting people."

"But you're a man, or about to be, anyway, and men need to be able to handle themselves and protect those they love."

"I guess."

"That's what you learn, how to survive."

"We're going to be late," Randy reminded him.

"Yeah, where are the guys?" David asked, going for the door. He looked around for his phone and flipped it open. "They're already downstairs, let's go." Randy stood up and followed David out of the room and to the elevator. Randy followed David to the lobby, where he found a group of men in a mix of smart suits and uniforms.

"Hey Cedric, you motherfucker." One of the men turned around and embraced David.

"Hey David, far away from the sandbox, right?" one of them remarked.

"Yeah, this is Randy Carruth, Eileen's son, soon to be my son, after today."

"Hi, how you doing?" Randy held his outstretched hand with a firm grip.

"You're going to be late," Randy reminded him again. Just as Randy spoke, the wedding planner appeared behind him. She held a clipboard in her hand and started shouting. "Oh my god, groom! Groomsman! Thank Jesus and just praise his holy name, come on we're late!" She spoke quickly, every word leaving her mouth on the heels of the last.

She started to herd the combat veterans towards the altar. Randy took his seat. Eileen processed with her daughter down the aisle in her white halter top satin dress. David watched, hands in front, until she arrived at the altar. Watching Eileen Carruth taking her daughter's hand. It looked perfect. The couple kissed and sealed the future together as Mr. and Mrs. David Bourden. It was far away from the sandbox, and David felt ready. Eileen and David shared their first dance as husband and wife. The champagne bottle popped open and David poured it into his mouth. The crowd cheered. His military buddies slapped him around like a flour sack. They clinked beer bottles and champagne flutes together. David poured out several glasses and handed the bottle to Randy.

"Drink up," David said.

Eileen countered, "No, David, he's too young." David turned his head towards her.

"I had my first fucking beer at ten, this boy at 15 can have some of this fucking French piss water, I mean, champagne. If I want to give my son a drink, I'm going to give my son a fucking drink."

Eileen stepped back, head down to her powerful husband, contrite and submissive. Randy tried to be cool and picked up the bottle. He looked at it for a minute and then took a sip. David held the end up, so he drank more than he planned. He grimaced a bit and then snorted some carbonation. Champagne didn't agree with him at first.

"Drink up, son." David looked at him, encouraging him to drink more. Randy drained the contents of the champagne bottle and the glass next to him. He set the glass on the white-clothed table. He wandered off into the party, looking for Kelly and looking at the people. The party swirled around him. Randy saw a group of kids standing together in a circle. He put his hands on his pocket and joined the circle. They expanded to include him. A girl with a mouth full of braces and a pink dress broke into a laugh when he stood next to them. Randy looked at the ground.

"Hey, what's your name?" She looked up at him.

"Randy."

"Bride or groom?"

"Bride, she's my mom," Randy replied.

"I thought so," she said, holding her arm behind her back. "Oh my god, where's my phone, I just got it, it was $200. I can't lose it." She looked around frantically before finding it at the table next to her. She flipped its lid open and pressed some buttons before putting it down next to her place again. Randy smiled at her.

One of the boys, in a suit that didn't fit his slim frame, grabbed one of the flutes of champagne and started to drink it before his mom hurried over and grabbed it out of his hands.

"Hey! Everyone else is doing it."

"That's everyone else."

"I had some, it's okay," Randy told him.

"I just wanted to have a drink and get drunk!" he said, weaving his body around wildly.

Randy looked around for Kelly. He poked his head outside of the circle. He separated from the circle to go around and look for her. Some people were dancing in the small dance floor area. Randy found Kelly sitting on a chair, watching the people dance.

"Are you tired?"

"Yeah, I am tired, and really full."

"Do you want to go upstairs?"

She shook her head up and down. Randy held out his hand and led her out of the reception and towards the elevators. They rode the elevator up to the room and he searched through his pockets for the key card and slid it into the slot. She changed into her pajamas and slid under the covers. Randy waited around until she was fast asleep before changing out of his suit and rehanging it on the hanger. He slid into bed himself and stared at the ceiling.

His head hurt a little and he let it sink into the softness of the pillow. He put his arm under his head for comfort. He thought about his Dad and the last time he saw him. Randy thought watching him drive away from their house. Randy remembered his promise they would meet up again but that had never happened. Randy only saw him in court during the divorce. Randy thought about that day. The hard benches and all the official language. Randy watched his Dad sign some papers and he seemed to sign himself right out of their lives. Randy didn't even get a hug from him. He just waved, tugged on his jacket and walked out of the court room. Randy kept thinking about what he had done wrong to make his parents get a divorce and why Mom had to marry David. Randy couldn't figure it out. He thought about it often. Mom kept telling him it wasn't his fault but somehow he still felt, in his belly, it was about him or maybe Kelly. He let these thoughts run around his mind before finally dropping off to sleep.

Chapter 2

David swung his hips around to keep the ball away from Randy. Randy reached up towards him to grab the ball from his hands. David swung around and went up for a basket. Randy jumped up and swatted the ball away sending it flying into the grass as it brushed off David's fingers. Randy jogged after it and threw it back towards the court where David snatched it from the air and dribbled it. David tossed it up and it sailed through the netting of the basket and back onto the concrete. Randy took the rebound and dashed down dribbling along the way to make a shot over his head. David noticed the front door of the house opening.

"Time!" David barked making a T shape with his hands. Eileen and Kelly walked out to the driveway with bottles of gatorade and a pitcher of lemonade.

"We come bearing liquids. I don't want either of you getting sick in this humidity." David took a cold bottle of gatorade and drank one quarter of it in one gulp. Randy opted for lemonade. Eileen and Kelly sat down on the concrete stoop near the driveway. David stood near them. Kelly stood up and held out a glass to Randy. He took it from her and sat down in the grass draining the glass. David walked over behind Kelly and put his arm on her back. David let his arm linger against her shoulder.

"You can come out and play with us. The exercise will do you good."

Kelly shrugged her shoulders. "You guys play fast. I like to watch Randy play." Kelly stepped forward to get away from his touch. She picked up the ball and tried to dribble it but it bounced away from her. Randy stood up again.

"Here."

Kelly tossed the ball over to him and he bounced it against the concrete. "Aim for your feet." Randy demonstrated as he bounced it again and then tossed it back to her in a gentle motion. Kelly reached for it and hugged it in.

"Don't chase it, let the ball come to you." Kelly tried bouncing the orange ball again and made two successful bounces before tossing it in the air towards the basket. The ball fell back to earth and Randy ran over to grab it, turned in his heel and sunk the ball into the basket.

David sat down next to Eileen and put his arm around her.

"You're sweaty!"

"Oh come on, you like it," David nuzzled her neck. "Keep playing kids, it'll do you both good."

Randy bounced the ball and began a slow game of basketball with Kelly. David joined in with them speeding the game up a little bit. Randy didn't play as hard and gave his sister a chance to score. David drove hard to keep the game moving. Eileen looked on at them, her elbows resting on her knees nursing her own glass of wine she had tucked around the corner.

The sun began to set lower in the sky. Randy let the ball bounce a final time before picking it up and tucking it under his arm.

"I'm hungry."

"Dinner should be almost ready. You guys were playing out here a long time." Eileen said standing up and wiping off her pants.

"I'll go take a shower." David said. David walked into the air-conditioned house and started upstairs. Randy yawned. "Yeah, me next."

Eileen and Kelly walked into the kitchen. Kelly disappeared into the living room and sat down and the TV. Eileen checked the meal simmering away on the counter. Eileen pulled on an apron. She tasted it. "Good," she thought before she took out the dishes for the meal. Eileen poured the meat and noodle mixture into a serving bowl. She opened the oven door and pulled out a cookie sheet of biscuits. She placed them in another bowl and walked over to the table.

"Kelly, come set the table! Dinner is ready!" She wiped her hands on her apron and pulled it off over her head. She looked over the table and smiled. She looked around for her wine glass. She found it and refilled it from the refrigerator. She returned to the table and sat down.

Randy sauntered into the room wearing his T-shirt and basketball shorts. Randy sat down at the table and stared up at the ceiling. David followed him a moment later in stocking feet holding a beer, fresh from his shower. Kelly quickly spread around forks and knives. The family settled down to dinner. David prayed over the food as they held hands. David passed around the serving dishes and everyone filled their plates. The family dug into the meal.

"Did you meet any new friends today, Kelly?" David took another forkful of the food on his plate.

"Dad! Are you coming to my demonstration this weekend in Kansas City?" Randy said quickly in between bites.

"Randy! Don't interrupt, wait your turn! Kelly, did you meet any new friends?" David snapped at Randy and re-directed his attention towards Kelly.

"No, not really, I mean, no one really interests me," Kelly said.

"There are plenty of girls at your school," Eileen said.

"They're boring. All they talk about are clothes and famous people, and boys." Kelly put contempt on the word "boys", as if other boys just didn't exist to her; not yet, anyway.

"That's what girls are supposed to talk about," David said after swallowing.

"I'm bored. I'm finished, may I be excused?"

"Yes, Kelly, go—" David interrupted his wife.

"No, no you may not. You need to work harder at making friends, Kelly. You need some friends." Kelly looked up at the ceiling, waiting for the requisite "friends" lecture to end.

"You may go," David concluded, and Kelly bolted from the dark wood table and ran upstairs to her small bedroom, where she promptly crawled under the covers and started to read a book.

Randy looked down at his plate and finished eating.

"May I be excused?"

"Yes, and yes, I'm coming to your meet," David said.

David and Eileen finished dinner. Eileen cleared the table and neatly placed the dishes in her new dishwasher. David came up behind her and gently cupped her waist with one arm and his hand grazed her ass. She looked over her shoulder at him with a smile.

"Why were you so hard on her?" Eileen asked over her shoulder.

"Just trying to have a normal family, Eileen. I'm worried about her."

"I know, I know."

David leaned against the laminate counter-tops, still shiny and new, in the color that Eileen had always wanted. He put his fingers on his chin. "I really like that table you picked out."

"Thank you."

"You've done a good job on our home, Eileen." David opened the fridge and took out a beer. Eileen finished gathering the dishes and started the dishwasher.

Eileen smiled and kept washing up from dinner. She finished putting the food and dishes away and walked past a pony wall towards the living room where David had sat into a large leather couch with a beer. She brought another beer with her and she curled up with him on the couch. The TV flashed on a sports program. David started changing the channel, looking for something else. He stopped on a sitcom. At funny moments Eileen would smile and David would grunt and nearly laugh before taking a sip of beer. Eileen leaned against him. The news played after the program was off. Eileen ran her hands over his legs and let her hand brush along his zipper. She slipped her hand under his t-shirt and rubbed his stomach.

"Do you want to try tonight?" Eileen asked breaking the silence. "We haven't really tried since Mexico. It's a good time, I took a test," she said, letting her hand run low again and rubbing his leg through his pants. Her hand neared his crotch.

"Not tonight, I've been really stressed at work." He moved her hands away from his manhood.

"I know, don't worry, it was a one-time thing, I think it'll be better tonight," she assured him.

David turned to her and looked at her. "I read, in a magazine at work, stress can cause problems. Let's get through this project at work and then we'll try again."

Eileen flashed a disappointed look, "I just thought that maybe it would be good to just reconnect. No pressure, just being together."

David let his head move freely on his shoulders for a moment. "Okay." He took her hand and led her upstairs. She moved closer to him and put her hands around his waist. He awkwardly climbed the stairs and walked into the bedroom. Eileen let her clothes drop on the plush carpet of the bedroom. David lifted his shirt off of his body and let his clothes drop off. Eileen climbed on the bed letting her feet dangle off the end of the bed. David lay next to her and kissed her on the lips. "Hi."

"Hi."

His erection touched her thigh. Eileen didn't draw attention to it at first as they embraced and let their tongues meet. Her hands roamed over his back. She began to gasp as he touched her and enjoyed the special rush that only he could give her. The worries and problems melted away and Eileen offered herself to him. Tonight, he took that offer and for a small moment she was grateful as her nails dug into the satin sheets.

Chapter 3

Eileen looked at the to do list she had for the day. The TV played morning television and she decided what she would tackle first. She decided that she would do some shopping first. She needed some ingredients for those cupcakes for Kelly anyway and she needed to stop in the pharmacy anyway. She grabbed her purse and found her keys. She stepped into her large SUV and pulled out of the garage and into the street. She passed by the other houses, painted in the same three colors and built in the same 3 repeating styles as she left her neighborhood and drove to the grocery store in the nearby shopping area. She pulled into the parking and slung her bag over her shoulder and started walking into the store. She plucked a cart out of the cart stand and began shopping. She selected a few items and wheeled around to the family planning section. She knelt down to pick up 2 pregnancy tests and placed them in the cart. Eileen completed her shopping. Eileen watched the tests pass by the cashier. The cashier smiled.

"Hoping for good news?" She asked.

Eileen nodded "I hope so."

Eileen drove home and she carried her items into the house. Eileen drank some water before she took out the cake mix and used the large mixer to make up the batter. She placed them in the oven and set the timer. She slipped into the downstairs powder room and took out the pregnancy test. She read over the box.

"They still work the same way." She said to herself. She let the pregnancy test sit on the sink and waited for the lines to appear. She waited for the required time and looked at the test. One meant not pregnant. Two meant pregnant. She waited and one single line appeared. Eileen looked at it and looked at the box again. She looked at the stick again. She pulled out the other test and repeated the process. The result was the same. Eileen's mind swirled. She counted days since they had sex, days since she should have gotten her period. She put the tests away and put them in the trash. She covered them and left the bathroom. The timer on the oven rang and she removed the cupcakes. She removed them and let them cool. She went back to counting. Eileen leaned against the counter. She was late, she should be late, this should have worked. Her mind drifted back to the tests in the bathroom trash. No result. Eileen dug through her purse for her address book. She found the number and dialed it on the phone. She waited for the receptionist to answer. She dialed through the phone tree.

"Hi, this is Eileen Carruth. I need to schedule an appointment. This week would be great. Okay, great, Friday is fine. Before 3 would be great. 11 am is fine. Great, I've got it down. Thank you."

Eileen hung up the phone. She tried to put her mind at ease. The doctor would be able to figure things out. She wouldn't tell David unless he asked about it. Eileen put the problem aside in her mind and began to work on other problems in her to do list. She heard Randy drop his bike and open the garage. She walked towards the front room of the house and looked for Kelly's bus. She saw the large, yellow bus stop near their street and a bunch of kids streamed out of the vehicle. Randy walked by her on his way upstairs.

"How was school?"

"Fine mom, I'm going to play playstation."

"Do your homework first."

"I will."

"Before playstation!" She shouted. Randy was already in his room. Eileen stood outside and waited for Kelly to walk up to the house.

"Ready for ballet practice?"

"I need to get my stuff." Kelly said.

"Alright, go change and come out to the car."

"Okay." Kelly said going upstairs. A few moments later she walked out to the SUV. Eileen followed her out and drove her to ballet practice. On their way home, Eileen picked up dinner for the family and walked in carrying 3 bags of food from the popular restaurant.

"David! We're home! I have dinner! Randy, can you get some plates and forks!" She shouted. Eileen dropped off the food on the dinner table. She let her bag fall on her arms and started taking out the food. David appeared with Randy in tow with the plates and forks. They distributed the food and ate.

"How was ballet?" David asked.

"Fine."

"Good. You look good in your little, whatever it's called. Dress"

"It's just a leotard." Kelly reminded him

"That's it." David said in between bites.

"Can I be excused?" Kelly asked. "I have homework."

"Me too." Randy added.

David nodded. "I want to see it after, no playstation!" David chided.

Randy and Kelly both disappeared upstairs. Eileen and David gathered up the food containers and dishes and carried them all into the kitchen. Eileen packed them all into the trash. David loaded the dishwasher. Eileen put in the soap and closed the machine. She opened the refrigerator and pulled out the fresh frosting she had made earlier. She pulled off her wedding ring and let it sit on the counter. She looked for a small spatula and after searching some drawers, found the tool and started to frost the cupcakes. She spread the frosting across the top of them. David opened a beer and looked on. "Those for school?" He asked.

"Yeah, Kelly has a school thing tomorrow, so she needed some cupcakes so I have to get these done before tomorrow so I can drop them off."

David walked up behind her and hugged her from behind. "I love when you do that. You're a good mom. And I want to make you a mom again." He ran his hand over her stomach. Eileen giggled. "I have to focus."

David kissed the back of her neck and walked into the living room and turned on the TV. He settled into his chair. Eileen finished the cupcakes and joined him with her own glass of wine in the living room. They watched shows together until the news came on.

David clicked off the news and lifted his arms above his head for a long stretch.

"Ready for bed?"

Eileen nodded and gathered his beer bottles and returned them to the kitchen. She picked up the ash tray and emptied it in the can. Eileen looked at the sink full of dishes for a moment and decided to put them in the dishwasher before heading up to bed. David stripped off his shirt and started upstairs. Eileen shut off the lights and checked the doors before going upstairs. David was already in bed. Eileen washed her face and used the toilet before removing her clothes and climbing into bed next to him.

"Maybe if I'm naked, that will encourage him," she thought as she passed her nightshirt lying on a chair near the bed.

Eileen placed her ass on his side. He stared up at the ceiling, ignoring the naked woman next to him. He turned over and put his ass on hers. He reached down and itched himself through the black briefs. He closed his eyes.

He struggled to sleep. When he closed his eyes, the eyelids served as a screen for those images. Those images were always there, playing at a cinema for one. The dark tunnels of Tora Bora, the villages, the poppy fields, and the explosions. It was like a neverending Michael Bay movie. In this film, the actors were his friends, his unit buddies, and dead comrades with no body left to recover or lost limbs. Slowly, as three tours passed, he couldn't eject the events from his mind. They invaded his sleep and that's when he became afraid. No one noticed, but he knew, and that was enough. The sand and the cold invaded his thoughts. The smell of gunpowder would come back to him. The blood against the ground and the bloody uniforms would come back to him. Watching humvees flying through the air would play over and over again until he couldn't take it.

His eyes flew open to the darkness in their bedroom. His mind went to the first time he had what the doctor described as a "panic attack." Those feelings started again. His heart was racing and his skin felt clammy. He had been working on 3-4 hours of sleep when the C-130 touched down at Joint Base Lewis-McChord in Washington. Coffee, energy drinks, and a friend's ADD medication were all that kept him from crashing, hard. He remembered that feeling; the racing heartbeat and the cold sweat. He could feel it in his feet. His hands gripped the sheets. He turned over and hugged Eileen into his body.

He thought about going down the hall. Eileen repositioned herself. What was down the hall was the only thing that made him feel alive. When he was driving, when he was at work, the fantasy of doing it again played quietly in the back of his mind and he couldn't escape it. When he thought about doing it, it made him feel alive again. How had the fantasy jumped from his computer screen into the real world? What was he thinking? What was he about to do? What had started as an escape in the corner, against walls, on his phone, on his laptop, waiting for the mortars to stop, now had become real. Just a few steps away, his fantasy lay quietly in bed sleeping. He rolled out of bed, adjusted himself inside his black briefs, the fabric stretched out in front of him, and walked down the hall. He softly opened the door and closed it against the frame. He dropped to his knees and crawled across the floor to her bed and reached up under the covers.

Chapter 4

Randy woke up when he heard footsteps. His body signaled that he needed to pee. He swung his legs over and walked down to the hall and lifted up the lid. The nightlight provided all the light he needed in the small bathroom. When he walked back out of the hall, he noticed Kelly's door was slightly open. Randy rubbed his eyes to make sure he was seeing what he thought he was seeing. It removed some of the grogginess from his eyes and his mind. He woke up more and stepped towards the open door.

"Why is her door open?" Randy thought, rubbing his eyes. "I'll close it back up."

The walls were dark, but the white laminate-wood doors reflected the light from the nightlights Eileen had carefully put along the floor. Randy pressed the door open. He saw David from behind, his muscular back stretched out, his head obscured by her princess blanket and sheets. He stood there for a moment, in the darkness, before his brain woke up again and finally began to comprehend what he was seeing. David pulled his head out from under the covers and wiped his mouth against his arm. He turned around to see Randy standing over him in the doorway. David was on his feet in a flash, barely human. He grabbed Randy by the arms and hauled him out into the hallway before carrying him back to his room. David forced him back into his room as quietly as possible. Randy protested, he tried to cry out, but David covered his mouth. Randy grabbed his arms but David was stronger and Randy couldn't break his grip. David slammed the door shut, closing them both inside.

"What—were you doing?" David asked.

Randy's chest heaved. "What the fuck were you doing?" David strode across the room and slapped Randy straight across the face. Randy stepped back and fell onto the mess on his floor.

"Don't you fucking use that language with me young man!"

David took labored breaths. He looked down at Randy, who was sitting on the floor. Randy stood back up. "Fuck you!" Randy said, "What the fuck is going on?"

"Forget about what you saw. When we wake up tomorrow, this never fucking happened. You hear? Everything, this never happened. Just go to sleep and tomorrow everything will be all right."

Randy looked at him and climbed back into bed. His eyes stared as

David closed the door. David turned around, and in the hallway, Eileen stood there in her thin robe.

"Did he fucking catch you?"

"He didn't see anything."

"He fucking caught you." Eileen pounded her fists on his chest. David held her wrists over his chest. David looked down into her eyes, almost like a chastened child who had been caught stealing cookies.

"He didn't see anything, I told him to forget it. Everything will be fine tomorrow."

"Are you ready now?"

"Ready for what?"

"To give me a baby."

David looked down at his crotch. "Not tonight. I don't know what's wrong." David opened the door to their room. The couple climbed back into bed. Eileen slipped back under the covers. Her eyes swelled up with tears.

"What does she have that I don't?"

"Nothing."

"Then why do you like her?"

David looked at the ceiling. "She makes it go away."

"I don't make it go away?" Eileen started to sob into her pillow.

David left the question unanswered. He didn't know himself. He didn't know why this wasn't enough, everything he had wanted. If he knew that, maybe he could sleep again. Maybe the unending war film in his head would stop. Maybe he would feel alive and not "just a piece of meat sent to go kill other pieces of meat called people" because someone told him that was his job. He had a craving and there was only one way to satisfy it. Eileen didn't go back to sleep for several hours. The couple faced away from each other

Chapter 5

Eileen's eyes popped open. She looked around and noticed that the alarm wasn't due to go off for another ten minutes. She rolled over to see David facing away from her. She rolled out of the sheets and walked into the bathroom. She sat down on the toilet and held her head in her hands for a moment.

Eileen flushed the toilet and stood up and looked at herself in the mirror that stood over the double vanity. She looked at her body for a moment. She started to poke at her stomach. She turned around and looked at the length of her hips and butt over her shoulder.

"I'm still pretty. Maybe I can lose ten pounds."

Eileen stepped into the shower and closed the door behind her. She started to wash when she heard the alarm go off. David walked into the bathroom and lifted the lid and started to urinate. He didn't flush the toilet and instead opened the door of the shower, slipped off his underwear and joined his wife under the hot water.

"Good morning babe," David said.

"Morning," Eileen said, ruffling her hair before reaching for the shampoo. She moved around him to start washing her hair and David ran his hands over his body.

"I need to rinse." David and Eileen moved around each other again. David washed his body and put shampoo in his hair. Eileen rinsed her hair and opened the door.

"Where're you going?" David said.

Eileen looked around. "I have to check on the kids."

She wrapped herself in a towel and walked through their room and into the hallway. Eileen looked out into the hallway. Satisfied, she returned to the warm shower and dropped her towel on the floor. David had rinsed off and he hugged her into him.

"The kids are going to be up soon."

"I know. I'll be fast." David kissed her on the lips. The water splashed all over their faces and bodies. David shut off the water and held her hand as they exited the shower for the bedroom.

"You're getting water everywhere!"

David pulled her in and pushed her gently onto the bed. "Finally!" she thought to herself. "He wants me again."

Eileen laid herself on the edge of their bed, ready for him. David finished inside her right as they heard the alarms ringing in the kids' rooms.

Eileen stood up from the edge of the bed and pulled on a pair of sweatpants and a T-shirt. David found a pair of underwear and started to gather his work clothes.

"That was fun," Eileen said. "We should do that more often."

David smiled as he pulled on his pants.

"I'm going to go start breakfast," she said, biting her lip. She knocked on Randy's door on her way to the kitchen.

"Time to get up!"

Eileen started cooking and one by one her family wandered down to the table. Randy slid into the table without a shirt on. His eyes were still bleary.

"Morning, Randy."

"Hi mom."

Eileen started putting hot food on plates for her family. David walked down the stairs. Randy looked at him and quickly looked back at the table. Kelly sat at the table, letting her legs swing. She wore a simple dress and cloth shoes. Randy wanted to hug Kelly close. David sat down at the head of the table.

"Randy, go put on a shirt."

"I will, after I eat."

"Go now."

Randy left the table with an eye roll and returned a short moment later wearing a shirt. A quiet took over the room as the family said grace and ate the hot breakfast.

David broke the quiet of the breakfast table. "Randy, get that form for Driver's Ed."

"Yes, sir." Randy quietly consumed his breakfast. "Mom, did you wash my basketball stuff?"

"Yes, it's on the stairs."

Kelly finished eating first and stood up to get her backpack.

"The bus is almost here!" she said, slipping on the straps of the purple bag. Eileen smiled at David and looked out the window towards the bus stop to see if the bus had arrived.

"I'm late, babe, I got to go." David kissed her and walked out to his truck. He pulled out of the driveway and made his way to work. Randy walked his sister and his bike to the school bus a short distance away from their quiet suburban street of similarly styled houses.

He hugged her extra that day and watched the yellow bus pull away before beginning his bike ride to high school. His hips swayed back and forth as he pedaled the bike and balanced his backpack.

Randy sat at his desk in home room and looked forward, but he wasn't paying attention. He was too busy doodling and rolling the image of what he saw last night in his head. He couldn't so easily forget like David told him to do. At the end of the period, Randy was ready to shuffle to basketball practice, but was briefly stopped by the friendly teacher.

"Randy?"

"Yes, Mr. Emmons?" Randy replied.

"You were really out there today."

"Yeah, I guess I just got a lot in my mind."

"Anything you want to talk about?"

"No sir."

"Are you sure?"

"No sir, I really have to go or I'll have extra relays."

"I'll see you tomorrow, Randy, with your homework."

"Yes sir." Randy nodded his head down and headed out the door for basketball practice. It was good that practicing basketball didn't require too much mental power. His mind was at home, thinking about Kelly. How could he keep her safe? How was he going to stop David? Randy walked towards the gymnasium where the basketball court was and dropped his things in his locker. The rest of the team stood around. 3 tall, lanky black kids leaned against the metal lockers.

"Here's the boy who thinks he can play ball." One of them said as Randy changed into his practice outfit. Randy ignored the remark and pulled on the team branded clothing. Randy walked past them, his head down as he walked out to the court.

"Layups!" the coach shouted. Randy took his place in line as the order shattered his thought process. 45 minutes later, he lifted tired legs over the frame of his bike and began the ride home.

Randy put his bike in the garage and walked through the garage door. He crossed the living room to go upstairs.

"Randy! I'm making some snacks before dinner, do you want anything?"

"Uh, what are you making?"

"Bagel bites."

"Yeah, I'll have some." Randy turned around and started towards the kitchen. Eileen put some more bagel bites out on the cookie sheet.

"How was practice?" she asked. Randy sat down at the counter.

"It was fine. I'm tired, though."

"Looks like you didn't shower either."

"Nah, the locker room is weird."

Eileen smiled, "Does it bother you?" she asked, putting the frozen food in the warm oven.

"Like, it didn't used to but now it does. It's weird."

"That is weird, but that's okay, you can shower here. Sometimes locker rooms are strange for boys your age."

"Yeah…" Randy's voice trailed off.

"Something on your mind?" Eileen said, looking into the oven. The cheese and meat bubbled.

"Did you hear David in the hallway? I saw him in Kelly's room."

Eileen looked up at Randy. She swallowed before looking away towards the refrigerator. She removed a bottle of blue liquid.

"I'm sure he was just checking up on her. Making sure she was in bed."

Randy shifted his body weight on the chair.

"That's not what I saw."

Eileen looked at the counter. "I don't know what you saw, Randy, but I'm sure it was fine." She turned around and removed the snacks from the oven and put them on a plate. She put the plate on the counter in front of Randy. She picked up the bottle of blue liquid and set it in front of Randy. "They had your favorite flavor of gatorade at Costco. I bought two cases."

"Did you get another tub of mayo for Kelly?"

Eileen chuckled. "I did, Helmann's, her favorite. But don't tell David, he hates how she eats."

Randy nodded her head. "I think he's trying to turn her into a beauty queen," Randy opened up the bottle and took a long swig.

Randy put the bottle down, "What would David be doing under her bed?"

"Checking for monsters, maybe. It's fine." Eileen smiled. "Eat up, then go take a shower."

Randy smirked between chews. Eileen poured a glass of wine for herself. She started to sip from the glass as Randy tromped upstairs to take a shower.

Randy thought about what happened. Randy stripped off his clothes and climbed into the shower still thinking about what he had seen. He washed quickly and sat down on the edge of the bed. Randy tried to put the pieces together on what he saw and why David wanted him to forget about it so bad. But what he saw and the reaction lingered. He turned on his PS2 and put the disc for Max Payne in the top of the console. He started to play but his mind kept drifting. Randy thought about he could learn more and figure out what was going on and why it was going on. Randy felt his belly get tight as he thought about what David was doing. Randy didn't like how he felt. He turned up the volume on the TV and kept playing his game.

Chapter 6

The coach blew his whistle. "That's practice boys, good practice, be ready for the game this weekend."

Randy finished his final drill and walked slowly around the court. His muscles ached. He high-fived his teammates before heading into the locker room. He dodged the showers and went for the lockers instead. He took out his stuff and closed the door tight. Randy left the locker room with his backpack slung over his shoulder. He found his bike and unlocked it from the rack. He put the other strap over his shoulder and started to bike home.

Randy pedaled the bike along the roads until the house came into view. Randy put his bike on the rack in the garage. Randy waved at his mom as he walked up the stairs to his room. He dropped his backpack on the floor and stripped out of his sweaty clothes, leaving them in a pile on the floor on top of the permanent layer of clothes, books, papers, and other items that supply an extra layer of covering above the carpet and below the feet on a teenage boy's floor. He reached under his bed for one of the magazines he had picked up around school. Randy lay on the bed and started to destress. Afterwards he tucked his magazine back under his bed and fell asleep for a few minutes. His nap was jolted by yelling. He slowly pushed up his torso onto his elbows and turned his head towards the door to see if he could hear anything.

"Stay out of the goddamn mayonnaise!" David shouted at Kelly. Randy heard her small footsteps up the stairs. Randy slid off the bed and onto the floor. He found a pair of shorts that were handy and slipped them on while opening the door. He walked out quietly into the hallway and towards the stairs. Randy heard Eileen and David's voices yelling from below. He stopped on his left foot and stood there, ears tuned to the conversation.

"I don't know what's wrong! I just—I want a baby but I'm just not with it right now. Can't a man have the fucking privilege to not have to perform?" David shouted.

Eileen let out a sob. "I don't want to make you mad. I'm not trying to pressure you. I just want to feel close to you and I know you want to start a family. You've done so much for us and I don't want to ruin it again!" Eileen crumbled into a full cry.

"You aren't ruining it. Just, leave me alone about it. It'll happen when it happens. Come here, don't cry, alright, you don't want the kids to hear."

Randy started to back up as he stepped back, Kelly walked up behind and hugged his waist.

"What are they fighting about?"

"Nothing, nothing, just go back in your room."

"Is it about me?"

"No, no it's not. Just go back in your room."

"Come play."

"I'll be there in a minute." Randy stood there for a few minutes more before tearing himself away. He crept down the stairs slowly.

"I don't know what to do, David! I don't fucking know how to please you. I don't know how! Just....love me, just love me." Randy heard her start to cry loudly.

"Shut up! The kids will hear!" David intoned.

"What do you want me to do!"

"I don't know!" David threw his beer bottle against the wall and Randy heard the glass shatter everywhere. Eileen cried out and bolted out of the kitchen into the living room and curled up on the couch. David's chest heaved and he followed her. Randy kept walking downstairs into the kitchen for something to eat and drink. He listened to them as he gathered his food. He was quiet. He could see and hear them past the kitchen and the small hallway. He was obscured slightly. He just focused on getting the food.

"Eileen! Eileen! Bring me another beer. I need to fucking relax."

"Has work been stressful?" She looked up at him from under her blanket and pillow.

"Yeah, things are crazy."

"Okay." Eileen stood up and wiped her face. She walked over to the kitchen and took out another beer and retrieved her glass of wine. Randy held some water and sandwich fixings on a plate. He passed her on the way back upstairs. Eileen avoided eye contact with her son. Randy say her walk around the island and hand David the beer. She sat down and drank a portion of her own glass. David couldn't look at her; he was absorbed in television. Randy started upstairs.

"Do you want her to join us? Would that help you?" Randy's heart raced and he stopped on the stairs. That moment stuck in his mind. Randy's mind raced with possibilities. But one stuck out. If they were trying for a baby and they were talking like that, could it be true? Randy froze on the stairs and kept listening.

"No, that would be inappropriate."

"What do you want to do?"

"I don't know."

She crawled over to him and laid her head on his lap. "The next time you go to her and you are turned on, don't finish, just come back to me. I'll do it whenever you are ready and we'll make love and we'll have a child. I want your child so badly, David."

He finally directed his attention to her. "Okay," he said in an innocent, puerile manner.

Randy's heart sank. His chest was knotted and his stomach flared with pain. His hands trembled with what he had just heard. The pieces fell together slowly. Randy resolved to walk forward. He climbed to the stop of the stairs and walked down the hall to Kelly's room. He pushed the door open and set the food down on her little table. Kelly was tucked in a corner on some pillows reading a book.

"Hungry?" Randy asked.

"Yup!" Kelly said putting the sandwich fixings on some bread. She slathered the mayonnaise onto both pieces of bread. She bit into the sandwich. She spread more mayonnaise onto the bread. Randy just stared at the food. He opened a chip bag and plucked out a couple pieces.

"Are you okay?" Kelly said in between bites.

"Yeah." Randy lied, "I'm fine."

"You seem weird. Did you talk to that girl in your class yet?"

"No. Not yet."

"Huh, you probably should." Kelly said.

"Are you okay?" Randy asked.

"Well, my book is getting exciting. The witch just cursed the hero, so I want to find out what happens next." Kelly bit into her sandwich again. The mayo squeezed out of the edges.

"I thought you wanted to play."

"We can play Sorry!" Kelly said putting down the sandwich and getting up to find the board game.

Randy crossed his legs. His body was calming down now. He dug into his own sandwich as Kelly setup the board. She finished her sandwich as they started the game. They played through the evening. Randy watched her carefully. The hours ticked by until it was time to go bed. Randy stood up and yawned.

"It's time for bed."

"Okay." Kelly said standing up.

Randy stood up and opened her door. Eileen stood in the hallway.

"Are you guys getting ready for bed." Eileen asked, her words slurred.

"Yeah, was just playing games."

"Did you have homework?"

"No." Randy lied.

"Alright. Off to bed."

Randy nodded at her and she tottered away towards her own room.

Randy turned back and looked into Kelly's room. He watched her again for a moment before closing the door behind him and returning to his room. He brushed his teeth, used the bathroom and climbed into bed himself. He stared at the ceiling and wondered if he would hear footsteps again. He wondered and listened, listened and wondered as sleep finally closed his eyes.

Chapter 7

Randy looked up from his drawing to look at the back of her head. He studied every hair and the way the skin on her neck looked in the sunlight. He didn't really remember what the teacher was talking about, but he was hoping she would turn towards her left so he could finish the profile picture he was drawing of her in his book. Randy was drawing and thinking about how to approach her to ask her about the Spring Dance. The poster for the dance hung on the wall over the shoulder of his teacher. Randy passed her in the hall and saw her in this class but otherwise, they didn't speak. He needed to make an introduction but it had to be natural. He smudged some pencil to smooth a line. He didn't want it to be weird or contrived. She wouldn't turn around, and before he could get any more sketching done, the bell rang. Randy stood up and left the classroom and headed straight for his locker. He made his way down the sterile hallway towards his wing of the building where his locker was located. Randy was annoyed about the long walk; thanks to a clerical error, his locker was farther away than it should have been otherwise. Randy rounded the corner to his hallway where his locker was, down at the end. A group of black kids stood between him and his locker. His pace slowed as he started walking towards them and one of the boys pulled at his backpack.

"What you carrying around so much shit for, white boy?" the largest of the boys shouted at him. "You're awfully skinny for all that shit."

Randy tugged the bag back and kept walking, and the boys walked backwards in front of him. He was trying not to look down. Other students milled around. The others whispered among themselves and pointed at him.

"Why don't you guys go suck a dick?" Randy threw the insult back.

"Why don't you teach us how, faggot?" One of them shot back.

Randy let his fists fly in a series of punches that had the taunting boy on the ground in less than a second. He was screaming, and it reverberated in the halls. The other boys immediately backed up.

"He hit me! He fucking hit me!" the boy screamed as two teachers ran up. They escorted Randy to the Principal's office. Randy remained there until David and Eileen arrived. David's scowl told Randy everything he needed to know. David and Eileen walked out of the school with Randy in tow.

"Suspended ten days for fighting, and benched for the season from basketball," David said. "I said defend yourself, not make him bleed!" David stamped his foot. "I need a fucking drink."

"Do you want to ride your bike home, honey?" Eileen asked him, rubbing his cheek.

"Yeah, that's fine, I'll see you guys at home," Randy replied. David and Eileen climbed into his pickup and he ripped out of the parking lot, tires squealing and with much unnecessary effort from his engine. Randy walked over to the bike rack and unlocked his bike. His swung his leg over it and started pedaling for home. His thoughts moved to the girls in his class. He just really wanted to take her to the dance, and now he would be sitting at home with no girl and no dance.

Randy pedaled slowly around the corner as he rounded the bend to his street, the large backpack shifting with his body as he rounded the curve. He walked his bike up to the house and placed it in the open garage. When his hand touched the doorknob he could already hear David screaming. This was becoming more of a regular occurrence. It seemed like the more they drank, the more they fought. It bothered Randy more and more. He thought it would be different this time, but it wasn't. His dad used to drink and the same thing would happen. Randy resolved to make the trip from the door to the stairs and from the stairs to his room. He steeled himself. Randy opened the door and walked into the kitchen. Eileen was leaning on the counter to hold herself up. David was standing, with his hands on his thin hips, looking at her.

"When I said I wanted another beer, I wanted another fucking beer!" His voice rose as he ended the sentence.

"I thought you said we weren't drinking on weekdays!" she sobbed.

"Fuck that, after what happened today. Oh look! Here comes the fucker now!" David said, acknowledging Randy's presence in the room.

"Leave him out of this, I'm sorry, I'm so sorry David. I'll do better I promise. I'll get you a beer, right now!" Eileen made for the fridge for the golden liquid. She tugged open the door and handed him the cold beer across the kitchen. David popped off the top with his belt buckle and threw the cap towards the sink and missed. Randy started walking again.

"All ten days boy, we'll be doing PT, I'll find work for your ass. You won't be spending it playing fucking video games!" He threw the remark over his shoulder as he sat back down in the recliner with his beer. Randy climbed upstairs and dropped his backpack in his room. He changed out of his clothes and put on some loose pants and walked down to the end of the hall. He knocked on the door.

"What?"

"It's Randy."

"Come in."

Kelly was sitting in bed in her pink pajamas, reading a book.

"You're dressed for bed early."

"I'm hiding from the drama downstairs. I thought it was going to be different this time."

"Me too Kelly, me too."

"What if he hits mom?"

"I hope he doesn't do that. It looks like I'll be doing a lot of pushups this week."

"Why?"

"Got suspended."

Kelly sat up. "Why? What did they do?"

"I finally punched out those kids in the hallway."

"Really? What happened?"

"They started talking, I punched one. The big guy, the one that doesn't smell so good."

"Huh, some girl told me about a fight, but I didn't know it was you. No one knew who it was."

"Yeah, I guess news travels fast, but I got suspended for ten days for fighting and I'm pretty much off basketball until next year so I'm in deep shit."

Kelly pulled up her legs. "That's no fair."

"That's how it works."

"Yeah, I guess so," she said. "That's okay, it won't be so bad. You can beat the monster that keeps killing you."

"Yeah, I don't know if I'm grounded or what. David said a lot, we'll see how much of it he remembers."

"Okay, I have homework."

"Did you eat?"

"No, not really. I had a snack."

"Was that snack more than mayonnaise? Do you want something to eat?"

Kelly beamed, "How'd you guess it was mayo? I'm kinda hungry, but I probably shouldn't."

"If you're going to keep your grades up, you should eat. I'll see what I can get." Randy stood up and Kelly jumped out of bed to give her big brother a big hug around his belly.

"Okay, okay, I have to find some food."

Randy walked down stairs and rooted through the freezer. He found a pizza and after reading the box put it in the oven. Eileen walked into the kitchen and opened the fridge and just looked at Randy and mouthed, "Thank you," and walked back to the living room with another beer.

The oven timer rang and Randy quickly stopped it and carried two plates with pieces for Kelly and himself upstairs with some cans of soda he found in the back of the pantry. Kelly opened the door and the two siblings sat on the floor, quietly chewing their pizza. When they were finished, Randy collected their dishes and returned them to the kitchen. He looked into the living room and saw Eileen cuddled on David's lap, her hands tugging at his jeans and her head resting on his plumper middle. She looked like she was trying to hang onto him and if she could grasp him strong enough she could save him, their marriage, this house, and maybe her kids. They stayed close as they went up to bed that night. Eileen kept her arms around him hugging his close as they slept.

David burst into Randy's room the next morning. Randy sat up to see David leering at him.

"Get up. PT, all 10 days you're suspended." David was dressed in workout clothing. Randy felt around for some shorts and a shirt. David marched him out into the garage where David put Randy through a grueling workout. Randy's face was covered in sweat. His arms and legs were sore from the workout. David looked at the time.

"I got work for you." David tugged on Randy's arm. He led him towards the yard. The morning breeze was cool on Randy's skin.

"See all this shit, leaves and crap. I want it all cleaned up and in bags by the I get home. You don't want to know what's going to happen if it's not. Go eat something and get to work."

Randy nodded as David marched away. Randy slipped into the kitchen and poured himself a bowl of cereal. His Mom walked in with Kelly in tow.

"Good, you're eating, that's good. I'm going to walk Kelly to the bus and run some errands."

"Cool."

"Did David give you a job for the day?"

"Yardwork."

"Alright, I'll check on you when I get back," she said. Eileen touched his arm as she picked up her purse and started towards the garage.

"Kelly, let's go, you'll be late for the bus and I don't want to have to drop you off."

"Coming!" Kelly said pulling on her pink backpack." The pair left through the garage leaving Randy alone with his cereal and his yardwork.

Chapter 8

David and Eileen sat on the side, waiting for Randy's fight. Kelly sat on the floor below with some other children who were half paying attention and half playing or running around. David rubbed his hands together with anticipation. The gym was hot on the humid afternoon, and the sun shining through the short windows wasn't helping the internal climate, despite the best efforts of the aging AC system. The first group of younger kids had all gone, and now it was time for Randy's group to have their fights.

"Go get me something to drink," David said.

"I'm hungry too! Can I have a hot dog!"

David nodded. "Go with your mother, but leave the goddamn mayonnaise alone," he warned.

Eileen stood up silently and made her way down to the concession stand. Kelly followed her. She returned with some plastic cups of lemonade. Kelly munched on her hot dog with ketchup and looked out towards the tournament. David drained the cup, crushed it, and let it fall to the flat metal bleacher below. Randy finally stepped onto the mat for his first fight of the day. Randy and the opponent touched hands and began their bout. Randy won handily despite his slight frame. Jiu Jitsu was an ideal form for him, and he excelled at it, something David approved of with a smile, especially with a win. Randy kept fighting the ring until the final round. David was shouting and cheering and Eileen looked on. She had what she thought she wanted, and while she was enthusiastic and seemed happy, anyone who looked deeper could tell. They could tell something wasn't quite right. The difference between true happiness and a woman who was acting happy because she felt it was her job to be happy with her husband. Randy finally won the long final round, and David jumped from his seat. David was waiting ringside for his son. He grabbed his hand and shook it vigorously and patted him on the shoulder. The other participants milled about, avoiding the display. David sent Randy off to change while they waited for the closing ceremony. Randy walked into the bathroom where the other boys were changing. Randy slipped his worn backpack off his shoulder and onto the ground. The fighter he had just pummeled rinsed his face.

"Nice fight."

"Thanks," Randy said as he started to untie his uniform.

Boys walked in between the sinks and the row of five stalls in various states of dress and undress. They pretend-punched each other and the scene generally devolved into a typical high school locker room. The smell of sweat and testosterone filled the air with notes of excess body spray and boyhood screeching. Slowly most of the boys filtered out, until the bathroom was occupied by Randy and this other boy who seemed to be wasting time.

"Do you have hair down there yet?"

"A little, I wish I had more. Some of those guys are hairy."

"Yeah, me too, it's growing though." Randy looked up and saw the boy inspecting his crotch in the mirror, hoping there was more hair than his 15-year-old body had yet produced.

"You know, you need to let that shit air out sometimes. Air flow is good for your dick."

"What?"

"Yeah, sometimes you just have to let it be free."

"I guess so." Randy pulled off his undergarments and slipped some bloused boxers over his thin legs.

"Hey listen, I got this magazine, from my older brother. Wanna see?" The boy motioned to Randy to join in the generous space of the handicap stall. He pulled out the prized contraband and flipped out the pages. He had marked his favorite pages of women kneeling on laundry baskets, lying on beds, and pleasuring each other towards the back. He was blatant and started pleasuring himself with his opposing hand as he flipped the pages.

"Come on, it's fun, just let go." Randy nervously slipped his manhood out of the fly and joined him. They flipped through different pages together for a few minutes and the other boy leaned against the wall. Randy leaned against the metal wall of the stall and closed his eyes, thinking about what he would do if he had a chance with the women contained within those pages. When Randy opened his eyes, the other boy was looking right at him and took 2 steps forward Randy momentarily let go of himself. The other boy leaned in for a kiss. Randy accepted the kiss with his eyes closed. He tasted like sweat. The spell was broken when David walked into the bathroom, shouting Randy's name. David saw the two sets of bare feet in the stall and knocked at the door. Randy quickly stuffed himself back in his boxers.

"Randy, get out of there, what the fuck are you doing?"

Randy hesitantly opened the door and David spied the scene. David yanked Randy's arm out into the open.

"What the fuck are you doing?"

Rand stuttered, words failed him. "He had a, uh, magazines, and uh, there were these girls, and I just…"

David cut him off with a booming voice. "Not here, not right now, and not with another boy. Get dressed, we'll talk about this later." David pointed right at his nose when he spoke the words with sniper precision. "And what's your name?"

"Beau."

"Get dressed and don't fucking touch my son again, you hear?" His finger pointed right at the boy's face.

"Yes sir." Beau looked down at his feet and hurriedly pulled his clothes on. Randy pulled on his formal studio uniform. He walked out into the crowd and stepped in line with the others from his group. They slipped the blue ribbon medal over his head in the closing ceremony. Randy looked straight ahead. His mind was back at the stall and the moment of that kiss. He didn't understand it, his young mind was confused. He tried his best to be present as everyone congratulated him. Randy finally broke away from the crowd and joined his family. The family went to a small restaurant in their town. The conversation stayed around the fight, and Kelly bounced up and down, gushing about her big brother. Randy sat in the back with Kelly during the uneventful truck-ride home. He was the first at the door, and dashed upstairs to his room to change and shower. A few moments later, David knocked on the door and walked in. Randy was sitting on his single bed, headphones on. The room was sparse, with a simple desk on a wall, his bed in a corner and a messy bookshelf opposite. There were a few posters on the walls and clothes and other items spilled out of the closet. There was a rug at one time, but it had long been lost under papers, books, and various clothing items. He looked at David and pulled them off.

David crossed his arms.

"What were you doing in that stall with that other boy?" His voice was gruff, barely below a scream.

Randy sat up. "I don't know."

"Don't give me that shit. What were you doing?"

"He had this magazine, it was just some girls, we were looking at them," Randy offered.

"Yeah, I could tell," he said sarcastically. "Look, if you want to look at porn I don't give a fuck, in fact, it's good for a boy your age. But you don't fucking look at porn with another boy and you sure as fuck don't jack off."

"I-I-didn't know. I don't know what I was doing."

"Did he touch you?"

"No," Randy lied.

"I better never catch you doing that shit again, you hear?"

"Yes sir."

"I'll get you something later."

"Okay."

David slammed the door behind him. Randy put on his headphones and closed his eyes. His contemplation was interrupted again when there was another knock at the door.

"Randy?" squeaked the small voice.

"Yeah, come in."

Kelly appeared in a cute little T-shirt and cut-off jeans.

"What was dad yelling at you about?"

"Nothing, it was stupid."

"Didn't sound stupid."

"It was stupid. What are you doing?"

"Nothing, reading."

"Okay."

"What about you? Your room stinks!"

"I'm listening to some music, trying to not be hungry." Randy picked up a nearby can of body spray and sprayed a little bit of the odiferous liquid into the air to counter the unmistakable odor of maleness.

"We just ate."

"I know."

"Want me to get you something?"

"That'd be cool."

Kelly ran out to the hallway and down the stairs. She returned a few minutes later with two peanut butter and jelly sandwiches and a small bowl of mayonnaise.

"PB for you and one for me." She ate the mayo first and then dug into the sandwich.

"I will never understand that."

"PB and J?"

"Eating plain mayo."

"It's yummy in my tummy!" she said, mimicking a much younger child's voice.

"You know David hates that."

"I know, but I don't care." She collected the plates and the bowl after they finished eating.

"It's bedtime," Randy said.

"I know, I have to present in Sunday school tomorrow."

"What are you talking about?" Randy sat up fully to look at her sitting on the floor.

"David and Goliath."

"Sounds like fun," Randy offered.

"Not really, it's boring," she said, hanging her head.

"It sounds exciting to me."

"Will you play Goliath? I can shoot a rock at you!" Kelly said with a broad smile.

"Okay, that sounds like fun."

"Okay!" Kelly jumped on his bed.

"Bed."

"I don't want to go to bed," she said, swinging her arms around.

"I know, I know."

"It's supposed to be our secret."

"It still is."

Kelly hung her head. "Can't I sleep in here with you?"

"You know David doesn't allow that."

"I know, but its cozy in here with you. You're warm."

"I wish we could," Randy said, flopping backwards on the bed.

"I'll see you in the morning," Kelly said as she closed the door. Randy walked down the hall into her neat room full of yellows, pinks, and greens. He leaned against the door frame while she slipped under her princess blankets on her bed.

"Night."

"Night, tomorrow everything will be okay."

"I know."

Chapter 9

Eileen sat up in bed. David laid stretched out next to her. She watched him breath for a moment. She noticed he had slimmed down a little. His stomach had reduced down a small paunch. She slipped out from bed and walked into the bathroom. She turned on the shower and let the water make its way up to the faucet. She flushed the toilet and walked over to the shower to test the temperature. Satisfied, she stepped inside and let the water run over her. She closed her eyes and slowly started to wake.

A moment later she felt a big hand on her shoulder. Eileen stifled a scream when she realized that David was standing behind her. He pressed his body against hers and the water splashed over them both.

"Good morning."

"Good morning," Eileen cooed.

Randy ran his fingers down her body. Her breath caught in her throat when he touched her.

"The kids will be up soon," she warned."

"I don't care," David whispered in her ear.

Eileen reached up behind herself and rubbed his head. She turned around and picked up some soap and started to wash him.

"We should get you ready for work."

David let the soap run down as he picked her up into his arms. Eileen held on, her gaze fixed into his eyes. Her nails dug into his back until his eyes closed in ecstasy. He set her down in the shower and she stayed close to him for a moment.

"We really need to get you ready."

David broke the embrace and started to wash. They traded places to get the water and Eileen shut it off once they were both clean. They dried off together into the bathroom. Eileen turned on the fan to circulate the air and the pair walked back into the bedroom to get dressed. When they arrived downstairs, Kelly and Randy were waiting in the kitchen.

"Mom, I'm going to be late." Kelly said with a pout.

"No, I don't think so, bus doesn't come for another 40 minutes. Plenty of time to eat some cereal." Eileen pulled down 3 boxes from the cupboard. Randy looked into the fridge.

"Would you like bacon and eggs?"

Randy nodded his head. "That'd be cool."

Eileen nodded. "David, do you want bacon?"

David nodded his head as he walked outside to find the newspaper. He returned to the table with the paper as Eileen took out a large cast iron frying pan and started to fry up the bacon. She placed paper towels on a plate to drain the bacon and took out several eggs from the fridge. Kelly took her cereal into the living room and turned on the TV to watch cartoons.

David looked over his paper towards the living room.

"Does she always watch cartoons before school?" David asked Eileen.

Eileen nodded, "It's fine, just kids shows. Keeps her busy while she eats her cereal."

David kept reading. Randy poured himself some orange juice and waited for breakfast to be ready. Eileen watched as the items cooked and started to pull the food from the big pan. She brought the plate of bacon and the eggs towards the table.

"Randy, get a plate for you and David so you guys can eat while I walk Kelly to the bus!"

Randy followed her with the items. Eileen set the food down and called for Kelly. She ran into the kitchen put her bowl in the sink and grabbed her backpack.

"I don't need you hold my hand Mom!" Kelly remarked.

"I won't, I'm just going to watch."

"I can do it myself."

"I know you can."

Eileen led Kelly outside and walked out to the end of the yard and watched Kelly walk to the bus stop. Eileen walked back inside once the bus had pulled away from the stop. David held out his arms and she walked over for a kiss.

"I'm out of here."

"Alright."

Randy followed David out to the garage. Eileen stood in the doorway and watched David pull his truck out of the garage and Randy take off on his bike towards school. Eileen closed the door and cleaned up the kitchen. She turned the TV over to another channel to watch morning programming as she went about her housework. She put the dishes in the dishwasher and cleaned the pan. She left it on the counter to dry after rubbing it in oil. Looking at the time, she realized she had a lunch appointment. She picked up her purse and left.

The house stood empty for the rest of the day until David and Kelly arrived back at home in the afternoon. Randy was happy that he had no after school practice. He was free to go home and play some games. Randy found his bike in the bike rack and started for home. His legs and hips shifted back and forth as he rode through the crisp afternoon breeze towards home. His mind turned around his day and highschool in general. He was already tired of going to school everyday and sitting in classes. Randy wondered if he should just drop out and find a job. It would be a good way to get away from David. But what would happen to Kelly if he weren't there? His mind turned like the wheels on his bike as he pulled up to their street. He thought about playing college basketball too. Maybe he could make Mizzou. He could be a Tiger.

Randy wiped his brow as he laid his bike down in the driveway. He picked at his crotch and shifted his jock strap. He unlocked the door and started pulling off his clothes to go shower. His shoes were flung against the wall behind the door. The stairs were in sight when the open refrigerator door in the kitchen caught his eye. Randy pulled his tank top on his body as he moved towards the kitchen barefoot. Randy looked at the group of empty beer bottles. Randy saw Kelly's legs struggling and David's knee firmly planted on her. Randy arrived at the fridge, covering the short distance in less than a second. Randy saw that Kelly's face was bloody and she looked smothered in a pink substance. Randy's mouth dropped open when the familiar smell hit his nostrils. Mayonnaise.

David held a spoon and was shoving the mayonnaise in her face. She was crying, attempting to breathe, and trying to struggle against him. Droplets of blood and mayonnaise spread around.

Randy stood there frozen in place until his hand felt heavy. He wanted to tell David to get off of her, to fuck off, but his mouth wouldn't form the words. The pan was in his hand. Randy couldn't think about how he found it or how he picked it up. It was just there. The normally heavy pan felt light in his sinewy arms. He stood there, shirtless now and ominous over David's head and body. His muscles tightened and tensed. He swung toward the dominant man right as David looked over his shoulder.

"What the fuck, boy?" David said as Randy slammed the pan onto his head with a thud.

The first blow stunned him and his mouth moved with gibberish. Randy didn't stop. He kept swinging and beat David's skill to a bloody mass of hair, bone, brain and blood. David lay on the floor, lifeless. As if by magic, Randy felt himself snap back into the present. His body went limp and he dropped the pan on the ruined linoleum floor. He dropped to his knees and pulled David off Kelly.

The metal refrigerator doors banged against the cabinets. Kelly was bleeding out; Randy picked up what was left of his sister and cradled her. Her body fell limp in his arms. He fell backwards onto the floor. He lay there, staring at the ceiling. His mind felt numb; he couldn't remember his name. He felt a blindness cover over him as he passed out. He was jolted back to life when his mother screamed at the top of her lungs. Randy's eyelids flew open at the stimulus and he stood up on his legs slowly.

He looked down, grabbed his face and screamed, "Kelly, don't fucking die!" He dropped to his knees again and spread his legs wide, lying next to Kelly's lifeless body.

Randy could hear his mother screaming and he didn't move. Randy heard her calling 911.

"Yes, that's right, there's been an accident," Eileen said. "My husband, and daughter, yes they're hurt, very hurt, please come quickly!"

Eileen hung up the phone.

"Randy, what have you done?"

Randy's mouth hung open but he didn't reply.

"Randy! What did you do?" Her voice was louder. The tears started to stream down her face.

"Randy! What did you do!" she screamed.

"I—I don't know," Randy croaked out. His voice was rough.

Randy didn't hear anything again until two police officers pulled him off the floor.

"Son, take off your clothes. They're evidence," the tall officer said. Randy stood there.

"Son?"

Randy looked into space.

"Let me help you." The officer started to pull on Randy's clothes. The officer stripped Randy and put his clothes in evidence bags. Randy stood in the kitchen naked until a female officer brought him a gauze gown. Both officers grabbed his arms and put his wrists in handcuffs.

"You have the right to remain silent. Anything you say can be used against you in a court of law. You have the right to an attorney. If you cannot afford one, an attorney will be provided to you." Both officers walked Randy out of the house and to the police cruiser. Randy turned around to see a gurney carrying Kelly's body out of the house.

When they arrived at the police station, they led him into a small holding cell and removed the handcuffs. After some time passed, a female office wearing blue gloves opened the white cell door and left him a green uniform. Randy looked at them for a while until he shivered and gingerly unfolded the items and pulled them on. The items were cut straight with no shape, but the simple shirt and elastic pants fit him. He sat there, just looking at what he could see out of the window, until he fell asleep against the wall of the cell.

Part 2

Chapter 10

Randy stood in line with a few other young men. He was already out of his suit he had worn to court and back into the green jumpsuit that the state of Missouri used for its prisoners. He was standing in line waiting for transport away from the court house. His hands were cuffed in front of him and his feet were shackled together. The chain was long enough for him to stand comfortably but not run or move very quickly. When the young men walked they shuffled. Randy looked at the other boys. Most of them stared straight ahead. Some of them looked young to him while a couple were obviously older. They leaned against the wall. 2 officers paced around the area. Randy noticed that the officers looked outside from time to time. They stood and they waited and they stood and waited some more. Randy's feet started to hurt. He stepped out of the rubber sandals and onto the hard floor. The change provided little relief. He squatted down first and slowly the other boys began to sit or squat against the wall. Randy looked outside when the officers looked. A bus rolled up to the doors and the officers made everyone stand up. They began their shuffle to the bus.

The boys sat in the bus and when everyone was seated the driver closed the door and guided the bus away from the court house and towards its destination. Randy didn't know where he was going or how long he would be there. He had almost no information to any variety other than his sentence: twelve years. It didn't seem like a long time but he also realized that he wouldn't be free until he was 20 years old and somehow 20 years old seemed along way away. The bus rumbled over the roads. Trees passed his window as the bus pulled away from town and out into the rural spaces between towns. One of the boys started to talk but the officer swiftly quieted him. Randy took that as notice not to say anything on the journey. Randy hadn't really thought about school or his friends or his basketball team until that moment. He wondered what everyone was up to or what they were saying. And there was the girl with the golden hair, her drawing still unfinished sitting in his room. Randy's mind had been to filled with the trial it hadn't occurred to him that just a few months back, he was in school. He was going to school everyday and he was on the basketball team. That was all gone now.

The bus rolled to a stop outside an aggressive fence with barbed wire. The officers stood everyone up and led them out of the bus and directly into the facility. The building was squat and made of bricks with a metal roof. Layers of chain link fence created pathways for people to travel to and from the facility. Serious people with scowls on their faces stood behind gates as the boys shuffled into the facility. They stopped the train of boys as the officers exchanged some paperwork. Randy kept quiet. Others started to ask questions or try to talk but the officers simply ignored them. Once the officers concluded their business, they took the cuffs and shackles off of each boy and placed them in a box. Randy rubbed his wrists. He was glad to be free to the metal restraints. They all moved their limbs to get feeling back in their extremities.

One by one, they were taken into a small holding area and searched. They stripped out of their clothes and were searched by a male officer. The search itself was degrading. Randy was examined by gloved hand all over his body. He flinched at the touch and looked away from the man as he held up his testicles and was forced to turn around, bend over and cough. Once the search was over, a large, female officer waved them into another room away from where they were. Inside where shelves of items.

"Take one of each and put it in these boxes, at the end you'll find a bedroom with towels, sheets, and a bed pad, carry all of that with you as we take you to your cell bock."

Randy carried a box of personal hygiene items, as well as his bedroll, with him down the hall. He followed the guard in her khaki uniform. It was neatly pressed and her belt was filled with tools and items.

"This block is for all you juveniles to stay at before you get sent off to one of the schools," the guard told him. "Make yourselves at home, you'll find out later when you're going to be moved.

Randy looked into the open cell where five other boys sat on the metal bed frames. An open toilet stood at the back of the cell with a metal sink. Randy sat on the floor, looking at the other boys. No one wanted to talk much that first night. It wasn't until they were let out into the yard that anyone was interested in talking. A tall, good-looking boy was the first to approach Randy.

"Hi, I'm Brad."

"Randy, nice to meet you." Randy's eyes shifted up and down his long frame. He was intimidated by him, but Randy felt intimidated by everyone, the system, the world, the moment that landed him here in the first place.

"It's chilly, let's keep walking to stay warm," Brad offered. Randy followed him.

"What are you in for?" Randy asked first.

"Drugs, possession and distribution. You?"

"Homicide," Randy said simply.

"Shit man, deal gone bad?"

"Yeah, you could say that," Randy said, not wanting to give too many details. The two walked around the perimeter fence of the facility. Some others had coats.

"How do you get a coat or anything in here?" Randy asked.

"You have to have money on your books, then order things at the prison commissary," Brad replied.

"I definitely need a coat, maybe some notebooks and paper. I don't know if I have any money or not. My mom might have put some, but I really don't know. I guess I'll have to find out."

"You might want to wait on that, man."

"Why?" Randy asked.

"You'll be moved soon, most likely, and you probably won't get your stuff. If you have money, hang on to it until you get to where you're going. You might be able to trade for some paper, if you have anything."

"It sounds like you've done this before."

"Yeah, I'm 17, this is my second rodeo. I was just like you my first time, though."

"I guess that helps," Randy said, rubbing his arms.

"Be careful in here. A lot of the older guys like to pick on the younger guys and take advantage of them. They'll try stuff, just be careful, try to find a buddy and stick with him. Don't be alone if you can help it." Brad looked around the yard and pulled a cigarette from his coat.

"This is contraband, illegal. Here, have some, you'll feel better."

"I don't smoke."

"You do now man, trust me, you'll feel better." Randy took the cigarette.

Randy inhaled from the cigarette. He choked a bit and coughed a bit.

"Thanks man," Randy said.

Brad looked around again. They traded the cigarette back and forth until it burnt down to the filter.

"See? Better," Brad said, smiling. Randy nodded.

"If shit is going to go down, it's going to go down in the yard. Just know that. We might end up on lockdown, you never know."

"What happens on lockdown?"

"We can't leave our cells for any reason other than medical emergency."

"Oh," Randy said, looking around.

"Yeah, it's not fun. They usually serve us sandwiches or whatever else they can come up with that's cold and easy to serve."

No sooner were the words out of Brad's mouth than a group of black inmates mobbed two white inmates. The corrections officers were on top of the fight in seconds, but it took several minutes to stop, and the alarms rang. Other officers barked orders for the other inmates to get inside.

Brad and Randy shuffled in the socks and sandals they were wearing over to the gate. The officers guided the young offenders to a separate line. The other men all lined up in one place. The corrections officers guided everyone to their appropriate cellblock and cell. As promised, no one went anywhere for the rest of the night. Peanut butter and jelly sandwiches were passed around by the staff later in the evening. Different groups of inmates were brought out several cells at a time. When they came around to Randy's cellblock he knew why: mandatory shakedown. A shakedown involved the officers removing the prisoners from their cells and having them sit in a common area while they tore the entire place apart. The officers shuffled Randy and the six other guys in his cell down the three flights of metal stairs and into a common area consisting of some metal stools and a round table that were welded together and bolted to the floor. Randy sat there as the officers rifled around. They were led back up the metal stairs to their cell. Their meager belongings were piled on their beds with no effort made for its organization or even assurance that the right stuff was on the right bed. Randy did not have much, so his pile was very small and he was able to find all of his items. Randy had a hard time sleeping with people throwing people's items back and forth and talking through the aged concrete walls. The blanket they gave him was thin and wasn't of much use. With seven guys it seemed like one of them was always using the small metal toilet at the back of the room. Between the noise of urine hitting the water and the loud flushing sounds, Randy only slept in 10-20 minute sessions. His eyes popped open. Randy took the friendly advice and tried to stay among people who weren't getting threatened and were peaceful. Even compared to his rough and tumble public school, the prison seemed like chaos. He clasped his arms around his shoulders and looked out into the dim light of the cell.

Chapter 11

The guards opened the doors in threes. Each group of boys stood outside of their cell, and Randy followed suit when the door on his cell opened. The guards let them outside to walk around. Randy made his way outside to the yard and braced himself for the cold air.

He hugged his shoulders in close as he looked around for Brad. Randy saw Brad leaning against a concrete divider, a cigarette between his fingers. Brad waved Randy over.

"Hey there."

"Hi." Randy nodded towards him. Randy leaned against the concrete and it felt warm on his skin.

"They're going to move me tomorrow. You too, probably. They're cleaning this place out."

"Why?"

"Need the space, this place isn't for long-term anyway. "

"How do you know all this stuff?"

"I listen. To the guards, the other inmates. If you want to make it, listen. Know your surroundings. See who does what." Brad threw his gaze across the yard.

Randy shivered and tried to look with those kind of eyes.

"Here, take a few drags. I put a little weed in that one."

Randy took the cigarette out his hand and inhaled three times in quick succession.

Randy kept as quiet as he could and did what he was told. He sat in the dark bus with the other young offenders. It almost looked like they were going to school. Without the circumstances that landed them in the system, they would have been. Randy's thoughts turned back to his classmates and the girl two rows up and one desk over in his class back at school.

"I bet she thinks I'm some sort of weird monster," he thought to himself. Randy resolved to let his thoughts of her go. He would probably never see or speak to her every again.

Two hours of knocking around and chains clanging against metal brought the offenders to their final stop. The officers escorted all the inmates off the bus in a fairly orderly fashion and led them into the facility. Randy didn't know what it was going to look like, besides what his last facility looked like and what he knew from TV.

Randy didn't expect what looked like a hamster habitat crossed with a science fiction movie. Randy gawked at the whole place; it was built in U-shaped pods, multilevel with stairs leading to terraced rows of cells.

The center of the pods was dominated by a steel and glass column that supported the command booth and formed the whole of the prison command. From those clandestine offices, they could keep an eye on the entire prison in all pods and send out teams to subdue the prisoners as necessary. Keeping humans confined, especially young criminal humans, took cleverness, resourcefulness and fear, as evidenced by the shotgun holes in the roof near the central command center.

Randy was led to a small processing center. The walls were white, and there was a pool of vomit and blood in one corner.

"Carruth, strip!" Randy removed his clothes and the burly officer inspected his entire body and searched all his cavities. The search was less degrading this time. It was the 3rd time he'd been searched like this and somehow, he was getting used to it. It was like a weird dance with a stranger. On command, Randy exposed his entire body in the same routine to check his armpits, mouth, balls, and ass.

Once completed, he was given a new uniform. The cut was the same but it was grey and white. He was led out of the processing room and into his cell. The cells were all separate but with solid doors and small thick windows. Randy was one of four inmates in a room that possessed only a metal toilet with a modicum of privacy provided by two panels on either side, as well as twin sets of wall-bolted bunk beds. Randy carried his pile of standard prison issue items:

1 thin blanket
1 sheet
2 pairs of socks
2 shirts
1 extra set of grey shirt and pants
1 toothbrush and a small tube of toothpaste
1 bar soap
2 small towels
1 wash cloth

When the door opened, the three other boys looked to see who would be occupying the empty bottom bunk. Randy was given a gentle shove into the cell and the door closed behind him.

The three other boys looked back at him as he walked in and put his small pile down on the empty bed. The boy above him looked to be about 16, and larger, with broad shoulders and an acne-filled face. The other boys on the other bunk looked up from their reading materials. The boy on the top bunk opposite looked younger, about 12 or 13, and the boy on the bottom bunk looked to be about 17, but was thin and so tall his feet dangled off the end of the bunk.

"Hi," Randy said when the door closed.

"Hey."

"What's your name?" the younger boy on the top bunk asked.

"Randy."

"Cool," the tall boy said as he looked back down at his magazine.

"Names?" Randy said as he spread out his blanket and put the clothes under the bed.

"I'm Josh," the younger boy said.

"Chris," the tall boy said.

Randy smiled at them and glanced upwards.

"Be nice, Jake, he's new," Chris said.

"I'm Jake. You better not fuckin' snore."

"I don't think I do, man."

"Good, cause if you do I'll fuckin' beat your face in. I like a quiet cell, we keep to ourselves and we don't like fuckin' talkin so shut up."

Randy laid down on the mattress and stared up at the metal frame of the bunk above him. The short hours to lights out passed quickly, and the lights blinked three times before being reduced to a low level to signal it was time to go to sleep. Randy noticed on his first night that the prison was always filled with an echoing cacophony of disembodied sounds and shouting. The steel and concrete muffled most of it, but that just turned the sounds into a din of white noise. Randy has spent enough time in confinement that he was even learning to sleep with the constant noise of doors opening and closing with loud bangs as they slid. The constant low light that permeated and the constant sound of people walking around or hanging out in their cells. Although everyone was supposed to be sleeping, the quiet whispers and talking between cells only added to the background of white noise.

Randy slept in sessions but also spent time staring at the metal above him. This would be his view for the next twelve years. Randy somehow still couldn't get his mind around it. He fell asleep again and in his groggy state he heard Kelly's voice.

"Come play! I'm hungry!"

Randy tossed a bit and mumbled in his sleep. He could see her running around in the yard and playing in the summer sun. His Mom was smiling and watching. It felt so real. He joined playing with her. He smiled at his sister. A wave of happiness passed over his body.

Randy was jolted awake when a loud alarm sounded. The other boys stirred and looked up.

"Someone must have got in a fight," Chris said.

Randy stood up and walked over to the door. Out of the small window he saw a team of people in T-shirts, vests, and squeaking sneakers run by the door to stop the disturbance. The team seemed to appear out of nowhere. Randy watched as someone was hauled out of the cell, to the end of the row and down the stairs. Randy noticed other eyes and parts of faces gawking at the scene. Just as quickly as the hubbub began, it ended. The alarm ceased, the lights were turned down low and the white din of background noise began again.

Chapter 12

The lights jolted Randy awake again the next morning.

Randy covered his eyes with his hands. He sat up on his elbows and looked around the cell. Jake jumped down first, scratched himself over his underwear, and walked over to the toilet in the corner and started to urinate into the metal bowl. Randy stood up next. Jake put his hand against the wall until the stream had ended. He pulled at his shorts when he turned around.

"Get out of the way, kid." Jake climbed back up into his bunk. Randy turned to let him pass before going to the toilet himself. Randy changed underwear and put on his other set of grey pants and shirt. He sat on the edge of the bed.

"Randy, go back to sleep," Chris said, putting his arms over his eyes.

"Why?"

"Breakfast isn't for another hour. Our floor is 2nd breakfast shift."

Randy swung his legs back into his bunk and looked up at the metal frame. He touched the edges and noticed that they had all been painted over and filed down to be smooth against his finger.

Randy didn't really go back to sleep so much as he closed his eyes and dozed quietly. He heard the doors on their floor unlock and some of the guards go by opening the doors.

"Breakfast, time to get up."

Randy swung his legs over the side of the bed and passed through the open door. Other boys from his block seemed to be walking downstairs, so he followed the crowd towards the cafeteria. Randy stood in line with the other boys and picked up a battered green tray. He collected a foam plate and the thin, plastic cutlery and started through the line. He scooped out eggs, oatmeal, and even a couple strips of bacon. He sat down on the plastic bench at a round table by himself to eat the simple, institutional food.

Randy didn't eat alone for long before three boys sat down at the round table. Randy didn't speak to them, but just kept on eating.

"You're new here?" one of them asked.

"Yes, yeah, I just got here," Randy replied.

"Cool."

Randy kept eating and scraped his plate clean. The cafeteria was quiet.

The rustling of fabric and rubber shoes dominated the space. Quiet conversation could be heard in the background. Randy stood up and returned his tray. A large garbage can stood nearby for the remainder of the dishes. Randy looked around the room and noticed a group of boys heading out another doorway away from the cellblock. Randy crossed the room and followed them. They passed two prison workers before being let out in the yard.

Randy looked around the yard. He took a hesitant step out onto the dirt as he studied his surroundings. He rubbed his arms after he felt the chilly air against his skin. Randy started to walk the perimeter of the yard. He saw four boys standing around smoke a cigarette. Randy approached them.

"Can I have a drag?" Randy asked.

A brown-skinned boy wordlessly passed him the cigarette. He took a long inhale before passing it to the boy nearest him.

"Thanks."

"No problem."

Randy kept up his pace after that and just kept walking around the perimeter of the yard. The boys just seemed to mill about. Randy noticed that the door was left open and the boys seemed to be able to come and go. Randy looked around the yard before deciding he was cold, and he started to go inside and back to his cell. Randy walked into the cellblock and made his way up the metal stairs until he found his place again. The other three were gone. Randy decided to lay down. He started to doze off before he heard a knocking at the door.

"Carruth, you got to see your counselor."

"Huh?" Randy replied.

The tall black woman waved her blue-gloved hand at him. "Just come with me." Randy looked around before he stood up and followed the woman.

"I have a counselor?" Randy asked.

"Everyone does, honey. She'll tell you when you need to come next, but you're new here." Randy followed her to a group of rooms. She showed him into one of the rooms. Randy saw the woman sitting on a normal-looking office chair in normal clothing, not the ironed uniforms that everyone else wore. He immediately noticed her beautiful appearance. Her long red hair rested neatly at her breastbone. She was beautiful with delicate and kind features.

"Hi Randall, I'm Allison."

"You're very pretty," Randy said.

Allison smiled. "People like to tell me that."

Randy smiled and looked at the floor.

"Happy Birthday," Allison said with a smile.

"What?"

"Today's your birthday, don't you remember?"

Randy searched his brain for a moment. "I lose day sometimes, that's cool, that makes me 16 now."

"I read over your file, Randall. Can I call you Randy?"

"Yeah, no one ever calls me Randall."

"Okay, I don't think you need to stay here forever," she said, leaning towards him.

"I got twelve years." Randy shifted on the plastic chair again.

"That's what it says here. But for juveniles, there's a couple things you can do to complete your sentence early and continue your life outside the system," she said with a smile.

"What's that?"

Allison picked up a brochure and handed it to Randy. He took it from her and looked at the tri-fold piece of paper. It had pictures of smiling young men in uniforms like him looking at the camera.

"There's six steps. Everyone is assessed and put into a stage when they arrive. That's what we're going to work on today. We also might look at medication with the physician. What do you think about that?"

"Don't I start at one?"

"Do you think you need to start at the first step?"

"I don't know." Randy rubbed his flat chest a bit.

"Let's work on this questionnaire and we'll decide. I think you'll like some of the privileges in step 2 and 3."

"Okay, so what can I do at step 2?"

"You can have more things in your cell. You can have a notebook and you can order from the commissary."

"I'd like that," Randy said, rubbing his thighs.

Allison started going through a survey and evaluating Randy. Randy had to think hard about the questions but answered all of them. Some of them were uncomfortable. Questions like "Have you ever felt sad?" or "Have you ever felt depressed?" bothered Randy.

"Have you felt violent?"

"No."

Allison looked up at him. "Really?"

"I'm not violent."

Allison looked down and kept going through the questions. "Do you feel suicidal?"

"No, I mean, maybe during the trial; I don't know."

"I need a clear answer, Randy. If you feel like you're going to hurt yourself then I have to let some people know some things so that we can make sure you stay safe."

"No, I'm not trying to hurt myself. I'm actually surviving. Yeah."

"Okay then, alright. Let's put you on step 2 this week and see how you do and then if everything goes alright, we'll see about upgrading you up to level 3."

"What does that mean?"

"Rec room privileges, you can go to school, but you're not eligible for jobs yet, you can order from the commissary and yard privileges, so you won't have to stay in the building at all times, and you can come and go from your cell during the day like the rest of the boys. Boys on step 1 don't get those things."

"Okay, um, okay," Randy replied. His eyes blinked as he tried to take in all the information and remember what she was saying. Why had it become so hard to remember things?

Allison stood up. "Do you hug?"

Randy looked up as he stood up from the plastic chair. It squeaked when he moved. "Uh, I guess?" Allison held her arms out. Randy hesitantly moved into her embrace. His hands couldn't quite touch her back. The embrace felt strange, but it was brief and they pulled away. Allison opened the door and let Randy out into the hallway and handed Randy's file to the guard. Allison spoke to the guard.

"So he's going to start out on Step 2, so he can join the others, he just can't do any jobs yet. He can go into the yard and the rec room and he can go to school. He also doesn't need escort everywhere he goes, so he can come and go."

The guard nodded and took the file. Randy was pointed where to go and he returned to his cell. When he returned there he found a pile of mail sitting on his mattress. There were several letters from his Mom and his Grandma. Randy started to open them. As he was reading, a guard walked by the open door.

"Do you want to go the rec room? Commissary order forms are there for you."

Randy nodded.

"Go ahead then." She held a gloved hand out. Randy picked up his mail and made his way to the rec room. It was mostly empty and a TV, covered in a metal cage, hung from the ceiling. Randy sat down in a blue overstuffed chair started to look over his mail. Randy read over all the letters and learned about how much Eileen was missing him and how sorry she was about what had happened. Randy was confused by what he was reading but he did find out she had put $200 for the commissary. He plucked up one of the commissary forms and started to see what he could afford to get. He put check marks by a coat, notebooks, pens, and some food items. Randy was already tired of the terrible food and was looking forward to something normal to eat. He looked for a place to turn it in. He put his name and his prisoner number at the top and he saw a small window where a sign had been posted: please leave commissary forms here. He put his form under the window and finished reading over his mail. Randy relaxed into the overstuffed chair. His mind was blank until thought started to bubble up. This was his life now. Commissary forms, counselors, privileges, and square cut clothes with officers around him all the time. That Jake guy was annoying. Randy resolved to try to steer clear of him. Josh and Chris seemed cool. Randy piled the letters neatly on his lap. David was dead and Randy had killed him. Somehow that hadn't sunk into his brain until this moment. Randy thought about those movies where someone asked if they knew what it was like to kill a man. Randy didn't have any special feeling like those movies. His chest felt numb. David was dead and Randy had killed him. Randy could barely put the details of the crime together in his mind. Where had that pan come from? Randy remembered bacon. The space in his brain where Kelly should be was somehow grey. He couldn't remember what she looked liked when it happened. Somehow he preferred it that way. Randy would remember her in life. Eileen had written about the funeral service, closed casket, for Kelly and where she was buried. Randy wanted to go see the grave site and promised himself he would the moment he was released. That still seemed a long way away. Randy hoped that his counselor would come up with something that would get him out sooner. He wasn't a threat, was he?

Chapter 13

Randy's eyes blinked open again with the lights slowly turning on around the pod. Randy jumped up and made his way to the toilet before Jake had time to stir. He sat down and put his head in his hand. He flushed the toilet and started to sponge bathe himself in the sink. Randy was halfway done when Chris stirred.

"Are you ready for your first day of school?" Chris asked.

"I guess. It'll be good to get back into school."

"I wouldn't call this school," Josh said through a tonsil-revealing yawn. "You sit around a lot, they try to teach stuff, but then you end up just doing worksheets. It sucks. I'm dropping out."

"How old are you man?"

"I'm 16," Randy replied.

"Okay, you can drop out if you want. Josh can't until next year."

"I'll try it out. It's something to do."

Josh looked at Chris for a second and bit his chapped lip, "It's really boring."

Randy shrugged his shoulders, "I'll try it out. If its boring then I'll drop out or maybe just sit around and draw."

Josh stood up and walked over to the metal toilet in the corner. The boys took turns at the toilet. Jake leaned against the door until it opened and the boys trooped down for breakfast. The breakfast area looked like a school cafeteria. The tables and chairs were all one metal piece. The tables were round and small round stools stood out from them. Randy found his own spot. Jake went to sit with some other boys but Chris and Josh sat with him.

"You can have as milk as you want," Josh said gulping down milk from his plastic cup. Randy nodded at him as he stood up to get another glass of milk from the large, brown dispenser that sat on a table against the wall. Chris chuckled, "That kid loves milk."

The boys finished breakfast and while Chris went back to the cell and Jake disappeared, Josh and Randy made their way towards the class rooms. The large classroom looked like any other American classroom except that everyone wore the same clothes in various styles. Some guys just wore a white T-shirt. Others had their uniform short open and still others had them wrapped around their waists. Randy just wore his white and grey clothes, neatly buttoned.

"Hey new boy!" Another student in the back shouted at him.

Randy pursued his lips and sat down at an open desk. Josh sat in the back corner and leaned against the wall. Randy sat farther up front. The teacher didn't wait for the room to settle down before handing out some reading assignments. There were no staples in the pieces of paper, they were simply folded at the top.

"Morning, it looks like we have some new faces. I'm Mr. Kimble. This class is for those who are studying 10th grade material, we'll be doing some reading and math today."

The teacher, a tall man with a grey goatee, passed out different packages of reading and math. Randy looked over the material. It didn't seem the same as what he had been studying in school before the trial. The trial had become one of those life events that becomes a hard line in the brain. There was life before the trial and there was life after the trial. Randy didn't even think about David, at least not often.

The class was as boring as Josh promised. The pattern was the same, read the instructions, complete everything in the paper and then turn it back in. Mr. Kimble didn't really take time to explain much. Randy noticed his casual attitude towards the class. There were people who weren't really paying attention at all. Randy easily completed the material. It didn't seem like 10th grade material. However, he noticed others were struggling. He looked around the room and noticed that some of the others weren't doing anything at all. Randy noticed that throughout the day, different guys left at different times. The room was a cacophony of people moving chairs, talking, and others coming and going.

Mr. Kimble stood at the front and waited for their latest assignments to be turned in.

"Come on, lets get this wrapped up. I can only care as much as you care about learning what you need to learn," his arms were crossed across his body. The boredom seeped out of his pores.

"How is anyone supposed to learn anything?" Randy thought to himself. The clock, secured behind some bent pieces of metal, showed that it was nearly lunch time. At noon, the class shuffled to the lunch room. Randy collected his juice, bologna sandwich, and stale crackers. The meal did not taste very good and Randy tried to force it down as fast as he dared. The group returned to the classroom and they repeated the morning routine again. More worksheets were handed out and turned in as the rhythm of the people coming and going continued. At 3:00, a bell rang and everyone stood up and started to leave. Randy looked around the classroom as everyone stood up and left the room. Randy made his way back into his cell and sat on the edge of the bed. Josh wandered in a few moments later.

"What did I tell you about that place? You dropping out?"

"I don't know. It sure is tempting, it was pretty boring. I don't want to think about doing that every day."

"Chris said it, you should just drop out. You're not learning anything anyway," Josh replied as he walked out of the cell and down the hall. Randy looked out to see where everyone was going. He decided to follow the crowd of guys.

Randy saw a small sign that read, "Rec Room." There was a group going, so he joined them and walked towards it. The room was painted white and the air had a stale scent of maleness that seemed to sit right over the slight smell of chemicals. Everyone spread out towards tables and chairs and busied themselves with games or watching TV. Randy draped himself over a chair until a young man with a brown face tapped him on the arm.

"Wanna play?" He had a deck of cards, and there were two other guys sitting at a table.

"I don't really play cards."

"We'll teach you, c'mere."

Randy unfolded himself from his chair and sat down at the table. The brown-faced boy started by dealing the cards to the players. The other two were noticeably younger.

"You're Randy, right?"

"Uh, yeah."

"You don't recognize me?"

"No, should I?"

"I'm in your class."

"Oh, sorry, what's your name man?"

"Alejandro, but everyone calls me Alex." Randy noticed how he aspirated his name with an accent. Alex explained the rules of the game and they played awhile. Randy picked the game up easily.

"What about you guys?"

"I'm Matt," one of the others said, looking seriously at his cards.

"Juan, but everyone calls me John," said the last one.

"Okay."

They boys kept playing cards and casually looking at the TV from time to time.

Matt stood up after they finished a hand of the game. "Is it dinner yet?"

Alex shuffled the cars with one hand, "I don't know man."

Matt walked his long, lanky legs around the table and poked his head out of the door to ask about food. He leaned back in and waved at the table, "Dinner!"

Randy stood up and followed his new friends out of the recreation room and towards the long tables of the dining hall. He looked around for Chris and Josh but didn't see them. He stood in line and got his food, served in a styrofoam tray. Randy sat at the table. Alex and Matt scooted in around him. Alex tugged at his clothes as he sat down.

"This shit again," Alex remarked.

"Same shit all the time," Matt added.

"Yeah, the good is pretty bad," Randy said taking a bite out of the hamburger and crinkle fries. Juan sat down and looked around.

"What you guys doing after food?" Juan asked.

"Nothing, probably TV," Matt said taking a big bite of the burger.

"You?" Juan said nodded at Randy.

"I think I'm going to check out the library."

"Ah, you on that reading shit. I get you, I get you," Juan nodded his head.

Randy ate his food and listened to the other guys. When they finished eating they placed their styrofoam boxes into large trash cans and filtered back towards the Rec Room. Randy walked back to his cell to get is drawing pad and made his way to the library to see about some books. TV never interested him much in the first place.

The smell of the library was stale and filled with old books. Randy started walking among the stacks looking at the various books on display. He gravitated over towards the fiction section and started to pick out some books. He piled 3 books on his arm and started to look for a desk to check them out. He saw a young man in a neatly pressed shirt and pants passing by and stopped him.

"Where do I check out these books?"

"You must be new! Follow me."

Randy followed him to a desk. He stood behind it and opened the books.

"What's your number?"

"23571."

"Here you go."

Randy took his books and walked out of the library and walked back towards the rec room. Randy sat down in one of the over stuffed chairs and opened his selections. He started to read and draw in his notebook. The lights flickered and Randy looked up at the ceiling.

"Bedtime, boys," a short white woman said as she opened the door.

All the boys stood up and started filing out and back to their cells. Randy followed suit and soon crawled into his bunk. He pulled out his notebook and started to write and doodle with the rubber-plastic pen. He sketched a simple outline of his teacher's face. Once he completed his sketch, he turned to the back of the book. The back pages revealed a half-finished but elaborate drawing of his therapist. Randy used the side of his pen to fill in her hair. Her eyes were still piercing, though they stood alone without the rest of her face finished to the same level of detail.

"Hey, uh, Randy." Jake leaned over the edge.

"Yeah?"

"You read right?"

"Yeah."

Jake sighed and let his meaty arm down over Randy's head.

"I got a letter."

"Yeah?"

"Can you tell me what it says?"

"I can read it out for you," Randy said laying his drawing aside for a moment.

"Cool."

Randy took the letter from his hand and started to read it out for him. Randy's voice was smooth as he read out what Jake's mother had wrote to him from rehab for her own drug addiction. Randy's brow furrowed as he finished the letter.

"That bitch, can't get clean or sober," Jake remarked, "Just like always."

Randy handed the letter back to him, "I get it. My Mom drank too."

"Yeah, it fucking sucks."

Jake disappeared back into his bunk and the lights dimmed for the night.

Randy started to yawn and tucked his notebook under his bedroll before going to sleep.

Chapter 14

Allison sat on her chair and looked at Randy for a moment, "I think you're ready for group therapy. I think it could be healing for you and it would help you open up to talk about things and what happened."

Randy shuffled his feet. "I guess. What's it like?"

Allison pursed her lips. "Everyone sits in a circle, there's a counselor there and he usually starts with some questions to get everyone to open and talk about their experiences."

"I don't really want to talk in front of other people," Randy said rubbing his arm across his body.

"It might really help," Allison noted with pressure in her tone.

"I don't want guys to know that I, you know."

"How can you heal and get out of here if you don't talk about it?"

"Why do I want to do that?"

"Because your life isn't over Randy," Allison replied turning her head and making a note."

Randy fell silent. "I don't know."

"It's time to end for today. I'm assigning you to a group therapy session. It starts this afternoon, at 2:00 P.M. I'll add it to your schedule but it might not make it to the team so do your best to go on your own. It is in room 223. Now hug me so you can go."

Randy stood up and gave her a hug across her shoulders and left her office. He returned to the drag classroom and the endless worksheets that comprised the education the state of Missouri required. A few minutes before 2:00 P.M. Randy stood up and made his way to the door.

"Where are you going?" Mr. Kimble asked, the sarcasm dripped off his words.

"I have group therapy now, she added it to my schedule," Randy's words were weak.

"Which room?"

"223."

"Fine." Mr. Kimble turned back to the rest of the class. Randy started walking. He walked up the stairs and found room 223. Randy opened the door and walked inside. The room, like almost all rooms, was devoid of most decor. The clock was covered in wire and the plastic chairs stood in a row. Randy saw a man standing with a clipboard of paper. Other boys started to walk in. Randy retreated to lean against a wall until things started.

"Everyone put the chairs in a circle. The last group did some activity so they moved the chairs," he started. "For the new kids who have just arrived, my name is Mateo and I'll be your group leader. This is an open space to talk about your problems, fears, desires, and I hope to help each other through this process so you can go back out and be a part of society."

The group leader was a large, gruff-sounding hispanic man that looked intimidating but seemed friendly enough to put Randy at ease. Randy sat down in one of the plastic chairs in the circle. Randy looked around at the group of teens. A few had bad tattoos, most had something pierced, at least an ear and others more. Randy listened as they talked about their problems. He felt like his problems were similar, but he didn't have nearly the drinking or drug problems that many of them expressed. Somehow he didn't feel like he belonged.

There was the boy who was still having withdrawals from heroin. His arms were covered in dots of red and other scratches that marred their smooth milky-white complexion. He shifted in his seat and kept trying to cover his arms as he talked about his usage. The instructor always used words like, "your use of drugs" or "your addiction." Randy couldn't decide if they were just bad people or bad people because they did drugs or if drugs were bad and robbed people of their lives. When it came time for Randy to talk about why he was there and his problems, he had a hard time expressing himself.

"How about you Randy, what happened that put you here?" Mateo started.

"Uh, well, not anything that we're talking about."

"That's okay, this is an open place."

"I, uh, I got convicted of manslaughter."

"Just a random somebody on the street?" the boy with the ruined arms said.

"Uh, no, my, uh, my mom's husband."

"Do you want to tell us about it?" Mateo prompted.

"No, not really, it's private."

"You can tell us, it's okay," Mateo assured him.

"I can't, I just..." His voice trailed off.

"Leave him alone, if he don't wanna tell, don't make him, shit, it sounds serious. He fucking wasted someone," another boy said.

"Okay." Mateo gave up on the line of questioning.

Randy stared at the floor and didn't look around or make eye contact with anyone. When the group was over, he began his shuffle back to his cell. When he arrived, the cell was empty save for Chris, who was lounging on his bunk.

"Did you fill out your commissary form?" Chris asked.

"No, I didn't even see them. I don't have any money anyway."

"Are you sure?"

"Yeah, I will probably have to write my mom or my grandma, but I haven't heard from them in a while."

"Your mail is probably behind you if she wrote you at your last facility."

"Okay.

"Do you need anything in the meantime?"

"I don't think so."

"I have an extra cup of noodles if you get hungry later."

"Thanks."

Randy flopped down on the bunk and just stared up at the metal frame for the remainder of the evening. The officers came to get them for the evening meal, and Randy also was able to retrieve a hefty pile of mail that had finally caught up to him. Randy ate quietly at a table with other inmates he didn't know. A few minutes later, the boy with the pock marked arms from his group therapy sat down next to him. Randy looked at him with some surprise.

"Hey."

"Hi," Randy said, taking a bite of the food.

"Not that great, right?"

"It's okay."

"Don't worry, you'll get sick of it pretty fast, but you're new."

Randy nodded and kept shoveling the meager food into his mouth. The boy did the same.

"I'm Dustin Bigelow, by the way," he held out his hand for Randy to shake.

"Randy, Randy Carruth."

"So why didn't you want to talk about it?"

"It's really weird. I don't want people to get the wrong idea about me."

"We're in prison, dude."

"I guess I'm still trying to be normal."

"You'll learn man, you'll learn."

The boys ate in silence and Randy took in the scene. It would almost looked like a regular high school lunch room, except for the fact that everyone was dressed in exactly the same green and white uniform and there were no girls. There were still cliques and certain people sitting together. The boys were given a few minutes to eat before they were shuffled off to their cells or other assignments.

Randy sat on the edge of his bunk and read through his mail, and found a collection of letters from his mom and his grandma. Randy used a few pieces of paper from his notebook and replied to them with his address and information on putting money on his "books." Randy read through the letters, which included lots of questions about him but little detail about what was going on at home. Grandma included some news and said that they buried Kelly at a cemetery near her house. Randy saved that letter under his bed. He folded it neatly in his notebook. He put the rest of the letters in a waste basket down in the common area. Just before the lights blinked out, Randy re-read the letter describing Kelly's funeral.

"We had to keep the casket closed. But they wrapped her head in gauze. We dressed her in a cute dress. There were lots of flowers." Randy thought about sketching some flowers. The lights blinked out and Randy tucked the letter away again and tried to get some sleep.

Randy was the first of the boys up the next morning. He looked around for movement before slipping over to the toilet. Randy started to empty his bladder when he felt a hand against his shoulder.

"Get out of the way faggot, a man's gotta piss."

Jake gave him a shove. Randy bumped his head on the wall as his foot slipped. It hurt, but he worked to not let it show. Randy stood up and waited for Jake to finish up and then took his turn followed by washing his face and hands in the small sink nearby.

Randy thought about how he should stand up to Jake. He had as much right to piss too. Randy was getting tired of Jake and his miserable attitude. Just like those kids in the hall. Randy finished washing his hands and sat down on his bunk to wait for breakfast. Jake climbed back up on his bunk. He let his foot almost kick Randy in the face. Randy leaned back. Jake chuckled at his movement.

"Don't be such a dickwad, dickwad."

Chapter 15

Randy's eyes blinked open again. He looked at the familiar metal springs from the bunk above. He rolled over and felt his notebooks and safety pens under his head. He moved them down towards his chest. His eyes adjusted to the low light and he stared up again, waiting for the lights to turn on signaling another day had begun.

Chris turned over and jumped down off the bed. Jake didn't stir. Chris made for the toilet. Randy followed him. They both gathered their shower supplies. Josh finally rolled over.

"You guys going to shower?" Josh asked.

"Yeah, I'd like to get clean," Chris replied.

Josh reached under his bed to find his soap and towel. Jake woke up and swung his legs off his bunk and jumped down.

"You faggots are up early."

"Shower man," Chris replied.

Jake grunted and used the toilet. Chris, Josh and Randy started towards the showers. Randy followed them towards the shower area. Randy looked over his shoulder and saw Jake walking after them

The long room was filled with booths, divided with cinder block walls with shower heads sticking out of the dividers. There were no curtains to be found. Each boy found an open booth and turned on the water. Steam filled the space and the cold air began to warm.

"You guys better wash good, I don't want to smell your asses," Jake shouted over the wall.

Chris chuckled, "You're the one who needs to wash after playing basketball."

"Fuck off," Jake shot back.

Randy focused on his own mission to clean. The air was warmer now but you could smell the faint stench of teenage males and mildew in the concentrated space. The showers fell quiet after a few minutes. Randy could detect heavy breathing from Josh's shower next to his. Randy focused on himself. He shut off the water and dried himself off. Chris leaned up against the end of his stall.

"Ready?"

"Yeah." Randy pulled on his clothes and followed the boys back to their cell. They waited for breakfast and ate quickly. Chris and Josh made their way out to the yard and Randy followed. The temperature was moderate but a slight breeze brought a chill across his arm. Randy looked for one of the basketballs. When he found the ball he kicked it up to his hand. The sides were almost smooth from use and any identifying marks had been practically worn away. Randy dribbled the ball and shot towards the basket. The ball bounced off the side and fell back down to earth. Randy kept shooting as he spied Jake and some other boys coming over. Randy let another shot fly towards the basket.

"Clear out Carruth, we're going to play some ball."

"I was already here shooting."

Jake walked towards him and towered over his head. "I said get out."

Randy didn't back down, "I can play against you."

Jake chuckled, "Fine, 1 on 4,"

Randy shrugged, "Not really fair."

Jake pointed at some other kids, "Anyone want to be on this dickwad's team?"

Two boys stood up and Chris started to walk over.

"There, 4 on 4, lets move."

Randy tipped the ball towards Jake. The players moved around the court and Randy made his first basket. Jake attempted to trip Randy but Randy would always step over his outstretched foot. Randy made another basket. Jake started to get red and started to run after Randy wherever he went. Randy was breathing heavy but Jake was nearly out of breath trying to keep up with Randy's every move. Although exhausted, Jake started to make consistent baskets and once he was in control of the ball, Jake favored his team mates and they began to score. Randy finally slowed to a stop and sat down.

"I'm done."

"You're fast little fucker Carruth."

"Yeah, you still won."

"Just goes to show who the real man in our cell is."

Chris sat down next to Randy, "Why'd you give up?"

"I'm tired and I got school. He's good."

"Gotcha. Yeah, no one's beat him while I've been here."

Chris stood up and started walking away from him. Randy looked around before standing up and starting towards class. Randy looked at the ground and resolved that he'd just be dropping out. Another day of those worksheets ahead felt crushing. He couldn't even really draw. Randy made his way to class and sat at his table, head on his hand just hoping the time would pass quickly. Randy relished the freedom of lunch and was happy at the end of the day when he could leave. He stopped at Mr. Kimble's desk on his way out.

"Uh...Carruth?" Mr. Kimble asked.

"Yeah, I don't think this is for me, I heard you could drop out if you're 16."

Mr. Kimble sighed, "That's right, you have to talk to the administrator down the hall."

"Cool. Thanks." Randy started to walk out of the classroom.

"At least get a damn GED," Mr. Kimble said leaning against his desk.

"I'll look into it." Randy said walking out of the classroom.

Randy made his way to his cell to see if it was empty. Randy felt like having some alone time. Randy stepped into the cell and saw that no one was around. He looked at his bunk and a box was neatly set on it. He opened the top of it and started to unpack the privileged items inside. The stuff stayed in the box but he smelt the brand-name soap. Randy felt excited to be able to throw away the generic, harsh soap he had used that morning. He carefully placed the box under his bed after organizing the goods.

Randy skipped dinner and opted to eat from his new box of snacks. He munched on his snacks when Jake arrived and clambered up on his bunk. Randy didn't look at Jake as he climbed up onto the bunk. Randy drew in his journal and stayed in his bed until near bed time when Chris and Josh walked back in and got ready for bed.

"Night," Chris said as he rolled into bed.

"Yeah," Josh said climbing above him. Randy put his drawing items away as soon as the lights blinked out. Randy tossed and turned looking for his usually inadequate amount of sleep. Randy lulled himself to sleep in between hearing the noises from other guys in cells or cell doors opening and closing through the night. He was dozing when Chris interrupted his sleep.

"Hey man, you up?" Chris said through the darkness.

Randy turned towards the open space between the bunks.

"Yeah?"

"Your commissary come in yet?"

"Yeah, it did."

"Good, that makes things easier."

"Yeah, it does, the food gets real boring."

"For sure."

Silence settled again.

"I heard you killed a man." Chris broke the silence.

"You heard right," Randy said.

"Why'd you do it?"

"I don't really talk about it."

"You should."

"I'm not ready yet."

"There are some nasty rumors running around man, if you started

61

talking about it you could stop that."

"Yeah, probably."

"What are you guys talking about?" Josh cut in. His bed frame squeaked as he shifted his small weight around on it.

"I'm learning about our cell mate," Chris said. "Trying to figure out what makes our guy tick."

"What are you guys in for?" Randy asked.

"I'm here for selling drugs, mostly at school," Josh said.

"I got in a fight, assault with a deadly weapon," Chris said.

"What happened?" Joshed asked.

"I'll tell you if you tell me first."

Randy slumped back onto the bed.

"I don't matter anyway. It's okay," Randy said.

"Okay man, I'm just saying, it'll be easier if you start talking about it."

Randy stretched out his arms. "It's pretty fucked."

"There's plenty of people who have done fucked things around here. It's prison, dude."

"Shut up, you faggots," Jake interjected. "Quit fucking talking. Tryin' to sleep."

Randy inhaled again and stayed quiet. The lights blinked on and Randy turned over to avoid the light to wait for breakfast.

Chapter 16

Randy waited outside his therapists office waiting to go in. Randy thought about all her questions. He wondered why she asked so many questions and why therapy had to be so invasive into his life. Randy looked around at other boys coming and going. Randy still was not used to having no privacy and no real time without other people around. The door on the office opened and another boy walked out. Randy walked in right after him, closing the door behind him. He sat down in the plastic chair again. Allison smiled at him.

"Hi Randy, how are you today?"

"I'm good. I like your hair."

Allison reached up and touched the bun. "It's just a simple bun."

"My mom used to keep her hair like that."

"Oh. This is an old favorite of mine. It was good for early morning shoots," she said, folding her hands in her lap again.

"Did you take pictures?" Randy shifted his body in the chair.

"No." She shook her head. "I was a model."

"That's why you're so pretty."

Allison smiled. "Maybe. I like it here, though." Randy looked down at the floor.

"So Randy, I want to talk about why you're here today. We don't talk about that much."

"Yeah, there's nothing to say. I got sent her after I got convicted."

"We've talked a lot but you still won't tell me about why you were convicted. Why is that?"

"I don't want to." Randy looked down at the pant legs of his green uniform.

"You talked about it at court."

"Don't they record that? You could read it or watch it I guess."

"I have."

"Then why are you asking?"

"I would like you to tell me, in your own way, what happened. But you need to talk about it."

Randy shifted in his seat. "What do you want me to say?"

"I don't want you to say anything. But I'd like you to tell me what happened on that day that put you here."

Randy shifted his seat again. "Okay."

"Why don't you start with what you were doing that day?"

"I was coming home from MMA practice."

"Okay, then what happened?"

"I got home."

"Okay." She pressed forward, unfolding her hands and brushing back her hair.

"Was it a good practice?"

"Yeah."

"What did you see when you got home?"

"I heard someone screaming."

"Who was screaming?"

Randy held his head in his hands. The veins in his arms bulged out and his arms vibrated. He looked back up at her with bloodshot eyes and a wet face.

"Why are you doing this to me?"

"What am I doing?"

"Asking questions! Doesn't anyone get it?" Randy's face turned red and he looked around the austere room. The plastic chair irritated his butt suddenly and he felt hot.

"What do you want me to get?" She was calm with her response and refolded her hands.

"I didn't want to kill him, it just happened. I don't even know how I got the pan. I—I just saw Kelly lying there and her face looked blue, I didn't even see if she was breathing. I was so calm. I just beat—I just...I don't know."

"You beat, what did you beat?"

"His head in."

"With the pan?"

"Yes ma'am."

"What did you do?"

"I—I beat his head in with a cast iron pan." Randy's words were slow and measured.

"How does that make you feel inside?"

"I'm sick."

The therapist leaned forward and her hair draped in front of her face. Randy could see the delicate lines on her face. She smiled. They were finally breaking through.

"Why do you feel sick?"

"I killed a man. I really killed a man."

"You were trying to save your sister."

"I'm 16 fucking years old! I'm in prison because I fucking killed somebody!" Tears streamed down Randy's face; his skin was red and stretched across the bones of his face. His teeth were showing and his arms were apart, opening his chest. He seemed desperate, vulnerable, and almost out of control. Randy's chest tightened as wave after wave of emotion came flooding back into his mind. The moment he had shoved deep in his brain was back. He inhaled short, shallow breaths. His lungs couldn't keep up and his heart raced as the tears flowed.

"Was he a bad man?" Allison asked.

"No---I mean---yes---he was---he was hurting her," Randy choked on his words.

"How did he hurt her?"

"He was stuffing her with mayonnaise. It was her favorite."

"Was that all?"

Randy shook his head and then put his hands behind his head, "He was doing stuff to her at night and I didn't know what to do. I couldn't save her."

"Alright, Let's calm down with some deep breathing. The hour is almost up, so let's just breathe for a moment," she said. She inhaled and motioned that Randy should do the same. The extra air helped Randy calm down. Randy felt reassured. His breathing slowed and his heart beat normally again. When he was calm, Allison leaned forward towards him.

"How is school?"

"A joke."

"That is what I've heard. It's sad that they don't take that more seriously. Do you read a lot?"

"I try to, whatever I can find."

"Why don't you find something to read and we'll talk about it next time?"

"Okay."

"I've recommended you for a job in the library. You just need to speak to Annie."

Randy perked up. "That would be cool, what would I do? Just stock books?"

"I think so. Other things she needs done. It's a good way to stay out of your room for a while."

"Okay." Randy stood up.

"Al lright, give me a hug and you can go."

Randy stood up on unsteady legs and reached out his thin white arms for her embrace. She hugged him quickly and opened the door. Randy walked out into the plastic-walled hallway.

"You can go back to your cell or the rec room." The black female guard smiled at him. Randy nodded his head and started walking.

Chapter 17

Randy walked out of the eating hall and made his way to the school administrator's office. He passed his classroom where Mr. Kimble was already teaching. They made eye contact for a moment. Randy broke the gaze but Mr. Kimble let his linger on Randy as he passed by the door of his classroom on his way to drop out of school. Randy kept walking down the hall until he arrived at the administrator's office. He opened the door and walked inside. He stood at the desk. The smell of office supplies struck his nose. It was an ordinary smell that wouldn't normally be something he would regard but somehow, in this space, for this moment, it didn't smell like prison. It smelt normal.

"Hi, I'm here to see someone about dropping out of school."

The lady at the desk had grey hair that fell around her shoulders. She had stuffed her body into the rolling chair from which she rolled around the small area and picked out some paperwork.

"Name?" she asked, her voice flat.

"Randy Carruth."

"Number?"

Randy gave her his number and she noted it down.

"Fill this out and you can sit over there. If you need help filling it out I can help you. I'll call your name."

Randy shook his head and took the clipboard with him to the plastic chairs. He filled out the form and held on to it. She looked over at him and waved him over.

"I'll call your name when he's ready to see you."

Randy returned to his seat. He waited and watched the clock. Over an hour passed until she called his name.

"Carruth? Carruth?"

Randy stood up and raised his hand. "Right here." He started to walk towards the desk. She pointed towards and office door. Randy walked into the office and took in the space. The office was small with a older metal desk, a worn office chair, and some knick-knacks near the front. On top of the desk stood a computer with a thick, flat screen monitor. Randy sat down in the familiar all-plastic chair. Randy looked at the tall man sitting before him. He looked adult but not old to Randy. The man sported a modest goatee. He didn't look at Randy at first, but the file in front of him.

"You're here to sign out of classes?"

"That's right," Randy replied.

"Any particular reason why our education isn't working for you?"

"It's boring and a waste of time."

"Education will be important after you leave the correctional system, it looks like here that you will be leaving at some point."

"I understand, I just don't think that it's for me."

The man looked over his file. "Alright then," he picked up a pen and signed the bottom of several forms. "Take this out to the desk and you can sign out of classes," he handed the file to Randy and pointed towards the door. He began looking at his computer screen as if Randy wasn't in the room. Randy opened the door and walked over to the desk.

"He said I need to sign some stuff," Randy said handing the file to the woman at the front desk.

"Here," she pointed at a line, "And here."

Randy signed his name to the bottom of another piece of paper.

The lady looked through his file. "All right, you've officially signed out of classes here at the school. If you want to study for the GED there's a study group in the library." She didn't smile at him. Randy nodded and took the copies of the papers. Randy made his way to the library. He found the information desk and waited for someone to become available. Randy approached the blue information desk.

"Hi, I'm looking for someone named Annie, I'm applying for a job here in the library."

A boy looked up from his book. "She's over there, man." Randy looked to where he was pointing and found the office. Randy walked over to the door and stood in the doorway. A middle-aged woman with red hair turned her chair around. "Hello, can I help you?"

"My name's Randy and I'm applying for a job in the library."

"Oh yes, well sit down. Do you like to read?"

"Yeah, and write and draw."

"Okay, are you still taking classes here?"

"No, I just dropped out. It was boring. I'd rather just read."

"Okay, let me take a look here," she looked up something on the computer screen, "I see here that you're down to level 2. So you can work as a page. A page stocks the shelves and makes sure the library stays organized."

"Okay."

"Do you know how to alphabetize?"

"That means putting things in order according to letter?"

"That's right."

Randy nodded his head.

"All right Randy, let's get you a cart and some books and I'll show you around the library."

Annie stood up. Randy followed her to an area out of view. Several brown carts were lined up and she pulled one out. "Grab a cart, and we'll find some books to file." Randy pulled a cart towards him and followed behind her. She was thin but attractive. Randy tried not to stare at her butt as she walked in front of him. "The boys leave the books they've read on these tables and then we pick them up and put them back. Same thing with the magazines. So all you have to do is collect them and just refile them where they came from." She picked up a pile of books and magazines and put them on her cart. She split the pile and put some of the items on Randy's cart. Then she started into the stacks. With each item she showed him how the books were organized. She opened a couple of the items and fanned the pages.

"Contraband, if you find anything left in the books, turn it in to my office. There's a bin outside."

Once her items were put away, she guided Randy on putting his items away.

"And that's all there is to it. Think you can handle it?"

"Yeah, I think so."

"Good. If there aren't items to put away, you're welcome to draw or read. Oh, and you get a special badge. I'll make one up for you. It lets you come and go after hours."

"Sound good. Is there a schedule?"

"There is, I'll have to put you on it. Check with me tomorrow after lunch." Randy nodded.

"Can I go now?"

"Oh sure, yeah, training complete! I'll put you on the schedule and I'll see you tomorrow, Randy, glad to have you on the library team!" she said, leaning on her cart.

Randy turned to leave towards the bookshelves.

"One more thing, Randy!"

Randy turned around for a moment. "Oh right," he said, grabbing the cart and driving it back towards the storage room. He put the cart away and started to make his way back to the library to look for another book.

Chapter 18

"How's the job in the library working out?" Allison tilted her head at Randy.

Randy shifted his weight on the plastic chair, "It's alright I guess."

"That's good. Last time we made some great progress in talking about how you got here."

Randy shook his head, "I don't know why you did that."

Allison sighed, "Hopefully to help you heal so we can find a way for you to live a productive life. You are young, your life is not over."

"I don't know..." Randy's voice drifted off.

"Just because you committed this crime doesn't mean your life is over Randy," Allison reassured him.

"I feel..." Randy's voice drifted off.

"What are you feeling?" Allison asked, "That's the first time you've said that."

"I don't want to be here. Just want things to go back to the way they were," Randy shifted his feet.

"What about Kelly? She was in danger and you were protecting her."

"I couldn't, I didn't, he was doing bad things and Mom was okay with it and I just don't..." Randy stopped himself and looked away from her at the wall.

Allison leaned forward, "What are you thinking about that?"

"I didn't save her. She's still dead and now I'm here. It's all over."

"What's over?"

"If I ever get out I'll be almost 30."

"You won't be here forever."

"You don't know that?"

"They'll transfer to an adult facility when you turn 19," Allison stated.

"I guess I mean in prison forever."

"Doubtful, you didn't get 1st degree murder and it was an accident. There is an end to this and we need to prepare you for that day."

"Why couldn't he just leave her alone? Why couldn't he just be a good guy?"

"What does that mean to you?"

Randy's face drifted back to Allison's gaze, "Not pressure her so much, he said so many weird thing about her weight and making friends and why did he have to do those things in her bedroom? That's fucked up, its just so fucked up."

Allison reached out and touched his knee, "I know."

Randy moved his leg away from her touch, "I couldn't do shit."

"I know."

"My Mom didn't do shit either."

"The adults in your life failed and now you are bearing the consequences of their inaction."

Randy rolled his tongue and looked her in the eye, "I guess thats how people like you say it."

"Did you get any mail from your family lately?"

"Not for awhile, I guess, I don't know. I don't care."

"Alright Randy, its time to end today, give me a hug and you can go."

Randy gave her a short hug and left the office. He started towards the library. Randy walked into the library and picked up his badge from a rack of badges near Annie's office. The library was quiet. A few boys read at tables. Randy walked to the back room to find a cart and begin re-shelving the books. Randy opened the door and saw Annie putting books onto a cart.

"There you are! Good, you can take these out and restock them where they belong. And you found your new badge." Annie bubbled with enthusiasm.

Randy nodded and started pushing his cart. Randy re-shelved 3 carts full of books before being able to rest. He replaced the last cart in the back room before looking for a quiet spot to read for himself before moving onto the next task.

Randy sat in the library at a table. He looked around for anyone needing any help. The library was deserted. Randy stood up for a moment and walked over to Annie's office. The contraband bin stood near the door of her open office. Randy leaned into the doorway and looked down. He opened up the contraband bin and looked inside. A pack of cigarettes sat on the bottom of the bin next to some mangled plastic flatware and some bundles of tape. Randy lifted the cigarettes out and secreted them in his pocket.

Randy collected piles of books that had been left behind and stacked them up in the back. Annie waved at him as he moved to the back room and put them on a cart. Randy waited for the cart to fill with books before pushing it out among the stacks. He finished empty another cart load when Annie tapped him on the shoulder.

"Could you wipe down the tables before you go to dinner?"

"Alright."

"And when you come back, if you could just wipe down the check out counter and stack any books on the carts in the back."

"Yes, ma'am."

"Have a good dinner then!" Annie said walking away.

Randy moved to the back room and found the cleaning supplies. He wiped down the long wooden tables, gathering books along the way and put the cleaning supplies back. He walked out of the library and across the building to the food hall. Chris and Josh nodded him over. Randy slipped in next to them. Randy picked the cigarettes out of his pocket and flashed them to Chris. Chris reached into Randy's pocket and took out the cigarettes and put them into his.

Chris began to eat but Josh picked at his food.

"Not eating?" Randy asked.

"New meds, I'm not hungry."

Randy shrugged and dug into the food.

"How's the library?" Chris asked.

"Fine, its cool I guess. I just shelf stuff and, like, clean."

Chris nodded his head.

"You going to the rec room?"

"Yeah, but I have to do some cleaning first."

"Cool."

The boys kept eating until their plates were clean. Josh picked along and only took a few bites. They returned their dishes and Randy separated to go back to the library. Randy tugged on the door just as Annie turned the open sign to closed and let him in.

"Thanks for coming back."

"It's okay, this is my job now."

"Just wipe down the check-out desk, put any loose books on the cart and then come find me. I need to find the keys for this door." Annie sauntered away from the door. Randy started for the back room and gathered the cleaning supplies again. He wiped down all the surfaces and gathered a pile of books. He replaced the books on a library cart. The cart was only a quarter full.

"I bet I could put these away quick," Randy thought to himself. He pushed the cart out to the shelves. Randy passed by the door as four boys entered the library.

"We're closed guys, go back," Randy said from behind his book cart.

The biggest one grabbed his crotch and looked around.

"We ain't here for books, man," his arms were covered in black lines. The veins in his neck popped out when he talked. His companions stood near him.

Randy pushed his cart towards them. "Then you'd better go back to the rec room. You can't be in here after hours."

"Listen kid, I need you to do something for me. I heard you were new here."

Randy looked down at his cart. "What?"

"There's somebody who's going to come looking for you. He's going to ask to see some books about birds. I need you to leave some stuff in some books for us."

Randy's pulse quickened. "What kind of stuff."

"Stuff like this."

The large one took some white lengths of paper out of his pocket. They were neatly folded long-ways and almost resembled bookmarks.

"Just leave these in those books. I'll bring you some every few days or so."

"And don't tell no one neither," one of the smaller boys chimed.

The large one turned around and smiled.

"Exactly."

"I can't do that. It's against the rules. What if someone finds out?" Randy said, pulling the cart back towards him. He tried to start walking towards the storage room, but the large boy grabbed his arm. "You don't want problems, man. It doesn't end well when we have problems with someone. But I know you're not a problem."

Randy tried to yank back his arm, but the grip was firm. "So, you gonna help us or do we have a problem?"

"Birds. We have books about birds. I'll leave them in the books on birds. It should be easy to find."

"Of course. It'll be easy, he'll ask for you." The big one let spittle fly into Randy's face with his comment.

"No, no problem. What do I get?"

The smaller one chuckled, "He thinks he's getting something. He's real funny." The larger one rubbed his arm, "You get protection. We'll make sure no one bothers you or anything like that and if you need something we might be able to help you out. Drugs, cigs, whatever."

Randy shifted his weight on his feet and sized up the boys. Randy knew that he couldn't fight them and if he refused they might be after him later.

"OK, it shouldn't be a problem. I'll do it."

"All right, I'll drop off to you around this time every night you work." The large one put five lengths of paper into Randy's pocket for him.

Randy nodded his head. The big one released him, and Randy made his way away from the boys to put his cart away. By the time Randy returned, they were gone. He placed the items in four books on birds. He noticed that they were lengths of toilet paper. The thin, 1-ply texture was unmistakable. But they were a bit thick. Randy squished them in between his fingers as he placed them in the books. Randy stood up and looked around. He replaced the other books and put the cart back in the storage room. He looked around for Annie.

"Annie? Hello?"

"I'm over here," she replied.

Randy started walking towards her raised voice, "I cleaned up and put some books back, there were just a few."

"Great, thanks," Annie lowered her voice just as Randy found her inspecting some books on a shelf.

"What are you doing?" Randy asked.

"It's a thing I do to keep contraband down. I'm ready to lock up. Let's get out of here," she smiled. She retrieved her bag from the check-out desk. She locked her office and picked up the contraband bin. She walked him to the door.

"See you tomorrow Randy."

"Yeah, see you tomorrow," He made his way out of the library and towards the rec room.

Chapter 19

Randy picked up his mail from the mail cart in the common room. He thumbed through the envelopes and noticed that all of them were returned letters to his mom. Only one from his grandma wasn't a returned letter. Randy inhaled and tried not to show his emotion, at least in the common room. He shuffled back to his cell and flopped in his bunk.

He unpacked the envelopes and took out a drawing of Kelly he had made for his mom. In the picture, she wore a little dress and looked down on the white page. He tucked it away in his notebook again. He placed the returned letters neatly in a pile and opened the only letter from his grandmother.

"How are you doing in there? Are you eating?" the letter read. "I should have some extra money for you soon. I haven't seen your mother in a while. I don't know where she is. I hope she calls. Please write to me if she writes to you or calls. I worry about her. I wish she would call me. I don't how she is taking all this. I saw her last time at the trial. She's disappeared and I worry. I worry about you too. How could this happen to us? We're good people. I think you are still a good person too. Some bad things happened to you and your Mom both. I think about you a lot. I visited your sister's grave again. The grass is starting to grow over it. The stone is beautiful. I will try to take a picture to send to you. It's pretty. Write me soon so I know how you are. Grandma." Randy folded the letter shut and put it in a pocket of his notebook.

Anger, there it was again, forming a tight knot in his belly. It was always there, latent, but present. It traveled up to his throat and produced a quiet sob. Jake hung his head over the metal frame that supported their thin foam mattresses and mocked him, "Are you crying for your mommy?"

Randy saw red. Randy punched him over and over using the power of his wiry arms against the boy. An alarm sounded but Randy didn't hear the alarm as it rang. Randy didn't even realize what he was doing until the guards were pulling him off Jake as he screamed. Randy kept his body tense as the officers subdued him and hastily shackled him. They drug him out of his cell as Chris and Josh looked on. Jake held his face, blood running down his body. Jake shouted at Randy as they carried him away.

The officers cuffed him and put shackles on his legs and put him into a small room. His therapist walked in and sat down in the plastic chair across from him. She opened a notebook and looked at him.

"So what happened, Randy?"

"He made fun of me."

"What about?""

"For crying."

"Why were you crying?"

"About Kelly."

"Okay, why did you lash out violently towards Jake?" she said, looking down at the notes.

"He called me a crybaby, I had it, I finally broke. Whatever, I don't give a fuck anymore, fuck him. He's treated me like shit since I got here so fuck him." Randy puffed up his chest a little bit.

"It looks like we have to levy a fighting charge against you and mark you down as guilty on that. That will extend your time here by a year. Inmates who are violent are sent to solitary confinement and have all privileges removed."

Randy just hung his head down.

"What do you think about that?" she said.

"Nothing."

"Okay then." She folded up the folder and notebook and walked out of the room. Moments later, two officers walked him to an austere line of cells. They opened the door to a small, grey 5x4 room with a small commode and sink with one bed on the floor, illuminated only by a solitary light on the ceiling covered by a grate. They gave him nothing to cover, wash, or clean with and nothing to eat for the first night. Randy found out that the sink did not work well and he had to use to his hands to cup the water into his mouth. The toilet flushed slowly, leaving a terrible smell. In the days that followed, meals were infrequent and he was fed once or twice a day. The first week Randy just sat there on the floor and looked at the wall and spent most of his time sleeping, pleasuring himself, or talking, except to eat. One night he just started screaming and couldn't stop until his voice failed. On week two, his mind just stopped. There was no poetry, no thoughts, memories, or even a desire to masturbate, just nothing. His mind hardly registered the night when the door opened and the guard walked in with a police officer. The men were older.

"Here he is. He's fresh meat though, should be fun.""

"How long has he been in here?"

"About two weeks."

"Good."

"Okay, bang on the door when you're done. I'll check on you in about 30 minutes."

The police officer handed a wad of cash to the guard, who stuffed it in a pocket without counting it and disappeared out of the cell, securing the door behind him. The police officer kneeled down towards Randy's bedroll.

"Hey."

"What?"

"You're cute."

"What?" The officer reached out and started touching him all over and pulling at his clothes. Randy tried to resist but the officer put him in a hold and turned Randy over, face down on the bedroll. Randy felt the burn against his ass as the officer entered him. Randy squirmed around to avoid the invasion. Mercifully, Randy blacked out. When he came back to consciousness, he was lying down on his stomach, his pants around his ankles, in tremendous pain and feeling very sick.

Time had no meaning in his box. By week four he had decided to call it a box, he was in a box. It was his grey box, no one else's box. The box produced food but he could never guess when the box would produce food. He wondered sometimes, in the moments when his mind would work, where the box got the food or if there were other boxes like his. The grey box became his existent universe. Randy decided to start tapping the walls, and he started to spend his time tapping every inch of the concrete. Starting with the floors and moving up the walls, finger width by finger width he tapped the concrete and studied it. He tried to count his taps but could never count more than 50 or so before the numbers were lost. He was working his way up the ceiling when the guards opened the door to retrieve him.

"Carruth! Get dressed!"

Randy just mumbled. His mind barely recognized his own name.

"Carruth! Get dressed!" The guard barked again.

Randy stopped tapping. He looked towards the door and shielded his eyes from the extra light. He picked up his clothes. They were stained and in poor shape, but he pulled on all the pieces, and the guards cuffed him. The box had opened and he already missed it. He didn't really understand the words going on around him. They put him back in the same cell. His belongings were sitting in a box on top of his bed. The bunk above him was empty.

Josh jumped down from the bunk and grabbed his shoulder, but Randy flinched at the touch.

"How are you? Are you okay? You were gone a long time!" Josh said, smiling at him.

"Yeah, man, it's been four months," Chris said.

"Huh?" Randy finally croaked out.

"Four months they had you in solitary. We might as well have been in solitary too, we were on lock down," Chris continued.

Randy heard the words but really didn't understand what they meant. He just nodded and sat down.

"Where's the fucker?" Randy said, breaking several minutes of silence.

Josh and Chris looked at each other.

"I guess no one told you," Josh said.

"Told me?" Randy said.

"Jake killed himself. After they put you in solitary, he hung himself in the kitchen."

"Oh shit."

"I don't miss him. He was a real asshole." Chris said, flipping through his magazine. Randy unpacked his things looking at them with a new light.

The conversation helped him regain his language skills, and he started to become more like himself.

Chapter 20

Randy stood outside of the office. He shuffled his feet in his plastic sandals. The hallways were always kept clear of objects. There were no real waiting areas. Everyone stood around in the halls waiting to go into offices. The guard leered at him. She was overweight but carried it well. That was something Randy could never get used to with prison. Always being watched. Someone or something was always watching everyone. Every movement and every behavior was tracked by a guard. One false move and someone was telling you to do something or not to do something. Randy contemplated that was probably the hardest part. Outside of solitary. Freedom wasn't just the inability to leave the building. Freedom was the ability to have some privacy and to do something without someone telling you what you could and could not do or how you should or should not do it. Randy reasoned that was the reason that everyone wanted to go home. It wasn't because home was that great. Randy had heard stories. Most of the guys in here didn't have a great home life. They were like him. But at least home offered a place where a guard wasn't looking at you all the time. It offered a chance to not have to be a building with strangers all the time.

She looked around the quiet hall. Randy kept shuffling his feet. The door opened and another boy exited. Randy noticed his tear-stained face and looked down at feet. The door was left open and he stepped inside. His therapist stood up and shook his hand. Randy sat down in the plastic chair near her desk and clasped his hands. Allison looked at him and they shared a silence for a few moments.

"How is it being back with everyone else? Have you been to the rec room?"

"Yeah, it's fine. It's whatever. Yeah, I went to the rec room. Everyone does."

"So what's going on with you this week, where are you?"

"Nothing, I guess Jake fucking suicided himself or something. That's what I heard."

Allison took a note. "How do you feel about that?"

"He was an asshole to me. Hopefully the next guy won't be such a dick." Randy never broke gaze with the floor.

"You aren't looking at me. Why's that?"

Randy shuffled his feet around before he answered. "I don't want to look at anybody."

"You've really shut down on me since your stay in Solitary, Randy, why is that? I know Solitary is hard. People come out damaged, especially after four months." Allison leaned forward and look down trying to meet his gaze with the floor.

"There isn't anything more to say. It sucked."

"What is going on? Is it something here? You know I can help you."

"No, you can't."

"I'm not convinced of that."

"No, not now but..." Randy finally volunteered.

"What were they doing to you?"

"I'm not telling you. So quit asking. Tell me about your daughter or something."

"I can't help you if you don't tell me."

"Help me get to level 1 so I can get me out of here."

"I might have another solution, but let's keep working together on it."

"Okay, sure let's try that."

"My daughter is good, thanks for asking. She wants to get into pagents. I'm not sure how I feel about that."

Randy looked over at the wall, "Like on TV? All those gowns and big hair?"

"Yes. Just like Miss America."

Randy turned his head and looked at the other wall. "I don't want that to ever happen again."

"What?"

"Solitary."

"I know."

"So much for my job at the library." Randy remarked.

"I'm sorry about that. Why did you decide to fight Jake?"

"Why does anyone do anything in here?"

"You don't strike me as the type."

Randy looked up at her and let his eyes bore into hers for a moment. "It was something to do. I didn't want trouble. I didn't want issues with no one. It sucks. I'm not even sorry about it."

Allison held the gaze with him for as long as he allowed before his eyes and head darted away again. "I know that guards do things in solitary Randy."

"Yeah?"

"Yeah. I hear things," Allison tried to reach out to him but Randy dodged the touch.

"That box becomes your whole world. It's like everything just goes away and it's just you and those same four walls over and over again like a movie that never ends. Same four walls. You even dream about those walls."

"How do you feel now that you're back in with the others?"

"It's fine. Didn't you already ask me that?"

"I did, but you were sort of opening up there for a moment."

Randy exhaled. "Why do you care so damn much?"

"It's my job. There are some genuinely bad guys in here. I don't think you are one of them. I think you had a bad set of circumstances."

"Yeah, bad circumstances. That's one way to say it."

"Do you feel anything about Jake?"

"No. Don't think I do."

"Why not?"

"He was just a mean bully. Treated everyone like shit."

"And now he's dead. Did he deserve that?"

"He did it to himself. Probably, honestly. Fuck him." Randy leaned back as far as the chair would allow.

"So, I think we should talk about working on getting you some privileges back like the yard and the rec room. That way you aren't in your cell all the time."

"What do I have to do for that?"

"I need you to go to anger management for at least 4 sessions. I think we could get you some privileges next month."

"I guess, whatever. I'll go."

"Alright, I think it will be good but you have to promise me you'll open up about how you feel about Jake."

"Sure."

Allison smiled, "Give me a hug and you can go."

Chapter 21

Randy's eyes blinked open in his cell. He looked down at the calendar in the back of the notebook. He looked around the cell. The grey metal bunk frames. the white walls and plastic floor. It didn't make for much of an 18th birthday. Randy sat up and slid into the toilet for a long piss. He leaned his hand against the wall. He flopped his body back on the bed to wait for the breakfast shift to start. Randy pulled out a small plastic mirror. He looked over his face. Randy noticed he needed a shave. He let his hand fall lower to his stomach with its own dusting of hair. He put the mirror away and kept waiting.

Randy enjoyed his breakfast alone until Josh sat down next to him.

"Happy birthday, man."

"Thanks," Randy said in between chews of cereal. "For remembering."

"I marked it on the calendar in my notebook a little while ago."

"That's a nice thing to do." Randy rubbed his arms below his T-shirt. He had left the green shirt in their cell. Josh unwrapped his from his waist and pulled it on.

"Little cold in here," Randy said.

"Yeah, it's early."

"So now you can work on getting out of here," Josh said, draining his bowl.

"That's the plan," Randy said.

"Yeah, me too, maybe."

"That'd be cool," Randy said, licking his lips.

"Yeah, figure out life and shit."

"I'm going to get my jacket and see if I can find a cigarette in the yard," Randy said, stepping out of the cafeteria table.

"Wait up, I'll come with you," Josh said. The pair returned their dishes to the collector. Randy walked up to their cell and retrieved his clothes. The pair then made their way outside to the grey cold. They walked the outside perimeter of the yard. Randy stopped at some people sneaking cigarettes and asked for one. After three meetings he finally reached his goal. He lit it off another and kept walking. Josh looked up at the sky.

"I've spent like two years in this place."

"More than that, because I've been here three years and you were here when I got here," Randy replied.

"Yeah, I guess. I wonder what I missed."

"Holidays."

"Yeah, my little sister is like 16 now. Probably driving."

"Yeah, Kelly would be in high school now," Randy said, gulping his spit.

"I didn't mean to bring it up."

"It's all right," Randy said through an exhale. "It's not like I wasn't already thinking about it a little bit."

The pair made more circuits around the yard. Eventually they drifted into the rec room and played cards until Randy was due at his therapist.

"Happy birthday," Alison said, folding her hands on her lap.

"Thank you," Randy said, slipping in his usual spot in her office, legs splayed wide. His compact frame had grown taller during his tenure.

"Now that you're 18, we can work on getting you out of here and with some kind of reintegration plan."

"Okay."

"I think I have a solution. It's called Juvenile Bootcamp."

"What is it?"

"Bootcamp is your best option for early release, Randy. I think it would be a good option. "

"What's it like?"

"Exactly as it sounds. Military training, lots of physical training, and you do whatever they tell you to or it's back to jail. However, if you pass, it puts you on the fast track to release. Kids exit the program and are home within days. It has a high success rate."

"All right. I'll do it."

Alison smiled. "I think this is for the best. I can't say you'll have a great time. It's bootcamp, but I think you'll thrive when you get out of here."

Randy nodded.

"Give me a hug and you can go."

Things moved quickly after his therapy appointment. Two days later, Randy packed up his few items and began the process of transferring to the Juvenile Bootcamp. The bus ride to the camp was quiet. The boys were all led out of the facility in two neat lines. Chris and Josh stood in the yard and watched Randy leave. Chris offered a wave as Randy walked onto the bus. The boys sat two on each bench. The windows were covered and let in only slivers of light. Randy sat in the bus and watched his facility fade into the background. The bus was filled with young men like him. Every one of them there on the hopes of an early release and home life.

The bootcamp began the moment the bus doors opened. The drill sergeant stood near the bus as it rumbled to a stop. They boarded the bus and stood all the boys up. Their voices boomed and seemed to vibrate the metals walls. Each boy carried his small sack of items as they departed the bus. The bus pulled away and Randy looked back over his shoulder.

"Eyes forward!" Randy's head snapped around to see a man's face inches from his nose. His chair was close cropped and sweat from the sun gathered on his brow.

"You look where I tell you, do you hear me?"

Randy nodded.

"Say sir yes sir!"

"Sir, yes sir," Randy replied. The boys were marched into the facility, sacks in hand for the next 12 weeks of training.

4 A.M. wake ups and shouting drill sergeants were Randy's life for the next 12 weeks. The bootcamp was run by ex-marines. They treated all the students just like marine recruits, including shaving their heads for the duration of their stay. They had no problem yelling, screaming, and giving fast orders. Looking into their faces, Randy often saw David looking back at him. Randy could hear his voice sometimes. The drill sergeant were scary but seeing David gave Randy chills. The cold Missouri air did not help.

Running in prison sandals was a painful and awkward experience. It was more a fast shuffle. But Randy worked hard to do what they said. His mind had disconnected and he did whatever someone told him to do. The instructors had a no tolerance policy for anything that wasn't physical training or life classes. The bootcamp marched his cohort through various classes on getting a job, how to fill out an application, and where to look for work once you were out. Randy could hear the words about discipline reverberating through his mind at night. They slept on simple mats strewn on the floor. They showered every other day and they took meals together in near silence. Every moment of every day was managed by the team. Randy just wanted to get through the process so he could leave the correctional system behind. Randy just wanted out. He didn't even want to go home, he just wanted to go. The 12 weeks were a blur for Randy but soon graduation day came. Some of the boys had family in attendance but Randy had no one. They gave him a little certificate before he left.

When the 12 week program had been concluded, Randy was returned to his original facility in Missouri. Randy stepped off the bus in the yard and was led back to his old cell. However, Randy discovered that Josh and Chris had both been transferred. Three other guys filled the beds. Randy returned to his familiar spot in the bottom bunk on the left side of the room.

His three new cellmates were all hispanic. They spoke Spanish and didn't speak to him beyond a quick nod. Randy kept to himself and tried to get back in his routine of eating breakfast and walking the yard. Randy was back at the lowest behavioral level and Annie welcomed him back to the library. He started his shifts in the library again and waited for word from his therapist on his application for release.

Randy waited two weeks before he was able to speak to Allison about his case. He sat up in his chair when he arrived in her office. He looked around eager for an answer. Alison opened his file and folded her hands on top of it.

"It looks like next week you can be released."

"Okay, that's good," Randy replied.

"Do you have somewhere to go? Usually we have to transition you to a place."

"Yes, my grandma's going to take me in," he lied.

"Okay, it looks like everything is in order then. I'll miss you, but I hope you do well."

"Thank you very much."

"Okay, hug me and you can go."

The week passed quickly. He jumped down from the top bunk. He took out the street clothes his grandma sent him. He started to tear the plastic they had been packaged in. He removed the green prison uniform that had adorned his body for three years. His cell mates were still asleep, facing the white brick wall. The wall that had held him in its cold arms and the walls that had become so familiar. He took his meager possessions with him in a paper bag: eight notebooks of poetry, one sketch pad, $500 cash, and the clothes he was wearing. All his letters and pictures were in the notebooks. He lifted his body up to the bed one last time to wait to be let out. 90 minutes passed and they seemed like an eternity. Finally one of the guards appeared.

Four hours of paperwork later, he scribbled his name too many times on his exit paperwork for him to remember. Six months of parole and he would be free from the Missouri state corrections system just before his 20th birthday. He was armed with a folder of resources, just pamphlets really, about reintegration into society. Smiling people splashed across the pages, looking like their lives were just fine.

All that was required was a once a week check-in with his parole officer and regular drug and alcohol testing and employment as soon as possible. The guards were walking him out to the parking lot.

An overweight female guard pointed her gloved hand to the door. As the final door released, Randy walked through the fence maze and into the free air. He poked around for any of his family. He looked frantically. He couldn't see a familiar face. He walked into the parking lot, struck by the cold of the winter air. No one was there. His head dropped down. A bank of aging pay phones stood nearby. He called his mom, but the number was disconnected. He called his grandma, but there was no answer there. He didn't have a number for his dad and didn't have contact with any other family. He was alone, all alone in a cold world. He started walking.

Part 3

Chapter 22

The Amtrak train rolled along its rails, the brakes screeching around the turns and the aging cars groaning as the train passed through another curve. The train wound through the mountains which mean plenty of curves and plenty of groaning.

Randy lay in his seat on the third car from the observation lounge. He had no seat mate on the Empire Builder as it headed east and he was enjoying being spread out.. The scenery passed by his window at a steady speed. He noticed the cars on the sides of hills where people had crashed. He was glad to be heading east. California wasn't everything people had made it out to be. Sacramento was hot, dry, and the work was sketchy at best. Randy had made enough money to get a coach train ticket on Amtrak back towards Missouri, which was easier than skipping on freight cars with hippie kids and weird people. Railroad people were weird, and Randy was ready to rest after a busy summer working at this and that in general labor and on farms.

He was looking forward to St. Louis, but first, this trip through the mountains of Colorado. His duffel bag was stored in the overhead compartment while his backpack was stowed at his feet. Like most of the single men who had picked up his train east, his bags held all his worldly possessions, and he wanted to keep an eye on them. He noticed a few other rough looking guys, alone, traveling the same way. A small duffel bag and backpack were all they had, just like him. The golden leaves passed by this window and kaleidoscope of color made him dizzy. Randy passed by time by reading a little, writing in his notebook and visiting the observation car. Randy always tried to jump in between the doors between each car. He didn't want to stay on those shifting plates any longer than he had to stand on them to move through the train. Randy noticed there were all kinds of interesting people on the train.

In the observation car, he met a guy who was like him, a migrant worker escaping the lackluster conditions in California and seeking out new territories and new chances elsewhere. He was from Bloomington and was looking to go home. Randy had a similar idea in mind. Randy let the miles pass across the northern part of the country, making stops at small towns and big cities until he changed trains in Chicago to make the short run down to St. Louis. By the time Randy stepped off the train with his bags in St. Louis, he had $60 in his pocket and nowhere specific to go.

"Hey, kid."

Randy turned around to see the other migrant worker waving his long arm at him on the platform. The man was missing some teeth and besides that had no other distinctive feature in face or body. He was the very definition of John A. Everyman. He hadn't brought attention to himself on the trip, but Randy did remember a short conversation he had with him in the observation car about a lake they had passed.

"Yeah?" Randy said, shielding his eyes from the sun.

"Randy, right?"

"Yeah. I don't really remember your name."

"Shane."

"Hey man."

"Do you need a place to stay?"

"Yeah, I do. I was going to see what was available in the parks."

"Wanna go in on a motel together?"

"Yeah, yeah that'd be cool. Maybe those cheap places over there?" Randy said, pointing to a distant group of vintage motel signs with various states of illumination.

"Yeah man, that works man, uh, let's go."

The two men started walking out of the train station and along the main road towards the motels. 40 minutes walking brought them to a place for $50 a night. At $25 each Randy could afford a night, maybe two if he conserved cash.

The two men walked up the metal steps to 203 and opened the door on the dusty room. The linens looked like something from the Reagan years, but it was a place to sleep. Shane put his bag on the floor and adjusted his hat. Randy put his things on the ground and sat on the edge of the bed. Shane found the small remote for the small TV and flicked it on. As the tube illuminated to life with pictures, he quickly found a sports channel to watch.

"I'm lucky man, the last guy I worked for paid me good. I actually have a little cash."

"You said you were going to Bloomington?"

"Yeah I'm headin' home."

"Me too."

"When do you leave?"

"I'm going to see about a bus. I didn't get a bus ticket so I have to figure that out. I dunno. Gotta find out tomorrow."

"Yeah, I don't think I'm gonna be able to afford a bus ticket. I think I gotta walk out, Maybe city bus at least."

"Yeah? Do you have a particular destination in mind?"

"Nope, but somewhere around the area. You know, whatever."

"Yeah, are you hungry?"

"Yeah, something cheap."

"Yeah, yeah, what's around?"

Randy looked out the window, towards the area right around the hotels. It was mostly fast food and a hamburger with some fries sounded good. He was tired of eating the snacks and cups of noodles that he had eaten on the train. Randy and Shane locked the room behind them as they left, walking towards the Hardee's across the street from the small motel. Randy and Shane sat down and started unwrapping their food when two young women in fitted t-shirts and jeans walked in. The shorter one had black hair that hung around her shoulders. Her friend had dark blonde hair that was held on top of her head by a pencil. They held dirty, beat up wallets and stood in line stretching their legs. Shane caught the eye of the shorter girl and looked at her for a moment. She turned away to whisper to her friend and motioned towards him.

"She likes me."

"Yeah?" Randy said.

"Yeah, I'm going to go talk to those girls when they get their food. Do you mind if they come sit with us?"

"Nah, go ahead." Randy focused on eating. Shane stood up and walked over to the ladies and motioned at the table. Shane, with the women in tow, walked back over to the plastic and metal table.

"Randy, this is Iris and Daelyn."

"Hi."

The girls held their trays and sat down, nodding at them. Iris, the shorter girl with black hair, said, "Hello." And then sat down next to Daelyn, who spent her first few seconds elbows out, adjusting her pencil bun. The girls dug in and a few minutes were spent in quiet chewing.

"Where are you boys headed?" Daelyn said first.

"Here for now, but I have other places to be." Randy said.

"Bloomingdale," Shane said. "If you girls are tired of driving, we have a room tonight. We were planning on getting some beers and watching some TV."

"Sounds like fun. I wouldn't mind getting off the road for a bit," Iris said, adjusting her glasses.

"Yeah, if there's beer, why not?" Daelyn said in between bites. "You guys seem cool enough to party."

The group finished eating and the boys pointed at the nearby hotel. The girls got their car across the street and into the parking lot underneath the door, and were followed a few minutes later by the men in question. The group of them walked a short distance down the long street towards a small building with a prominent "Liquor" sign. Randy wanted outside smoking a cigarette with the girls while Shane went in to buy a case of beer with the scraps of money he and Randy put together. Girls and beer in tow, Shane led the party back to the hotel room, put on the TV and started cracking open beers. Randy sat on the edge of the bed and took a generous gulp of beer. Randy could already tell what Shane had in mind for these girls and he looked forward to it, if the gamble worked out.

Randy had never seen such a smooth operator before. Shane just kept talking and kept the beer flowing. Pretty soon Daelyn had draped herself onto Randy and Iris had draped herself on Shane. The night progressed into the early morning, and a pile of cigarette butts later had landed both men in bed with their respective women. Randy was over eager to explore a new experience but didn't want to seem desperate or inexperienced. He took a few deep breaths and followed her generous and pleasurable lead.

Randy's feet were cold on the concrete while he busily inhaled a cigarette. He passed the glowing bit of paper and tobacco over to Daelyn, who inhaled deeply. Randy grabbed his arm and watched his breath condense a little in the early morning air.

"I guess we better get some sleep," Randy finally said.

"Yeah, we had better. When do we have to be out?"

"Noon," Randy said.

"Yeah, we better crash," she said, flicking the butt into the parking lot below.

Randy held the door open, and the pair walked in and crawled under the sheets back to back, and let sleep wash over them.

The next morning seemed to arrive almost instantaneously from when Randy fell asleep. He woke up to a tapping on his shoulder. He finally came to and opened his eyes slowly to see someone in a button down shirt shaking his bare shoulder.

"Hey, hello? Hello?" the man said in a strange European accent.

"Hi."

"It's noon, you need to get out of the room, was another man with you? Nevermind, you need to go, now."

Randy assessed the situation quickly. His backpack and clothes were on the floor. Shane had already gone and the girls with him. Randy was the only one left and he quickly stood up, covering his manhood. The man exited and closed the door behind. Randy pulled on his clothes and checked around to make sure he had everything. He checked his pocket for his money. It was still there, which surprised him a little bit, considering Shane had ditched him. Randy knew how the road worked. It was easy to lose stuff and it was easier to lose cash. Randy left the hotel room, the strange european man stood outside tapping his foot as Randy left the room. Randy walked down the metal stairs and looked around. He picked a direction, west, and started walking. Randy didn't want anything more to do with the man with the thick accent, and he didn't want to talk about any bills. He was content to get back on the road. Randy found a nearby bus stop and started studying a route to the north and west of town. Randy navigated three busses to get to a far end of town. The bus passed some rail yards before it let him off. He walked towards the rail yard and waited for nightfall so he could find a train heading somewhere.

Chapter 23

Randy pulled himself up from the makeshift camp he had made in the trees near the rail yard. He gave the can of beans he had eaten a kick and it flew into a bush. He gathered his blanket and stuffed it into the top of his backpack and slung his duffel over his shoulder. He unzipped his pants and let urine fly into a tree. He zipped up and ran his hand over the scruffy hair on his face. His blonde facial hair stuck out of his chin in all directions.

"I should have shaved back at that hotel when I was in the shower," he thought to himself. But the hair made him look a little older. It was better to look a little older sometimes. The hair also protected his face against the wind and cold in the winter. Spring meant warm days but colder nights. He started walking towards the train yard. He reached the edge of the trees. A sign cautioned anyone trespassing onto railroad property. Randy tapped it with his hand.

Randy took the opportunity to look at what trains were headed west. He looked down the tracks and read the signs to look for a train. Randy hoped for a box car but knew that the end of a hopper car was more likely. Hoppers were open on the end but there was usually room to sit and he could scoot down beside the cowling and not be noticed. Picking up rail cars in the yard was dangerous. The words of the traveler who had taught him how to jump trains seemed to whisper behind his ear.

"Stay the fuck out of rail yards, rail boss will beat the shit of you man."

Randy didn't have a choice at just this moment. He just needed that westward train. He hopped over another set of rails and kept walking. Randy was looking around the trains and ducking security when he rounded the end of a train and saw another couple walking on the loose gravel.

"Hey!" Randy shouted.

The couple was dressed in all black mostly and the girl had some beads in her matted hair. She hung onto her man, a thin fellow of medium height who looked like someone perpetually was pissing him off.

The man turned around but didn't reply. Randy jogged down towards then and shouted again. This time the man stopped and looked at him.

"Shut up, man, you don't want them to hear us!" he said, biting his words.

"Have you seen or heard about any west-going trains?"

"We're trying to go west too," the girl said.

"I think this one, maybe later, they were tapping the wheels," the young man replied. He licked his snake bite piercings.

"Anything open?"

"Yeah, we're on our way to the car."

"Can I follow you?" Randy asked. The sun was beginning to set and the yard was filled with looking shadows. Distant shouting of workers and the tapping of wheels started to fill the air.

"I don't, uh, yeah, sure, come on," the man said. He started to move quickly and after a short ten minute walk he stopped at a brown box car. The handle controlling the door had vibrated open, and using his body weight, he was able to open the heavy metal door. The car was empty but clean on the inside. He clambered up into the car, and after helping his girlfriend, held out a hand to Randy. He moved the door mostly shut and then joined Randy and his girl in the back corner of the car, in the shadows, where no one could see them. The three sat on alert for what seemed like an eternity until the train started moving. Once the car was in motion, Randy stood up on shaky legs and moved to the other side of the car.

"You don't have to sit over there," the girl said.

Randy pursed his lips, "Thanks for the help."

"Yeah, you have to help people out here," Darwin said.

"I'm Randy," he offered.

"Alyssa, but everyone calls me Lyssa," she said, looking down and smiling at him while consistently pulling on her hair.

"I'm Darwin," the man said with a sigh, swiping his flat, long brown locks of hair out of his eyes. His teeth pulled on his piercings again.

"Hey don't be like that," she said, chiding him with her finger.

"Where you guys going?"

"California," Lyssa said.

"Just came from there," Randy remarked.

"Did you like it?"

"Nah, there wasn't much work, even construction, I was in Sacramento."

"We're going to L.A." Lyssa stood up and crossed over to him. She kept her balance easily as the train rhythmically rocked back and forth. She sat down next to him. Randy scooted over to keep his distance.

"It's okay, I don't bite," she cooed.

Randy nodded at Darwin, "But I bet he does."

"That's my brother silly," she put her hand on Randy's arm, "I'm excited for the beach."

"I didn't get down there, probably better."

"I hope so, I really hope so."

Randy took out a cigarette, lit it and offered it to Lyssa. She took a long drag and handed it back to him.

"That's good, what do you smoke?"

"Whatever I can get my hands on, I bummed this from a guy in a suit so it's probably expensive."

"Nice, do you have any to trade?"

Randy nodded. She waved at Darwin and he slid her pack across the floor of the box car. The pack didn't make it all the way and she crawled to get it.

The train hit a bump and knocked everyone around for a moment until it returned to its straight and smooth course on the rails. Lyssa took out some toiletries and some snacks and put them in her lap.

"Any of this for a couple of cigs?"

Randy looked at the selection, "I'll take a couple of those bars."

"Can I get 3?"

"Sure."

The pair traded their items. Lyssa lit her own cigarette immediately and inhaled deeply, "That feels really good."

"Good."

"Where are you from?" Lyssa asked.

"I'm actually from around here but I haven't been here in awhile."

"That's cool."

"What about you guys?" Randy said snuffing his cigarette.

"Originally? Florida," she said ashing the cigarette.

Darwin stood up and opened the door slightly for some air. A chilly blast quickly filled the car, but the new air was refreshing nonetheless. Randy pulled the blanket off the top of his pack and covered his legs. He pulled his jacket close. Darwin let the air hit his body. He left the massive door cracked open until the air had cleared before sliding it closed again. Lyssa stood up and rejoined her brother. She spread out some things from her pack for a moment. Silence fell over the car as the party let the train take them through the night ever westward.

Across the train car, Darwin and Lyssa pulled out a small light that illuminated their side of the car and broke the darkness. Randy let the train rock him into a trance. Darwin and Lyssa shared some trail mix and what looked like a granola bar, but thicker than Randy remembered them.

Many things had changed while he was in prison. He was still getting used to the subtle changes that had occurred around him, especially the ones people didn't talk about. It seemed odd that people spent all that time looking at their phones texting or doing whatever else, and if they weren't texting they were talking, and girls seemed to spend more time flipping open phones than flipping their hair.

He aspired to get a cellphone; it was on his list of things to get once he got steady work and a steady place to live. California hadn't worked out and that had been hard. He had hopes for that, but like a lot of things, it didn't work out. Although he hadn't had time to really think about it, Randy did feel like he had come home. No matter what, the flat fields and small towns spoke a language of familiarity that he couldn't find anywhere else. He slept fitfully, trying to keep an eye for light.

He would start looking at towns, trying to figure out where to disembark his ill-gotten transportation. The train slowed several times and Randy had started to doze heavily when cool air struck him. He opened his eyes to see the door of the box car flung open.

Darwin and Lyssa stood there. The train was slowing down. Randy stood up and the train kept slowing. Randy rolled up his blanket and stuffed it under the straps. Darwin and Lyssa looked around and decided to jump. Lyssa threw him a little wave as she and Darwin disappeared out of the door. Randy shook his legs as he stood by the door. He could see the signs for the rail yard. He saw a patch of grass coming in a few seconds and he braced himself. The grass patch was at the next car as he leapt from the moving train and onto his stomach, using his duffel bag to break the fall. Randy stood up and looked around to get his bearings on his new location. Across a field he could see a small collection of buildings that formed the town.

Randy started the trek over towards the town. His cheap plastic watch told him it was 10:30 by the time he walked into the town. The main street, from what he could see, was fairly empty except for a diner, a bar, and a small convenience store. Randy decided to keep moving. As he walked through the town, different people looked at him and his strange appearance. He looked a bit strange carrying a backpack and a large duffel over his shoulder. He waved at the people, but kept moving anyway, looking around for any signs of work or even a good place to rest. His long walk brought him towards the edge of the town, where he found a large hardware store in amongst some other chain shops near a major road.

Randy finally got to the edge of the parking lot and decided to just walk around to see if anyone was looking for some work, someone he could meet and maybe find a place to stay indoors tonight and if he was lucky, a shower. Randy sat down on a curb and pulled off his pack. He looked around the parking lot for anyone looking for work. He sat on the curb and stared into the parking until the sun went down. The cars and trucks passed in and out of the space with him hardly being noticed. Randy noticed that right away, if you were homeless or a traveler people didn't really notice you. If they did notice you, it wasn't a good thing. He was grateful for the lack of a parking lot security guard. As the sun set, he started to think about where he could sleep for the night and try for some work the next day. He walked into the store and used his last few dollars to buy some snacks and soda before making the trek back out to the edge of the parking lot. He walked around the edge of the property and found a small, wooded area near a large power box. Randy waited for dark to cover the area and for the store to close. The parking cleared out leaving only random cars spread through the expanse of asphalt. He took a few moments to see if anyone else was rough sleeping in their cars or elsewhere around him. The area was quiet. Randy tucked in and kept catching sleep throughout the night.

Chapter 24

The morning sun beat down on his brown hair, and when he ran his hands through it they came back damp from sweat. Randy stood around the parking lot, looking for guys in trucks that looked like they needed work done. The parking lot was quiet for the first few hours of the day. Trucks and a few cars came and went. Randy did his best to look ready for work. He sat on his stuff and waited nearer the store. Some other men were also loitering around the parking lot. Randy presumed that they were looking for the same thing. He kept a sharp eye out for any opportunities. Randy was nearly ready to give up for the day until a man in an old beat-up pickup parked his truck and looked around the parking lot before going in. Randy decided to wait until he came out and then approach him to see if had anything that needed doing. A few minutes later, carrying a small sack, the man returned. Randy made his approach.

"Afternoon, sir.'

"Hi."

"I was wondering if you had any work that you needed some help with. I'm new here, and I could use some work."

"How'd you get here? The bus don't usually come in until later."

"I didn't take the bus."

"Hitchin'?"

"You could say that."

"Yeah, I could have some work for you. What do you do?"

"Anything, labor, landscaping, trimming, clean-up."

"I have some brush that I need cleaned up and put in the truck."

"I can do that."

"Good. I'm Bob."

"I'm Randy." He held out his hand.

"Climb in boy, we'll get out to the house."

Randy put his bag in the back of the truck and climbed into the front seat of the truck. Bob put it into reverse and pulled out of the fading parking spot. Randy cranked down his window a bit to get some relief from the oven-like conditions inside the cab. Bob lit a cigarette and offered one to Randy. Randy took it and the pair sat in silence. Bob turned on the radio to a country station, and the truck rumbled out of town and across some roads until Bob turned down a dusty lane and after a few minutes pulled into the driveway of a squat rambling house on some land with some grass kept at various lengths. There was another late-model car in the driveway and Bob pulled up next to it.

"Here we are, Randy. Welcome." Randy followed Bob towards an area on the east side of the property. "This is what needs cleared. I'll bring the brush hog over. That's the easy part."

Randy put his backpack and duffel on the ground by a tree and rolled up his sleeves. Bob returned a few moments later with a large machine with handles and blades. He filled the gas tank.

"You can come up in the house and find me when you're done. Take your shirt off, it's hot out today." Bob tossed the remarks off his tongue.

Randy looked around at the brush and where Bob had marked. He kept his shirt on at first as he used the sharp blades to attack the brush, but the sun beat down on him and he began to sweat. He removed his shirt and tucked it into his pants and kept cutting.

By noontime the brush was whacked down and Randy used his hands to start to gather it into piles until Bob brought him a rake. Randy raked it all into a pile and used a nearby wheelbarrow to haul the brush into Bob's truck. The pile of brush stood over the sides.

Bob walked out of the house to see his handiwork. The area had been neatly cut down and Bob looked around with a smile.

"That's real good. You know how to burn?"

"I do, you got a barrel or a field?"

"We do, out over there." Bob said pointing off in another direction on the property. Randy started walking across the grass toward the area where Bob pointed. As Randy approached the area the scorched pit lay away from some trees. Randy waited for Bob to bring the truck over and he unloaded the brush into the pit. Bob took out a lighter and helped Randy get the pit going. As the flames burned, Randy stood near the pit and waited for all the brush to burn down and turn to ash. Once the bulk of the plants had burned up, Randy wiped his brow and pulled his shirt back over his head.

"Thank you," Randy said.

Bob pulled out a wad of cash and plucked out four $50 bills and handed them over to Randy. Randy felt them in his fingers and pocketed them. Randy looked over his shoulder and saw the sun getting low in the sky. The blue sky began to turn matte shades of pink, orange, and a tinge of purple.

"Can I get a ride back into town?" Randy asked.

"You need a place to sleep?"

"I guess, but all the motels are in town."

"You can stay here tonight, we have a room."

"Really? How much?" Randy replied, picking up his backpack.

"Nothing, gratis."

"Oh, okay, cool, that'd be great."

Randy followed Bob into the house. The house was older and looked tired. From the front door there was a small sitting room, with a large picture window obscured by a large TV and a stand containing dusty media opposite a low couch. Stairs to the upstairs hugged one wall near a bench with shoes and coats spread around. A short hallway to the back, down which Randy followed Bob, revealed a kitchen with a table in it, a back porch with some mesh screens, a room with a closed door and an open mudroom. Bob opened the fridge and took out two beers. Randy and Bob sat down at the table in the cool air of the house.

"This'll cool ya down."

Randy rook the opened beer and took a long swig, enjoying the golden liquid pouring down his throat. The beer was cheap, but it was cold and made Randy shiver a little bit. The cool liquid took an edge of the temperature of working outside all day. Randy looked up when another young man walked into the room. The large pants he wore were faded blue and looked tired. They hung low on his hips and barely covered the demarcation line of hair that led lower to his manhood. His medium-length hair rested limply on the back of his head, almost touching his shoulders. He was shirtless, revealing the small random tattoos on his chest, side, and arms. The artwork moved between shapes, crown, and barely legible quotes. Randy read, "No one but God can judge me" tattooed across his shoulders.

Bob lifted his beer towards the man, "Good to see you up D."

"Hey there, uh?" D pointed at Randy.

"I'm Randy, I just did some work outside."

"Yeah?" the young man said, stretching his arms upward, revealing two solid tufts of underarm hair and his rib cage.

"This is D, he'll show you where you can stay. Take Randy, show him the place," Bob said pulling out a cigarette.

"Come on kid," D said. "Bring your beer with you."

Randy stood up and took a swig, lifted his pants, and sauntered after D. The house rambled on the property. It had been built in bits, pieces, and sections. The main room where they were at was connected to the rest of the house by a short hallway that revealed a line of bedrooms. D turned Randy away from that route and led him up a short staircase to a grouping of small rooms. D pushed open a door to a simple room.

"You can sleep in here. Shower is down the hall." D pointed at a white door.

"Thanks."

"I'll let you get settled in and take a shower. I saw you working outside. Do you like to party?"

"Yeah, I can party." Randy took his hands out of his pockets again.

"All right, I'll come get you in a little bit."

D left Randy in the room. Randy looked around the simple space. A double bed took up one corner. It was covered with a quilt. A chair stood in the corner opposite. The walls were covered in yellow paint but the ceiling looked to be missing some paint. Randy opened his bag and took out his shower kit from his duffel bag. He opened the door and looked right and left. He guessed where the shower was and found the bathroom at the end of the hall. Randy took his shower and washed off the day. Randy toweled off and put his clothes back on. His hair dripped onto his shoulders and he rubbed his head with his towel. He walked back down the hall and laid on the bed. He looked up at the ceiling for a moment until sleep overcame him.

Chapter 25

D knocked on the whitewashed, solid wood door. He knocked with his fist first and then kicked at the bottom indent of the door with his skater-shoe-clad foot. Randy opened the door to reveal D standing in the hall, his lean torso covered in a muscle shirt and his jeans sagged at the hips.

"You woke me up."

"I figured. You want another beer?"

"Yeah, I'm thirsty."

D pulled out a beer bottle from his back pocket and handed it to Randy. D used his belt to pop the top and traded the open bottle for Randy's unopened bottle.

Randy took a swig of the yellow liquid. D leaned against the door frame for a moment.

"Where you say you're from?"

"Missouri."

"Ah, and how'd you end up in my yard?"

"Picked up at Home Depot."

"Yeah, I saw you workin' out in the yard. That all you do?"

"Sometimes, I do any work that needs doing."

"Don't we all. That's life, Randy. Do you like to party?"

"Yeah, I party…"

"Good, come over here."

D walked the hallway and down the stairs. Randy followed him. They descended another set of concrete steps into a basement. The wood paneling covered the bottom half of the wall like wainscoting. The drop ceiling was composed of six-inch squares. Some of the tiles were missing in places and some others were stained brown. Randy detected the quiet hum of a clothes dryer. The glass table and some low couches were held up by an aging linoleum floor and occupied one half of the dark basement.

Even the basement was a series of rooms and the largest of them was dominated by weight equipment. Randy gravitated towards the machines in the room. The lights seemed to turn themselves on. He ran his hands over the free weights.

"We work out a lot here, usually a couple hours a day," D said, drinking his beer.

"I'm a fighter, MMA, cage fighting."

"Awesome."

D took a long swig of beer.

"You like to fuck?"

Randy looked at him. "What? Yeah, if she's hot, I guess." Randy moved around the room. D smiled at him and set his beer down. D took out a pack of cigarettes and in one swift motion removed a cigarette, placed it in his mouth, straight from the pack, and lit it.

"What do you guys party with?" Randy asked.

"All kinds of stuff, come on, I'll show you."

D led Randy to another room in the basement. The distinct chemical smell filled the air. D flopped down on the couch. He pulled a box out onto a glass coffee table. Randy saw two other young men working but they didn't notice him there. D picked up a glass pipe. The delicate glass had a blond piece punctuated by a glass globe at its base with an open top. D picked it up and with his long fingers twirled it between them. He opened a small wooden box. He took out a bag with some crystals and filled the glass pipe with them. He looked for a lighter. D produced a blue Bic lighter from his pocket. He set it on the end of the table and when he reached for it again it fell off to the floor. Randy casually picked it up. D took it slowly and looked him straight in the eyes as he melted the crystalline substance. His chest expanded as he inhaled the opaque, white smoke into his lungs. D closed his eyes; the high would soon enter his bloodstream. D repeated the process a few more times and then loaded the glass for Randy.

"I'll help you man, it's your first time!" Randy put the pipe to his crimson lips. It was light in his delicate fingers. D held the lighter under the bowl and the "ice" started to melt. Randy smoked a little more than D, and the rush came on quickly. He felt it go down to his toes and reach slowly up to his chest arms and finally his head. The room was spinning. He lost balance on the couch, but D grabbed his arm.

"Careful bud, don't get too excited." D walked over to a small fridge and grabbed a beer. He gave it to Randy. Randy popped the little metal top off with the lighter and poured the light golden liquid down his parched throat. Randy let out a sigh of relief. The beer fixed the burn in his throat. The high started to hit him. His body was tense and then loose all at once. The rush made his heart pound. He felt good, alert, and ready to do everything all at once. D lit a cigarette and exhaled the first puff.

"How do you feel buddy?" D inhaled again.

"I'm okay, I think, my body feels weird."

"That's normal, drink some more beer."

Randy had a few more sips. D pulled off the white ribbed tank top that covered his torso. He drank some beer and they sat down on the floor. He refilled the glass globe and smoked again. Randy took four deep inhalations. His whole body buzzed. He took his shirt off.

D kept smoking. Randy was flying. D took him up the squeaky steps to a small bedroom. Part of the ceiling was missing and a sheet—stained with water— covered the missing part. D sat on the side of the bed and Randy sat down next to him.

"Have you ever had sex?" D took his shirt off. He stood up and looked around.

Randy was floating. "Yeah man, uh, a couple times. Are you trying to find something?"

"With a real girl?"

"Yeah, I've fucked a real girl." He tried to sound macho about it.

"I'm looking for the remote; I want to watch SportsCenter."

D finally recovered the missing remote. Randy's head rolled around on his shoulders. Randy looked intently at the TV and shook his hand free hand while holding on to the remote. D packed another pipe with marijuana. He took several inhalations before handing it to Randy.

"You need this, it'll calm you down a little."

"Okay, okay, okay," Randy said quickly. He smoked the familiar plant and enjoyed its effect. Randy looked up at the ceiling when he heard footsteps on the floor above.

"Who's that?"

"Don't get paranoid, that's one of the boys taking a guy upstairs."

"Other guys live here?"

"Yeah, we'll stay down here tonight, I'll introduce you tomorrow. They're working."

D kept flipping channels once his program was over. The light from the TV flickered against the floor. Randy stretched out on his end of the couch and just watched the pictures go by. Randy and D passed cigarettes back and forth.

"What time is it?" Randy asked.

"Don't know," D said. "Morning soon, I think. I lose days sometimes."

Randy leaned back and looked at the ceiling.

"I feel, like, flying."

"Yeah that sounds right."

"What do those guys do?" Randy asked.

D turned over towards him and put his hand on his leg.

"They work for me, they, uh, they have sex with guys who are into sex with guys."

Randy recoiled. "The fuck?"

D smiled. "Don't get weird on me, dude."

Randy sat up straight and shook his head. The high was hitting his brain and he struggled to accept the information.

"Wait, are you gay?"

D shrugged his shoulders, "Any port in a storm. Why not?"

Randy settled down a bit and relaxed his body, "Yeah, I got in trouble for that once."

D laughed, "You get caught suckin' dick?"

"More of a mutual jerking thing."

"Ah," D replied, "You experiment?"

"No, I mean, I saw it a little in prison but that was pretty low key." D put his hand on Randy's leg again. He rubbed his thigh for a moment. Randy didn't like it at first but it felt good.

"Do you want me to stop?" D asked.

"No, it feels good, it shouldn't but it does."

"Okay."

D let his hands run farther over Randy's body. Randy didn't really want him to touch him like that, or did he? Randy didn't stop D from touching his legs and then his chest and then running his hands through his hair. D carefully helped him remove his shorts and D slid his pants off. Randy instinctively took his manhood in his hand. D unbuttoned Randy's pants and helped him slide out of them. The naked men looked at each other for a moment. D didn't say a word as he broke the gaze and moved his head lower on Randy's body. The men embraced. The drugs made everything D did feel better to Randy. The sensation was overwhelming and after trading back and forth they both climaxed. D stood up and pulled his jeans back on.

"I need a fuckin' cig after that, you're hot as shit." D stood up and pulled on his clothes. Randy followed him outside after pulling his pants over his legs. Randy sat on the floorboards of the porch in his jeans. His feet were bare and he brushed his hair back. D relaxed and settled back against the porch. He lit another cigarette.

"Most guys that come here aren't like you," D remarked after a long drag of his cigarette.

"What do you mean?"

"Most guys that come here are addicted to drugs and they need their fix. Sex is how they, uh, pay. Sometimes they come from bad homes or prison but most often they are orphans that have been shuffled through the system."

"Now they work here? Suckin' cock?"

D exhaled his cigarette drag. "Yup, pretty much, and more."

"More?"

"Yeah, sometimes more."

"That's fucked up."

"Sex sells man, I guess you were just here to do yard work though."

"That was the plan, now its' time for me to move on I guess."

D flicked his cigarette out into the yard, "You don't have to go if you don't want to; I could use a guy like you around here."

Randy nodded his head back and forth, "That felt really good."

D turned towards Randy, "You should always feel good man, that's what life is about, just feeling good."

Randy looked out into the dusk of the evening and wondered just where he had ended up. What did D mean?

"I could stay for a bit," Randy said puffing on the last of his cigarette.

"Yeah, you should, come inside, we'll keep partying. I'll get the beer."

"Alright," Randy stood up and walked towards the door. D ran his hand across Randy's shoulders as they disappeared inside.

Chapter 26

Randy and D stood on the porch, smoking cigarettes. The blue-white smoke curled up to the wood and disappeared into the air. The humidity hung in the air as the yellow rays of sunlight pierced the morning sky.

"So, is Bob your father or something?" Randy asked.

D flicked his cigarette off into a nearby bucket.

"That's tough. I was orphaned when I was 11. My parents didn't have any family to take me so I ended up in child protective services. At least that's what they told me it was called. It's basically foster care and I bounced from family to family. Some of them thought I was evil. I hated that church shit. They got rid of me quick man, so quick. "

"Wow, what did your parents die of?"

D looked around for a moment. "Drunk driver. What about you? Where's your mom?"

Randy exhaled his cigarette and looked down for a moment. "Yeah, my mom's dead, uh, haven't seen my dad since I was a kid," Randy lied.

"Typical, parents man, fucking worthless."

Randy nodded as he flicked his ash into the old coffee can.

"You want to meet my boys?"

"Sure."

"Chris! Josh! Come out here, I got someone for you to meet."

Two lanky guys without shirts sauntered out in flannel pajama pants.

"Hi, I'm Josh," the shorter one said holding out his hand. Randy noticed his handshake was limp. He stood with his weight on one hip and his arm tucked across his lean body.

"I'm Chris." Chris was taller and licked his lips. His ears were pierced. His body was solid and Randy looked him over to notice he was a little soft around his stomach. His pink lips seemed to be dry.

"D, you want to eat?" Chris asked.

"What do you have?"

"Some cereal, I guess."

"Do we got any milk?"

"Yeah, Bob picked some up."

D flicked his cigarette into the bucket and turned to go inside. Randy, Chris, and Josh did the same and followed D to the rear of the house where the kitchen table stood. Chris poured out the cereal in mismatching bowls and splashed each bowl with some milk before replacing it in the fridge. The boys ate quietly until they finished and dropped their bowls into the sink.

"Someone is on dishes later." D said. Josh raised his hand. "I'll deal with it."

Chris leaned against the wall. "So where are you from?" Randy looked at him. "Missouri."

"Local boy then." Josh said sitting at the table again.

"Yeah I guess so." Randy said.

"That's cool." Chris said. Chris sat next to Josh at the table. Randy's attention turned to the door as D returned.

"House cleaning day, we have a party coming up and we don't want the place to be filthy," D announced.

Chris and Josh looked at each other for a moment. Josh raised his hand. "I'll do the kitchen since I'm already on dishes."

Chris inhaled for a moment. "I guess I'll clean my room then and do the living room."

D smiled, "Randy, you can help me outside. We need to talk anyway."

Randy stood up. "I'll get a shirt." Randy walked downstairs to the basement and found his shirt. He slipped it on and found D on the back porch plucking cigarette butts out of the yard. Randy joined in. They gathered all the butts and put them in a steel barrel on the edge of the yard. Randy looked around the yard. The grass was a mixture of what was once sod and now mostly saw grass. The broad blades of grass created a mixed texture with the original sod. Randy noticed that an old trailer stood at the back of the property. Randy didn't remember seeing it before but it must have been there. A short fence separated the yard from the forest and meadow beyond. Randy stood in the yard with the sun beating down and looked around before walking back to the porch to escape the hot day.

D walked out of the house carrying an old broom and motioned Randy over toward him.

"Sweep this out so it's clean enough. I'm going to burn some trash. D walked inside and gathered up some bags of trash. He emptied the bags into the barrel and started the fire with his lighter. Randy swept the porch and looked up at D from time to time. Randy didn't really understand what was going on here but it felt good and there was some money to be made. It was a place to sleep and it was far better than sleeping in a parking lot with no car. Randy didn't have anywhere to be and here seemed like a good spot, at least or now. Randy swept as much dust as he could find and straighted up the chairs and odds and ends on the porch as best he could. Randy say the flames from the burning trash reach over the top of the barrel as he finished. D lit a cigarette from the flames and invited Randy over.

"Do you want to make some money tomorrow night?"

"Like Chris and Josh?"

"Sure," D said taking a drag and offering it to Randy.

"I don't know if I could do that." Randy looked down at the ground. "I'm not, you know," his voice trailed off.

"Gay?"

"Yeah."

"You don't have to be gay, you just have to help the guys feel good, they like guys like you, young, fit, and good with your mouth," D put his arm across Randy's shoulder. Randy kicked the dirt for a moment. D scratched his stomach and hugged Randy close to him.

"You'll be high, it'll feel good, most of the these guys are looking to take it, so it's like a girl, sort of." D exhaled. He pulled out a cigarette for Randy and offered it to him.

"It's easy money, easy drugs and you get off. It's nice work. I'll make sure you're okay. I'm really into you and I know that these guys will be too. Most of these guys are cops and shit, they're real gentle, they just get tired of their wives. You'll like 'em. It's fun, I promise and you get paid without having to slave out here on whatever."

Randy dropped his cigarette butt into the trash barrel.

"Okay, I guess."

"You'll have fun, I'll watch over you. After you smoke, you'll want to do it even if you don't want to right now." D smiled at Randy and put his hand on his shoulder. "It'll be, our parties are fun."

Randy looked up at D. "All right, I'll try it."

"That's a good boy," D said, rubbing his shoulders. "You'll have fun. I'll make sure of it. I take care of my boys."

"Okay."

"There's a few things you should know. These guys are gentle as long as things go their way but if you hold back or whatever, things can get rough so just don't hold back. Do what they want, make them feel good and you'll feel good too. You jerk off a lot?"

Randy nodded his head, "When I can, can't so much when I'm traveling."

D nodded his head, "Makes sense. You can get off here as much as you want."

"Just like a girl huh?" Randy asked.

"Yeah, basically, the mechanics are the same, you just have to get hard and do your thing."

"What if they want to do it?"

D rubbed his shoulders and leaned in close to his ear, "Then you give them what they want," D ran his hand down Randy's back to his butt and gave it a squeeze.

"What if I can't?"

"You can, I believe in you. You're a nice kid," D released Randy from his embrace and watched the flames for a moment.

"Need to shave though, these guys like their boys to look like boys."

"Yeah, I keep the beard for the road, helps with wind."

D chuckled, "I guess that makes sense," D poked the remains of the trash fire. The ashes smoldered in the barrel. Randy looked inside at the ashes of what remained. Satisfied, D left the barrel and walked toward the house.

"Come on, let's go check out Chris and Josh."

Randy followed D into the house. The living room was tidy and neat. The couch was clean and the side tables bare of anything on them except a lamp. The TV and the collection of movies around the base were neatly stacked and the space was dust free. D walked into the kitchen just as Chris and Josh put the last dishes into the drying rack. Chris wiped down the counter. D looked around the house for a moment.

"Rooms?"

"That's next up I think, then I want to watch Aladdin," Josh said. Chris nodded his head in agreement.

"Good, good," D said heading towards the basement, "I got shit to do, Randy?" D waved him toward him, "Come with me man, we're going to hang out."

Randy followed D downstairs to the basement again. D picked up a few things and put them on thin, wooden shelves. Randy followed his lead. D put many of the items on the work bench away. Randy stood near a wall and watched D work. D started to wipe his work surface.

"Do you know what the number one rule is for this party?"

"What's what?"

"Don't pull back."

"Don't pull back?" Randy turned his head as he asked the question.

D walked over to Randy and put his hand behind his head and leaned in for a kiss. Randy turned his head away for a moment.

"Like that, don't pull back from anyone," D tried again and Randy accepted the kiss. D's lips were rough against his. D let the kiss linger before pulling away.

"Remember, just don't pull away. Let them touch you and enjoy you. Just don't fucking pull away," D walked over to the bench and picked up a small glass pipe. "Let's smoke."

Chapter 27

A few trucks started to pull up around 9 P.M. Their lights lit up the yard as they arrived. Different guys, usually older, started to walk in one by one. D had given Randy some clothes. He was wearing a white T-shirt and some tight jeans. DC shoes completed the look. Skater shoes didn't fit him, but it gave him a young look that guys liked, at least according to D. He was afraid, he shuffled around. Would he freak out? Would he be too afraid to get through with it?

The first of several men finally walked in. They were all smiling. Josh and Chris stood nearby and different men drifted towards them. Randy noticed that Josh and Chris already seemed to know them. The air was already getting tepid with smoke from cigarettes and drugs. Some of the men had boys in tow. Randy shuffled around in the foyer of the house. He tugged at the clothes. A voice came up behind him and said, "You look uncomfortable in clothes, boy."

Randy looked up to see a man with a mustache and a bit of a pot belly.

"They're new, uh, just got out of prison and, uh, I'm not used to regular clothes yet."

The man walked up to him and graced his cheek with his hand. Randy clashed and almost brushed it off.

"Don't be shy, boy. I'm Dan."

"Hi, I'm Evan," Randy lied. Everyone lied about their names.

"Let's go smoke downstairs and then have some fun," Dan said, smiling.

They descended the stairs into the basement. Dan seemed to know the place and helped himself to a pipe and some more crystals.

"Where'd you go to high school?"

"I'm not really from around here," Randy offered.

"How long were you in prison?"

"Two and a half years, close to it."

"What for?"

"Uh, I, uh."

"It's okay, boy, I'm just curious." Dan had filled the glass with the crystals and began to melt them. "I'm cool, you know?"

"Uh, I killed someone."

"Why did you do that?"

"It's a long story."

"It always is. Here, have some."

Randy inhaled the opaque smoke for the second time that day. The day always started with smoking of various things. Randy was beginning to forget what normal felt like. The high was becoming his normal.

His body was buzzing incessantly. Dan leaned over and kissed him. Randy loved the contact, but his stomach began to churn. He kept his cool.

"Just, don't pull away," the advice D had given him flowed up into his mind again.

"Let's go upstairs," Randy offered. Dan smiled.

Randy led Dan by the hand up the stairs to one of the bedrooms. Randy took his shirt off and slipped out of his shoes. Dan grabbed him from the back and started kissing his neck. Randy's head rolled on his shoulders. He turned around and put his hands down Dan's pants.

"I like that. Tell me how much you want my ass," Dan intoned. Randy ran his hands over the man's body. The two fell into a sensual cuddle on the bed. Randy kept his eyes closed and remembered to never pull away. The men finished and Randy sat back onto his heels. Dan lay spread on the bed, his body heaved from heavy breathing. Randy laid down next to him and sleep washed over him.

Randy felt Dan roll off the bed and onto the floor. Dan stood up with a smile on his face. Randy was still asleep naked under the over-large fuzzy blanket that was draped on the bed. The blanket over Randy's body had some generic psychedelic design on it like the blankets commonly sold on corners and streets. Dan slipped on a pair of jeans and hoodie and walked down the creaky stairs and out onto the front porch. He lit a cigarette and started to inhale. Dan looked out into the dusky evening. The cacophony of insects were beginning to sing.

"Got a light?"

Dan turned around to see Randy standing there. "Have a good nap?"

"Yeah I did."

"Good." Randy took out a cigarette of his own.

Dan hugged Randy close. "How was it?"

"It was all right. My high is dying."

"Yeah? Well get back in there, champ, I bet there's another guy ready."

Randy flicked his butt into the dark of the yard. "Okay, have a good night." Randy sauntered back into the house. He looked around. He felt embarrassed. His mind had began to analyze what he was doing, what he had done. The tinge of hate rose up in his chest. On the back deck there were a few guys standing around. Randy joined the circle. The pipe was going around. A few more guys joined the rotation.

"What's this?"

"Primo."

"Okay." Randy didn't know what a primo was, but the combination of marijuana, cocaine, and meth took him quickly. Randy took a hit, and as the feeling overwhelmed him, he left the circle and sat down against the exterior wall of the house that faced the porch. The siding didn't make it comfortable but Randy couldn't stand much longer. Randy started to grind his teeth a little but it didn't hurt.

"Hey there buddy are you all right?" asked one of the nameless older guys standing around mindlessly. Randy noticed he was tall, or seemed tall from his lower vantage point. He had a long face with a brown mustache accented with a hint of grey.

"Yeah, I'm okay, I guess."

"Here, have some beer."

Randy took the cheap beer and drank a big gulp out of the can. The man sat down on the concrete next to Randy. His cowboy boots stuck out in front of him, his legs resting on the heels of the nice boots. Randy put down the beer can between them.

"I'm Rod." His baritone voice announced his name.

"I'm Josh." The lie was easier this time.

"Nice to meet you Josh, do you want to get out of here?"

"You want to go upstairs?"

"Nah, let's go out to my car."

Randy followed Rod out to his car. They climbed into the generous beige leather back seat of the Cadillac. Rod slipped his hands under Randy's jeans. Randy was buzzing in his mind and he felt that his whole body was vibrating. Rod's touch was different than Dan's. It was rough. Randy tried to cover himself. Rod insisted with his hands and mouth, while pulling down his dark jeans, revealing his manhood. Rod wrapped his body around Randy like a snake and moved the squirming boy around and took him. Randy cried out but Rod covered his mouth. A few minutes later it was all over. Randy's brain could hardly understand what was happening or that it was over until Rod opened the car door and drug Randy out. Rod left Randy in the grass in the yard with his pants around his ankles. Randy was mumbling but wasn't able to shout. He wanted to scream but his mouth would not work. Rod calmly touched his forehead.

"Thanks for the good time, kid." He calmly stepped into his car and casually drove off.

Randy lay there in the yard. His eyes just rolled back into his head and his world faded to black. The blackness was sweet to him. His consciousness was free from his body and just seemed to roam. His imagination ran wild with colors, images, and old movies. He saw the pan again and the blood spattered everywhere. The image passed. His body was gone, but he felt so free, like a balloon floating away into the ether of existence. His mind floated towards that blackness, the velvet embrace, experiencing the gentle touch. He felt so free, so beautifully and wonderfully free, it was unlike anything he had ever felt. He could stay here forever. Existence was so beautiful and never-ending. The exploration could go on forever in this stillness of time. Randy didn't move in the grass as the night passed over his body and turned to day. One by one the trucks began to leave. No one noticed Randy lying in the grass blissfully unaware of his surroundings.

D stood on the porch, smoking a cigarette. The sun was just beginning to illuminate the haze of the Missouri morning. D casually smoked until the sun finally rose high enough in the sky he noticed Randy's body in the yard.

"Fuck!" he said to himself as dropped the cigarette and ran down the short stairs of the porch and out into the yard. D kneeled down into the dewy grass and shook Randy.

"Randy! Randy! Wake up man! Wake the fuck up!"

Nothing D did worked, Randy was non-responsive. D needed help. He sprinted back into the house.

"Chris! Josh! Get your asses out here! We need to get him inside!"

Chris's elongated body was mostly naked except for a pair of shorts that covered his long thighs. His body was draped like old clothing on the couch, and from that prone position he sat up slightly and looked in D's general direction. "What?"

"Randy, Randy got left in the yard last night!" Josh walked out from the kitchen. Josh yawned, brushed his black hair aside and reached his light brown bare arms over his lighter-skinned bare chest. His sweatpants fell lower around the hips of his compact frame of 5 foot 8 inches.

"Who?" Josh said in his effeminate voice.

"Randy, that new kid that came here last week," D said.

"Oh yeah him, what happened?" Chris said in a baritone voice, sitting his pale-skinned body up from the couch.

"He's laying out in the yard ass naked! Come on!" D ran out of the living room and out into the yard.

Josh looked at Chris, shrugged his shoulders, and sauntered out into the yard. Chris ran his fingers through his medium-length brown hair, lifted his body up from the couch, and followed Josh.

D was leaning over Randy's body. D shook his shoulder, but Randy was still not responding. D shook harder. Chris and Josh finally walked up beside D.

"Let's get him in the house," D said.

"Let's pull the man's pants up first," Josh said as he kneeled in the grass and pulled up Randy's jeans and stuffed his legs and manhood into them and pulled the fly shut. D stood up and lifted up his shoulders and head. Chris and Josh each took a leg. The men hauled Randy into the house and up the stairs into a bedroom and laid him out.

Chris and Josh stood over the bed on one side while D kneeled next to the bed on the opposite side. The room was small and very bare.

"Is he breathing?"Chris asked.

"I don't know, I think so, we can't take him to a hospital."

"You should go wake up Bob, we'll keep an eye on him," Josh said, sitting on the side of the bed. "Babe, go get me a shirt."

D and Chris left the bedroom. D walked through the small hallway and through the back mudroom out towards the back yard. D approached the metallic RV at the back of the property. He was regretting his lack of shoes as he winced over every rock and sharp plant in the ill-kept yard. D finally reached the door and knocked on the dented metal surface. He knocked more urgently. He heard the floor start to squeak and the trailer began to rock back and forth.

"What!" a man's voice yelled.

"It's D, Bob. Open up!"

Bob opened the door.

"D, you had better need somethin' real important or want to suck me off I just got to sleep and I—"

"It's the new kid, he smoked a primo last night and went out with a guy. I think he's almost dead or dead. What the fuck do we do?" D interrupted him.

"Fine, fine, let me get my robe, get the poppers and some water, we'll see if we can wake him up."

The two walked back into the house together. D went to the kitchen and took a bottle of water from a case on the floor next to the fridge. He opened a cabinet and took out a small shaving kit bag and made his way up the stairs towards the bedroom where Randy still lay. Bob was looking for Randy's pulse when D laid down the water and the shaving kit bag on the bed.

"He's still alive, but his pulse is weak and his breathing is shallow. Give me a bottle."

"Which one?" D asked.

"Don't matter none." Josh stood up to see how effective this would be.

Bob held the potent liquid under Randy's nose. He stirred. Bob put a small amount under his nose. A few seconds passed with no response, and then Randy's eyelids flew open and he promptly rolled over and threw up as Josh backed up to avoid the fluids. Little came out of the boy's throat but he kept dry heaving.

"There!" Bob declared. "We're doing O.K."

Randy calmed down and flopped back onto the soft surface of the bed, gasping for air.

Chapter 28

D breathed fully for the first time in 20 minutes. Josh and Chris stood against the wall on the far side of the room.

"Good, no dumping of any bodies today," Josh declared.

"Yeah, I'm glad he's okay. We were worried about you!" Chris said in a caring tone.

"Thank you," Randy said, coughing.

"I'm going back to bed. I'll see you later, Randy," Bob stood up and shuffled out of the room.

Randy sat up for the first time.

"Cigarette, buddy?"

"Yeah, that would be nice."

D stood up and opened the door. Randy swung his legs over the side of the bed and stood up. He was unsteady, but took the first few cautious steps. D grabbed his arm. They made their way down the stairs one at a time and out onto the porch. Randy leaned against one of the 4x4 posts that held the porch up. D helped him light his cigarette. His throat was raw, but he welcomed that first puff. Chris and Josh sat on the railings and took deep inhalations. Silence fell over the porch and Randy started to tremble.

"Don't you guys have some work to do?" D said.

Chris and Josh looked nervous and flicked their butts in the coffee can and went back indoors.

"You had me scared back there."

"Really?"

"Yeah man, I mean, a lot of guys don't care but you're new. I like to watch out for the new guys. What happened?"

"My body was buzzing, I didn't—I didn't want him to touch me. I just was trying to do it and I freaked."

"Ah ha, remember what I said rule #1 was?"

"Don't pull back."

"Right." He took a puff and exhaled. "I had that happen to me. I didn't black out like you, but he hurt me pretty bad. He wanted my hole and he got it. After that, I knew that I needed to be nice and high when I went with a guy and that I needed to go all the way, no matter what, even if I didn't want it. We need to survive, Randy, we have to."

Randy let a tear roll down his cheek. "God, I'm getting fucked by dudes like a bitch! Fuck!"

D grabbed his shoulders and turned Randy's body towards him. "Do you want to live? Or is your pride so big that you can't take a little butt sex to survive? You told me you walked out of the slammer alone. You've been struggling. You don't have to struggle here. For a little sex you can live. It's just sex, man. Sex is sex. It's not you, it's this fucked up life. None of us put down 'boy toy' down in the 1st grade as a career but life sucks, man, life just sucks sometimes. Look at Chris and Josh, they've been doing this since they were 12 when some fuckhead from child protective services dumped them. They're addicted too. You're lucky you're 19, you have a chance they don't. I don't have what you have. I'm all that's left for me. If I'm lucky I might make enough to get out or go live with some dude. But my days are numbered, man. I'm 27. I have nowhere to go and I have basically no money to show for it all."

"Why don't you leave then?" Randy said through his tears.

"Where would I go? What would I do? I know too much. I'd get dead real quick."

"But why do this shit to yourself?"

"It's only sex man, it's only sex."

D flicked his butt toward the coffee can and missed. The sun was fully risen and beat down onto the lawn. D sat down on the porch steps and invited Randy to sit down with him. D hugged Randy's torso to his bare hairless chest.

"Don't end up a faggot like Chris and Josh. Be strong."

Randy reached his arm up tentatively and hugged D. Randy left the embrace and clasped his hands. D looked out into the yard.

"Wanna smoke?" he said, breaking the silence.

"When in doubt."

D and Randy lifted themselves up and walked down into the basement. Chris and Josh were busy. D walked over to the work bench and deposited the crystals into the glass again. Randy walked over to him and stood next to him. D heated the glass and breathed in the opaque smoke. D shook his head back and forth and as he welcomed the high into his body. He helped Randy with the lighter.

"I feel better already," Randy declared with a smile. He felt alert and ready-to-go. D took the glass around to Chris and Josh and then again for himself.

"Let's go upstairs and smoke some weed." Randy and D went upstairs. The TV was flickering some unknown program. D turned it to another channel to catch up on sports. Randy and D sat down and passed the pipe back and forth, quickly smoking the bowl of marijuana.

D's pocket vibrated. He pulled out his phone and flipped it open.

"Ah, someone is coming by for a delivery. Stay here. I'll handle this."

Randy sat into the couch and let it swallow him up as he stared at the TV. He picked up the remote and flipped through the channels. An indeterminate amount of time passed, and D settled back into the couch with him.

"Hungry?"

"Not really."

"Let's eat anyway."

"I think I have $10."

"Awesome, let's hit the Waffle House."

D stood up and disappeared upstairs for what seemed like hours to Randy on the couch. D came back downstairs, fully dressed and with a set of keys. He walked to the basement door.

"We're going to Waffle House, you guys want to come?"

"Yeah, I'm kinda hungry, are you hungry babe?" Chris said.

"Yeah, let's go eat. This needs to cool anyway. Do you have cigs?"

"Yeah, we're coming D."

Randy was numb despite the flurry of activity. Chris and Josh pulled on t-shirts and jeans and slipped on tired shoes red with mud. D stood by the door.

"Okay buddy, time to go."

Randy finally stood up and rubbed his eyes. He checked his pockets. "My wallet," he said simply.

D looked around. "There, it's in your backpack, go get it."

Randy walked over to the backpack and dug around a little bit. He found the scrap of velcro and cloth that held his last few dollars and ID. He stuffed it in his back pocket and followed D out to his tired Sedan. The four men piled in and pulled out onto the blacktop to head over to the Waffle House. Randy loved the wind against his face that flowed in from the rolled-down windows as everyone smoked, texted on their phones and cast their gaze outside from time to time. The radio was on but Randy couldn't hear what was playing. D pulled the car into the small parking lot off the highway. There were a few guys milling around outside, but D ignored them and went straight into the Waffle House. It was in the afternoon, the lunch rush was fresh over and there were only two tables with anyone sitting at them. Chris, Josh, D, and Randy lined up at the counter and sat down in the brown laminate seats at the linoleum counter.

"Water for you boys?" The waitress was pleasant. Her teeth had bad overbite and her hair was pulled into a kind of sloppy bun. Her black company apron was stained from serving all day. She held the ticket book.

"Yeah, that's fine," D said.

She pulled out four menus and placed them in front of the young men, and put out the thin tri-fold napkins and silverware. Randy was reeling. Everything looked so good on both sides of the laminated menu, but he was craving pancakes all of a sudden, and some sausage. Hash browns, smothered and covered.

"Hon? Hon? What'll it be?"

"Pancakes, sausage, hash browns, smothered and covered," he said, like a waterfall of words falling out of his mouth.

"Anything else to drink?"

"Nah, I'm good thank you."

Randy sat at the table. He wasn't even conscious of what the others were doing. He was fascinated by what the waitress was doing and what the cook was doing with the food. His eyes just kept following their movements.

"Randy? Randy."

"What?"

"Chris asked you how you were doing? Are you alright? We don't a repeat of earlier."

"Yeah, yeah I'm fine. I was just watching. It was cool."

"How cute! You got mesmerized!" Josh said.

Chris chuckled. "This one is fresh."

"Be nice," D chided. "We all were that way one time too."

Randy turned towards them. "What was it like?"

"What was?"

"The first time."

"Ah ha," Chris said.

Josh leaned past D towards Randy. "Story time after we eat."

The waitress started to lay down the food at the places on the counter, reciting the order of each man as she placed the plate down. The white plates with brown accents around the edges clinked as she set them down. After reciting the final order she put down the check.

"Any refills?"

They all shook their heads no and dug into their food. Randy inhaled his food. He ate it so fast he hardly tasted it, but he loved the full feeling in his stomach. It seemed so necessary. He loved eating. He downed his water and enjoyed the feeling of satisfaction. D took his last bite and gulped down some coffee as he picked up the check. He held out his fingers for cash. Randy pulled out his wallet and his fingers rubbed against the sparse pieces of paper-linen in his wallet. He found one that said "10" with a picture of an old guy with a wig on it and gave it to D. D gathered up the money and got up and moved the few steps to the counter and the manual register. The waitress took the money and punched into the machine and asked about change.

"No change, it's for you." She smiled and pocket the extra money in her apron. She shoved the drawer shut and D took a toothpick and went for the door. Chris, Josh and Randy in near unison stood up and followed him out to the car.

"Have a nice day now."

Everyone took their places in the car and D pulled back out onto the four-lane road. He made a right down the highway and then made a U turn and started driving back towards the house. The afternoon sun was warm on Randy's skin. D seemed to drive randomly. He stopped the car at a small park that overlooked a small river. The car came to a stop in the small dirt parking lot. An amalgamation of wood and metal for children occupied one part of the park and was surrounded by some gravel and grass beyond that. Josh jumped out of the car and ran over towards the playground and climbed up the old metal jungle gym. Chris unfolded himself from the front seat and walked over towards the wood and metal playground. His sneakers crunched on the gravel as he swung his tall frame onto the play set. Chris ran through the play set several times. Josh sat on top of the jungle gym and looked out over the playground until he clambered down and joined Chris running around the play set. D lit another cigarette and Randy looked at the scene. D passed the cigarette back to him and he took a long drag.

"See those two?"

"Yeah?"

"They are still 12 years old."

"What do you mean?"

"They just never grew up, it's this life man."

"Oh." Randy didn't know what to say. He opened the rear door and walked over towards the swings and sat down on one. D eventually opened his door and, flicking his butt into the parking lot, walked down towards the stream. One by one they gathered around D at the stream. They situated themselves along the banks of the stream and D casually skipped rocks across the shallow water.

They all stared into the water for a moment until Josh finally broke the silence.

"I'll never forgive them."

"Josh…." Chris said, his voice trailing.

"It's true. I trust him, babe. Randy, I said it would be story time. So here's your story. Chris and I met when were 12. I had been in the system since I was five. They took me away from my mom because she was, how did they say it? An unfit mother. I don't know what was wrong with her, but there was no one to take me, so I was sent to a foster family. They were terrible. There were nine kids in the house and I think the lady did it just for the money. I was in a room with five other boys and it was just terrible. Anyway, I was sent to a few other foster families. I never did that well in school and I just never cared. I was still waiting for mom to show back up. I didn't know what was going on. I just wanted to leave where I was. That was until I met Chris. We both ended up in the same orphan home. I remember the first time I saw him. I was in love. At nights he would crawl down from his bunk into mine and we would cuddle. Then as time went on we did more. I finally felt love. I was so happy. They tried to keep us apart but no matter what we stayed together. The home we were at got shut down. I guess they weren't following some regulations or whatever. So anyway, they had to find places for all of us. That is when things really got weird. This nice man, a policeman said he was going to take us someplace we would like. Chris wanted to go with him, but I wasn't sure about it. I didn't really trust him. Babe, can I get a cigarette?" Chris pulled out a pack and gave him one.

"Basically, he sold us into a kind of slavery. The place he took us was pretty bad. Mostly a place where guys just wanted to do drugs and have sex. No one cared who we were, where we came from, or anything. A couple ran the place. The wife was kind in her way to us. She made sure we went to school and ate sometimes. But no one really checked on us. That's when we learned how to make stuff and sell stuff. We would sell drugs to the kids at school and by some miracle we never got caught. I dropped out at 16, Chris too. By that time we were doing all right. Then they busted that place for drugs. It was bad. They arrested us. Chris and I both did some time, but we were minors, so it wasn't long. I missed him so much!" Josh pressed his hand into Chris' arm. "I thought I'd lost him forever, but he wrote me and we managed to stay in touch and he was there to greet me when I got out. I was amazing! And we've never been apart since. I don't quite remember how we met D."

"I met you guys at that guy Nate's place up north," D said.

"Oh yeah, I forgot about that," Josh said. He pushed his cigarette butt into the bank.

Randy looked at them. "You said you'd never forgive them."

"Yeah, the last couple that quote fostered us. They took me away from Chris. That really sucked. I could put up with jail but I couldn't put up without my Chris."

Randy shook his head, tossing his blonde hair around. "Thanks for taking care of me this morning. I appreciate that."

"It was no problem! You're with us now, we try to keep things as safe as possible." Josh smiled at Randy.

"I take care of all my boys," D said.

The sun began to get lower in the sky. A gentle breeze pushed across them and ruffled the pleasant water.

"I need to smoke some weed," Chris said, breaking the silence.

D stood up from the bank and pulled Randy up. Chris pulled up Josh and they crawled their way up to the parking lot. They all sat down into the car and rolled up the windows. Chris packed the small metal pipe with the small green leaves and started to pass it around. Everyone had their hits and D fired up the car and they made their way across the country roads back to the house as the sun was beginning to dip below the horizon. D parked in the yard and the doors closed with a metallic thump.

"Can we watch a movie?" Josh asked.

"Sure, which Disney movie are you going to make me suffer through again for the millionth time?"

"I don't know yet babe, probably one of the usual."

D opened the door and walked towards the back of the house, disappearing. Josh busied himself looking for a movie. Chris flopped onto the couch and Randy sat on the floor. Josh selected a tape and shoved it into the aging VHS player. The sound modulated as the tape started. Josh curled up on the couch with Chris and they stared at the flickering screen. D reappeared and joined Randy on the floor. D leaned up against Randy and put an arm around his shoulder.

"Anyone coming over tonight?" Josh asked.

"Probably, it's Saturday night. We have time, though."

"Okay, any new boys coming?"

"I haven't checked my phone in a little bit. Probably, though."

"Okay. Let's watch!"

The four lost themselves in the story playing out on screen. When it ended, D stood up for a long-needed cigarette. He stood in the doorway looked at his phone. "Looks like a few guys will be coming by, maybe a couple boys too. Get ready kids."

Josh uncurled himself from Chris' embrace. "I'm going to take a shower then."

D exhaled and walked out to the porch. Randy joined him and leaned against a post.

"Are you going to be okay?"

"I think so."

"Okay, I need you tonight. I need you to be good. Okay?"

"Okay, I got it. I'll be good D, for you, I'll be good."

D put his hand on Randy's shoulder and offered him the cigarette. "Good, I know you will be. Take a shower after Josh."

"Okay, D." Randy inhaled several times from the cigarette. They smoked it down to the filter and flicked it into the can. Randy sank the butt right into the can and D smiled.

Chris and Josh sat shirtless in threadbare flannel sleeping pants around an aged, tilting kitchen table, eating cheap cold cereal from a bag. Randy came upstairs from the basement, rubbing his eyes. The sun was high in the sky. The brass clock behind the couch in the front room read 1:33. He couldn't remember what day it was. He remembered the weekend. Maybe it was Monday? He felt sore all over and jittery. The air felt hot, but he felt chilled. Randy sat down at the table on the side nearest the refrigerator. The early quiet was broken when the trio heard D start crashing through the house. D felt heavy, like his limbs would not respond. His mind was foggy but he had to find his laptop.

"Which one of you fucking bastards stole my fucking laptop!" D knocked about the house, looking for anyone to blame that he couldn't seem to find his laptop. Chris stood up in a smooth motion mid-bite and walked out of the kitchen and down the short hallway into the front room of the house. Chris looked around on the floor and spied the familiar white plastic of the laptop. He picked it up and made his way back. D was in the mudroom over turning shoes and unused coats.

"Dude."

"The fuck! Fuckers!"

"Look."

D let the coats fall back to the small wooden bench. A thin wooden door flapped open. He stared at the white textured plastic of the laptop and then in a swift motion seized it from Chris and hugged it close. He slid down the wall onto the mudroom floor. D was staring into space when the door swung open slowly. Bob stood in the doorway with a sour look on his face.

"We're in trouble boys."

"What's going on, Bob?" Chris asked, walking back towards the table and his cereal. Bob followed him and set about making some coffee.

"I got the tax bill on the place. $1,800. $1,800 I don't have right now and I only got 30 days to come up with it. Got filters?"

"In the drawer there."

D finally seemed more calm and joined them in the kitchen. He reached under a cabinet and found a plastic bottle of pure grain alcohol. He opened the top and poured a generous amount straight into his mouth. He put the bottle down and turned the cap back on.

"I thought you paid that in two payments," D said.

"This is the second payment."

"Shit."

"If we don't pay, we're out, and when they see what's going on downstairs they'll come after me."

"How much product do we have?" D asked. His mind was elsewhere but something was making him respond.

"Not much, I'm afraid. We've been short materials," Josh said.

"What if I got you stuff?"

"Three days," Chris said, slurping up his milk.

"And we still would have to move and come out $1,800 ahead," Josh remarked.

"What else can we do?" Randy offered.

"Me'n Rich talked about running some checks and maybe some paper."

D put his laptop down on the floor. "Yeah, but Rich's paper is crap." He rubbed his eyes again. "Okay, okay, let's get another batch going. Randy and I will go get some more stuff. I'll pick up those boys from this weekend, whatever the fuck their names were. We'll go get some and then we'll get a batch going and we'll see what we can do."

"Do you want me to call some people?" Josh asked.

"Yeah, yeah, get some guys to move this shit. And listen, no fucking fronts, okay? We got burned on that shit the last time. I'm fucking tired of it." D stood up on unsteady feet and walked towards the stairs. Randy stood up and followed him.

Chris and Josh flipped open their phones and their thumbs started dancing across the keyboards.

"Did you text that other Josh?"

"Yeah, and that weird Alex guy."

"Do you have Dan's number? That Dan who hooked up with Randy?"

"No, maybe Randy does," he replied.

"Do you want to watch a movie?" Chris said, never looking up from the black rubbery surface of his phone.

"Always!" Josh said, looking up from the silvery flip phone whose outer surface had seen better days.

"What do you want to watch?"

"Something fun."

"Always fucking Disney. Fox and Hound?"

"Too sad, I'm not in the mood to cry."

"Okay, how about Aladdin?"

"My favorite!"

"Okay. Would you like something to smoke?"

"Always!"

Chris and Josh moved from the kitchen to the couch. Chris stuffed the tape into the VHS player. The sound modulated and he sat back down on the couch. Josh curled into him close and enjoyed his supple skin and light dusting of body hair against his shoulder. Chris put his arm around his boyfriend and hugged him in close.

Randy followed D into his room and dug through his backpack for a T-shirt.

"Here, just wear this." D threw a muscle shirt at Randy and Randy slipped it over his thin frame and lithe body. He stuffed his pockets with his wallet and a little bit of money.

D dropped onto his belly and rooted around under the bed. He pulled out a metal lunch box. He stuffed the lump of green bills in his pocket and as he stood up retrieved a thin hooded shirt and slipped it over his shoulders. "Let's go. I'll explain what we have to do in the car."

D and Randy stomped down the stairs with inconsistent steps. D walked out the front door and Randy followed, looking back at Chris and Josh sitting on the couch.

"Bye," Josh said.

The car lurched to the driver's side when D sat down into it. Randy pulled up the handle and sat down carefully.

"Okay, here's how this works. We have to grab stuff that has the chemicals we need, I'll go with you on the first couple, show you what to get. We'll do a few ourselves. Just buy one or two boxes or whatever, don't draw attention to yourself. When you check out, don't talk a lot. If anyone asks any questions, your girlfriend is sick, your sister, brother, mom, dad whatever. Got it?"

"Yeah D, I got it."

"Okay, we'll go hit a few places and then we'll go grab those kids and send them out. I really appreciate how much you're helping me out with this." D started the car and pulled out of the yard. The car rolled down the road towards the first town.

"No problem, D. Thanks for letting me stay at your house."

"I help out where I can, man. I really like you too, that helps."

Randy smiled for the first time since he could remember. He rolled up his window and lit a cigarette. D started to roll up his window and pulled out a small glass pipe.

"Under your seat." D pointed between Randy's legs. Randy bent down and reached under the seat. His hand found the small plastic bag and he pulled it out. He pinched off some of the green leaves and deposited them into the pipe. They passed the glass back and forth and the car started to fill with smoke. They breathed it again and again, reaching to new heights each time. By the time D pulled into the first pharmacy, they were relaxed. Highly focused and ready to do what they had to do. D and Randy walked into the bright building. The cashier greeted them and they walked to the cold medicine aisle. D slipped $20 in Randy's pocket and took two boxes off of the shelf. Randy did the same. D walked towards the pharmacy and Randy walked to the front of the store.

"Hi," the young, pretty cashier greeted him. Her hair was pulled back in a simple ponytail with a fabric hair tie. Her nails were broken and oddly shaped.

"Hi."

"$12.67."

Randy took the worn bill out of his pocket and put it on the counter. The cashier swept it off the counter and punched the buttons in the machine, put in the drawer, made change and then handed him the bag, receipt and his change. Randy tried not to make eye contact with her, but he noticed she looked tired. Randy took the bag and change and walked out of the store.

D walked out a few minutes later.

"How was it?"

"It was okay," Randy said.

"Did she ask for your ID?"

"No, was she supposed to?"

"Technically yes, but it's better if they don't."

D unlocked the car and they drove to the next store. This time Randy went to the back of the store and D went to the front, but they encountered no resistance or questions. D was happy. They smoked more marijuana and D drove over to a squat motel in another town.

"According to my guy the boys are staying in #16, down at the end."

D parked the car in front of the door and looked around to make sure no one noticed them. D didn't stop the motor and just opened the door. D knocked on the door. A tense few seconds passed. D knocked again. A young man finally came to the door. His hair was very dark. His skin was light brown and his face was an interesting cross between hispanic and Asian. He was shirtless from the waist up and his eyes were heavy.

"Hey, you must be D."

"Yeah, are you guys ready to go?"

"Uh, yeah, uh. Wanna smoke?"

"We kinda need to go actually."

"Oh, oh, yeah sure. Uh. Hang on."

D walked into the room but left the door open.

The room was sparse and smelt of chemicals, a tinge of marijuana, maleness and sex. Just a few backpacks on the floor. The beds had been slept in and there was still someone in one. A small water pipe was situated on the dresser and the TV blinked away silently. The body in the bed farthest from the door finally moved and sat up. His chest and stomach were flat, accentuated by large nipples and a light dusting of dirty blonde hair that matched his head. His skin was pale, except for his arms and neck, which were only slightly darker.

"Who the fuck are you?"

"I'm D, I'm here to pick you guys up. You're coming to stay with us for awhile."

"Again? Fuck'n ass man. I'd just like to be chill for a little while."

"What's your name kid?"

"Nate."

"What about your friend?"

"That's Joseph."

"Why do you have such a bad attitude?"

"Uh, oh, uh wow. I don't have a bad attitude."

"Sure you do. You were talking shit when you woke up."

Nate looked sad. "Hey, look, I'm sorry, I didn't mean anything by it."

"Yeah, be nice. My associate and I are trying to be nice to you."

At that moment, Joseph walked out of the bathroom.

"Be nice, Nate. He's going to let us stay with him for a little bit."

"I know, I know. I just felt weird.

"It's okay, you don't have to be weird about it. Just get your backpacks so we can go. I need you two to help me with something."

Nate stood straight up out of bed, revealing his naked body. His clothes were on the floor and he started to pull the clothes onto his average frame. Nate wore clothes that looked a little large for his tall body. Joseph's clothes were dark and tight on his smaller body. D watched them dress and felt the urge of attraction. He was looking forward to tasting these boys later. A few minutes later, the boys were packed. D opened the truck of the running car and they dropped their backpacks in the trunk. They opened the back doors and folded themselves into the car. D turned towards the back seat and explained the situation.

"Who is this guy?"

"That's my buddy Randy."

"Hi," Joseph said.

"Hi," Randy said quietly.

"I hate doing this shit. But whatever, I mean, let's get to work. Do you have money?" D smiled.

"Randy, pack a bowl. We have a lot of places to visit today."

They repeated the process of acquiring materials over and over again for the rest of the day at different pharmacies and stores in five different towns. The sun was leaving by the time D started to make the 2 1/2 hour drive back to the house. D started to yawn.

"I really need to teach you how to drive," D said in between yawns.

"That'd be awesome," Randy said.

"When this shit is taken care of. We'll do it. And we need to get you a phone. Someplace cheap, we'll figure that out," D said as he shifted his body in his seat. He turned up the radio and rolled down the window to ash his cigarette again. D guided the car down the darkened highway and finally arrived back at the house. He parked the car in the yard under the white yard light.

"Wake up kids, we're home."

Everyone stirred and started to move. They opened doors and started picking up the many plastic sacks that had gathered all day long that had surrounded their legs on the road trip to the house. D opened the trunk for Nate and Joseph. D put his arm around Joseph's waist and smiled at him.

"You guys wanna party?"

"Yeah, yeah we're always partying."

"Good. We're gonna have fun tonight."

The four made their way into the house. Randy went into the kitchen, leaving the others in the front room. Chris and Josh were still ensconced on the couch.

"How did you guys do with sales?" D asked.

"Not so great," Chris said.

"Yeah, everyone is busy or wants fronts because they don't have a lot of money right now."

"All right, I got stuff, you two need to get mixing. We'll front a little to the guys we trust."

"Okay." Chris started to move, forcing Josh to sit up. Josh looked up at him with puckered lips and they kissed. Chris started examining the bags. Joseph and Nate stood near the front door. D kept showing Chris what they had to work with. Chris seemed happy with his materials. D turned around towards Joseph and Nate.

"Randy?" Randy reappeared in the front room from the kitchen.

"Show these guys upstairs, there's a room on the end they can crash in." Randy was pensive, but led them upstairs and showed them the white door. He opened it and let them in. He walked back downstairs and lifted his arms behind his head.

"Randy, I need you to take care of whoever comes by tonight, okay? Can you do that? I need you."

"Uh, yeah, no problem." Randy stood nearer to him.

"You know what the means, right?" D put his arms around Randy and moved his face within inches.

"Yeah, I know."

"No freakouts this time."

"No." Randy put his arms around D.

"Okay, you're strong, you can do it. I know you can. You're a nice kid. They like you."

Randy looked down at the floor.

"Hey, bud, this will all be over soon. We'll get through this. I promise. I meant what I said earlier."

"Why do you like me?"

"What?"

"Why?"

"I guess I see a lot of myself in you. I know how on weekends we get a lot of guys in and out of here, and boys like you come and go and come again. But since I saw you walking along I wanted to take care of you. I guess that's why."

"It's weird. You're a man, I'm a man."

D lifted Randy's head up towards him. "That don't matter. Look at these guys that come in here with their little boyfriends. Cops, lawyers, stock guys, shit, they're society's measure of normal and successful. But guess what, they like to fuck just as much as we do. So fuck it."

Randy smiled a little and hugged D tighter.

"And now that we've had the heartfelt faggot moment for the day, I need to help Chris and John. Clean up a little, grab out those cans, get ready and keep an eye on those boys upstairs."

"Okay." Randy released the embrace and walked up the stairs for a hot shower to clean his body inside and out. Randy came down a few minutes later in another of D's shirts and started to pack up the trash while keeping out the aluminum cans for later sale. 45 minutes of cleaning brought the house to some semblance of cleanliness, despite the thick dust and dated appearance. He was taking the bags out to the barrel when he heard an engine shut off in the yard. He was ready to go, whatever came, whatever he had to do, he was going to do it for D. He couldn't harmonize the feelings he had for D as a friend, for these new feelings he felt in his body that sought out that buzz, and the first pangs in his heart. Did he love D? How could he love a man? His head felt twisted like something was wrong. But there was no time now. Randy walked back into the house, his face, his body, and his mind steeled for whatever he had to do. Randy greeted the first guy that came in and invited him upstairs.

Randy walked down the narrow concrete stairs to the basement. The foul chemical smell filled the air. Randy sat down, leaning his bare back against the workbench.

"Make much progress?" Randy said as he wiped his forehead.

"Yeah, we're doing good," D said. He took off a mask and sat down next to Randy on the floor. "How was your night?"

Randy exhaled heavily. "Four guys is a lot of fucking."

"Yeah, was it all at once?"

"Mostly, yeah, like we had a freak fest up there."

"What time is it?"

"5, man, sun is almost up. Maybe 6:30."

"It's getting later, a little. Chris, Josh, finish up here. I'm gonna go have a smoke."

D pushed himself up and offered an arm to Randy. Randy grasped his forearm and pulled himself up. They walked up the stairs and out to the porch. The yard was dark except for the white glow of the yard light. The cacophony of insects sang like a disjointed symphony and flying insects darted around. D took his plastic lighter out of his pocket and lit a cigarette, and then offered a cigarette and the lighter to Randy.

"Where's your head at?"

Randy flicked the lighter and lit his cigarette. "Nowhere."

"Still feeling bad?"

"I guess. I don't know what I'm feeling. Just numb, I guess, and a little sore."

D put his arm around Randy. "I need you now, more than ever. The next few days, we've got a lot to do. We need to move this product, fast." D hugged him close.

"I don't know anything about that. I sold a little weed but nothing serious."

D smiled. "Don't worry about that. I'll take care of all that. I just need you to help me, whatever I need, and to just be there."

Randy smiled as he inhaled. "I think I can do that."

"It's going to be fast, a little dangerous, big time if we get caught."

"I know."

"I'll make sure you get paid, high, and laid. You think you can sleep?"

"Probably."

"Let's smoke first."

D and Randy walked out to the porch.

"What about those guys we picked up?" Randy asked.

"They're someone else's boys. Someone'll come to pick them up in the next couple days. Were they okay?"

"Yeah, they were okay," Randy said.

Despite the high he was having, Randy was able to let sleep take over in between the end of the high and the dullness of sobriety. He was feeling, but he didn't know what he was feeling; he just knew there was fear.

The next morning, D shook his shoulder. Randy woke up bleary-eyed.

"What?"

"We have work to do, bud."

"What?"

D laid down on the bed and put his hand on his stomach.

"Product's done and we need to make some deliveries and some sales."

Randy moved his feet past D and onto the floor.

"Okay."

"I love you when you're like this."

"What's that?"

"In the morning. You make me almost..." his voice trailed off.

"What? I make you what?"

"Nothin' man, let's get out of here." D stood up and closed the door behind him.

Randy and D stood out on the porch in their usual places, Randy leaning against one of the 4x4 posts and D usually sitting against the house or leaning against the house as if he were holding up. Anytime they went out to smoke, they gravitated to these spots. D did something different this time; he stood up and leaned against the railing with Randy. They smoked in silence for several minutes. Just as D re-lit another cigarette, he broke the silence.

"Let's tell war stories."

"What do you mean?"

"I've never asked you about your story, how you came to be in that parking lot."

"That's heavy, man."

"It always is."

Randy inhaled a few more times and stared at his shoes.

"I'll start," D volunteered.

"I was born in Illinois outside Champaign. My dad was a drunk and he liked to beat my mom when shit didn't go his way or whatever reason he found. If the Bears or the Cubs lost, he beat up on my mom. If he was mad at work, whatever the reason. He wasn't a bad guy, but give him some whiskey or cheap beer and it was a problem. My mom sent me from place to place, relative to relative until no one would take me. I was 12 years old. I guess someone at school got suspicious because CPS or Child Protective Shit as my mom used to call them got involved and they put me in a foster home. It was a nice family in a nice town, except for the father. The father, he was an All-American football player two years in a row. He liked me, and not just in a fatherly way. I guess I just accepted it because it was more loving that what I was used to. But as they say, sick is still sick. I'm sure the ladies of his wife's garden club would be a little surprised and never believe it that he liked little boys. I liked the nice clothes and the quiet neighborhood. He bought me a car when I turned 16. I didn't love it as much when he fucked me in the back of it. So I ditched it all. I dropped out of high school and walked with a backpack and the clothes on my back. I just couldn't take it anymore. I ran. After that I traveled from place to place by foot or train, occasional hitchhike, and then I ended up back here. I saw some beautiful country and I did some interesting things."

"That's just—I don't know what to say." Randy looked him straight in the eye. "You were raped?"

"Straight up the ass, man."

"But, but do you think you're gay? Like, have you ever been with a girl?'

"Yeah, I got with a girl, but it wasn't the same. I'm not saying I'm gay, it's just, I don't know. It is what it is." D exhaled the white smoke and it curled into the night sky.

"That's really tough, I mean, I'm sorry that happened to you. I still don't know what to say," Randy offered.

"Your turn," D said with a smile.

Randy flicked his cigarette butt towards the can and missed. "It all started with my sister. I wanted to protect her so bad. I don't even know where she's buried or if she's buried."

"Your sister is dead?"

"Yeah. I loved her so much and because of me she's dead." The words just fell out of his mouth.

"You left because your sister died? Seems a little extreme."

"Yeah, I guess it does. But considering I murdered our stepfather, it doesn't sound so bad now."

"What?—Shit? You killed a motherfucker?" D almost dropped his cigarette and stood straight up.

"Yeah." Randy admitted it again quietly.

"So what, you ran? Are they looking for you?" D asked.

"No, nothing like that. I was only 15 when it happened. I was arrested, had a stupid trial, went to prison, and when I got out no one showed up to get me or see me. So I started walking." Randy sat down on the steps.

D relaxed and finished his cigarette by flicking it into the metal can and landing the butt there perfectly.

D crossed his arms and looked at Randy. "That is some shit. What's it like to kill somebody?"

"I don't know. I guess, it's scary, it's sickening."

"How'd you do it? Shoot him? Stab him?" D said, turning around to face the yard. His eyes were already off in space. His mind was on tomorrow.

"I beat him."

"With what?"

"A cast iron frying pan."

D was plain-faced. "Get some sleep bud, we got shit to do in the next few days." D walked into the house, letting the screen door bang against the frame.

Chapter 29

Randy put on jeans, T-shirt, hoodie, grabbed his backpack and slipped on his shoes. He stomped downstairs and into the front room. He went into the kitchen and poured out a bowl of cereal. They could be robbed, caught by the cops which meant major jail time, and they could be killed anywhere along the way. If they were going to survive with their freedom and their lives then they had to get through the next few days with no accidents and no problems. Randy finished his cereal and threw the foam bowl away. He walked through the house and out into the yard.

"Should we put more in the back seat? I think the trunk is sagging too much," Chris said.

Josh crawled out of the truck of the car and looked at it. "Yeah, a little more, four bags, two on each side." Chris and Josh kept arranging the packages in the doors and hollow areas of the car so that the car would look normal.

D flicked his cigarette into the yard. "Let's get out of here."

"Are you sure about this?" Chris asked him.

"As much as I'll ever be," Randy said trying to sound confident.

"It's not so bad, it's not like we haven't done this before," Josh offered.

"Yeah, but in the past we've had help, we've had runners, you know."

"Yeah, but we don't have time for all that right now," D said. Josh closed the back door of the car and slowly walked over to the two men.

"Okey dokey then," Josh said, folding his arms and leaning next to Chris.

D looked around. "Randy?" he said. Randy walked over to the group and joined the circle.

"It's going to be dangerous, but it's going to be fun, I promise! And we'll be waiting here for you when you get back," Josh said with a broad smile, holding out his arms to take Randy's hands.

"Okay guys, enough, we have to go." D broke the circle and threw open the door of the car and got in head first.

The next 10 days, "Was it 10 days or longer?" Randy tried to remember but the days blended together in a blur of time. They drove all around Missouri, Arkansas and even as far as Illinois, dropping off, dealing, smoking, not sleeping, barely eating, and most importantly, making money. Randy tried hard to keep track of the days, but they blurred together. Randy sat in bathrooms, bedrooms, and cars with strange people of all kinds smoking. Some people brought their kids and would leave the kids in the car or in another part of the house. Randy would look at them sometimes. So innocent. He thought about how they had no idea what their parents were doing or that one day they might end up doing the same. The car got progressively lighter as D sold off the product and Randy stuffed their backpacks with the money. The journeys from place to place were long on the dirt county roads they took to avoid the police and the competition. Whenever it was time to move, D drove, day or night. Randy knew they were playing a high stakes game.

They were on the move again, on a dark country road with only the light from the headlights and the iridescent glow of the interior lights of the car. The car headlights illuminated the trees that hung over the road. From time to time Randy could see a pair of eyes staring out at the road from the trees.

"I love this car man."

"Why?" Randy said as he took a hit of cannabis.

"Stiff suspension and a good engine."

"I got something stiff for you."

"Oh really? I told you I don't bottom," D said with a chuckle.

"I'm horny as fuck, pull over, man, let's fuck."

"You're pretty forward tonight, young man."

"Yeah, yeah, I'm horny, man."

D reached over and rubbed Randy's thigh, and let his hand wander as he traveled down the road. D passed a dirt pull out.

"Let's see if we can stop there and sleep. I'm tired." D stopped and backed the car down the road until he found the pull out and backed the car into it. D got out of the car and felt the night air hit his face and several insects swoop in for the attack on his exposed skin. He opened his phone and waved his hand at the bugs.

"Shit," he said under his breath. He opened the car and sat back down.

"We got to keep moving. These guys are looking for their delivery tonight."

"How much are they getting?"

"Depends on how much money they have."

Randy nodded. D started the car and drove faster down the road with his hand firmly on Randy's thigh. D followed the instructions in his phone and eventually the car pulled up to a vine-covered trailer. D and Randy both stepped out of the car, Randy with backpack in hand. D gave the metal door a knock. A face passed before the thin window and the door opened.

"Hey," D said.

"Come on in, boys."

The customer was a pot-bellied fellow of about 35 or maybe 40. A white muscle T-shirt stretched over the paunch and his hairline had just begun to recede. A pair of tired jeans were tight on his legs.

"Babe, they're here." He stuck his hand into the back of his jeans and pulled out a wad of bills. "That's $150."

"Awesome," D replied. Randy opened the backpack and pulled out a few grams in pill bags. He took what Randy handed him and smiled.

"Smoke?" the pot-bellied man asked.

"Sure."

He prepared the pipe and passed it around. D sat on the couch, Randy sat on the floor.

D inhaled a long breath and then exhaled. "We were wondering if we might crash here tonight. We've been on the road for a few days."

"No can do bud, my wife'll be pissed at me."

"That's right." A bleary-eyed woman in a white T-shirt and some cotton shorts walked out of a bedroom, carrying a baby sucking a pacifier in only its diaper. "Ain't nobody sleepin' here tonight." Her mid-south accent was thick and she disappeared back into the bedroom as silently as she had come out. As the pipe was passed around, she joined the group and smoke with them silently, legs crossed on the end of the couch. A thin smoke began to fill the trailer. The baby started to cry from the bedroom. The woman stood up.

"What'd I tell you about smoking around the baby?" she said in a huff, and she went to the bedroom. Her husband stood up and opened a window.

"Weed?" Randy asked.

"Load it, man," D said.

The men kept smoking and the small trailer filled with smoke and conversation about early season football prospects.

The woman reappeared and put her hands on her hips. "Give me that!" She took a hit of the pipe. "Now get out, this smoking is making the house smell and the baby cry."

"Babe, we'll go outside."

"No, no, get them out of here. I don't want them in the house."

Randy stood up and slung the backpack over his shoulder. D stood up and held up his hand and walked towards the door. "Later guys."

D and Randy walked towards the car. D backed out of the driveway and pulled back onto the road.

"I have a bad feeling."

"What do you mean?"

"I just got a bad feeling about this. Something isn't right."

D kept driving. He saw lights up ahead. The lights turned off the desolate road. D sped up the speedometer, reached 70, then 80, then 90. He kept going until he saw the trucks blocking the road.

"Get the fucking gun Randy."

Randy reached under the seat and pulled out the 1911 pistol. He handed it to D as two men with shotguns surrounded the car. D rolled down the window slightly. The larger of the two men put the shotgun right at the edge of the window. "You know what we want."

D looked away. "We don't have anything."

"You just dropped off, we know you got stuff."

D sighed. "Randy, give'em the backpack." Randy reached unto the back seat and handed him the backpack. D rolled down the window and handed the backpack to the large man.

"That it?"

"That's all we have," Randy offered.

"Trunk!" the large man said. D released the truck lid. The two men moved to the back of the car. D reached for the gun. Randy put his hand on it.

"Don't do it, it's not worth it."

D tried to pull it out, but Randy held his hand firm. "Give me the fucking gun, man." The two men rifled around and closed the trunk. Wordlessly, they walked back to their trucks, threw their weapons on the seats, and drove off, leaving dust behind them and the road desolate once again. Randy let his hand off of the gun and reached down and pulled up his hoodie to show D where he had stored the money. D smiled.

"You're a smart kid, let's get the fuck out of here."

D put foot to metal and the car lurched forward and down the dusty road. D plucked out his phone from his hip pocket, flipped it open, and started texting.

"I think I found us a place to sleep tonight."

"Where?"

"Motel, off the highway we're coming up to."

"How many people?"

"Don't know, I'll ask."

"Just a woman."

"Is she hot?"

"I guess we'll find out."

The car sped down the road. D turned onto the highway, and an hour later, the sedan pulled into the small, ill-kept parking lot of a motel whose pool was closed.

"We're looking for room 211," D said as he cruised the parking lot. He found the room and parked beneath it. The men grabbed their backpacks and walked up the metal stairs to the door. D knocked at the door. A short round faced woman with stringy black hair that barely touched her shoulders answered a few seconds later. She held her lips open, showing her blackened teeth, and waved them in with a whole arm gesture.

"Come in, come in, Brad said you were coming."

D and Randy stepped into the hotel room. It was clean enough and the beds were made up. Everything was brown and gold, the carpet, the worn crown wallpaper and the furniture. "I had to clean the room, it was filthy, just filthy, when I got here. That's why Brad sent you boys over here. I'm Barb, by the way."

"Hi Barb, I'm D and this is Randy." Randy reached over to her extended hand.

"Thanks. I don't really have any food or much money but we might be able to go to McDonalds or something."

"Uh, it's fine, we have money, it's no problem," Randy volunteered.

"Let's go eat. I need a cigarette," D said.

The young men dropped their backpacks on the floor of the aging carpet and followed Barb out of the room. "You know, I'm kinda the mom," Barb said as she locked the door behind her. "I'm kinda the frat mom. I take care of all my young ones like you two. I try to keep everyone safe."

"You do good work then," D exhaled as he opened the car door. "Randy, open the lady's door." Randy opened the door behind him.

She sat down in the car. "Let's go over there, it's a nice place just American."

D pulled the car out of the over-chip-sealed parking lot and drove towards the direction she pointed. The car traveled a few blocks down the highway. "That's the place!" Barb said, pointing at the squat restaurant. D made a fast right turn off the road and into the small parking lot. The restaurant had large yellow-glass lanterns and the exterior looked like it was made of heavy sawed wood beams in a medieval style. The windows were painted with the specials in large bright neon letters. The group walked inside onto the brown laminate floors, the edges of which had seen better days. If you looked closely you could find the foot patterns of hundreds of diners over the years that had walked through this restaurant looking for a bite to eat. The metal sign said, "Please wait to be seated."

"They have good food here!" Barb reassured them. From the sign they could see the red booths, wooden chairs with short arms, larger lanterns in the same style from the vaulted ceiling, and laminate tables with napkin dispensers and condiments distributed on them. A waitress in a turquoise dress complete with white apron, clearly at the end of her shift, led the "party of three" to a back booth. The waitress was older, used a good deal of eye makeup, and held up her mousy brown hair with two pencils. They slid into red vinyl booths and picked up the menus the waitress had left behind. Barb and D sat together, facing Randy. A few moments later, the waitress came back.

"Something to drink? Iced tea?"

"I'll have iced tea," Barb said.

"Sweetened or unsweetened?"

"Sweetened."

"How about you boys?"

"Sweetened," D replied.

"Unsweetened," Randy said.

"Three iced teas, two sweetened one unsweetened, coming right up."

"I'm thinking about that steak special I saw on the window. It sounds yummy!" Barb announced when the waitress had left.

"It does," D said. He looked around at the menu. The waitress returned with cheap plastic glasses full of the required sweetened and unsweetened liquids on thin napkins that served as coasters. She set them down on the table and the sides were already moist with condensation. Barb picked up her glass and put salt on her napkin. "That way the glass won't stick." The waitress stood there with her almost-empty ticket book. Barb ordered the steak special, Randy ordered a bacon cheeseburger with the regular fries, and D completed the order with another steak special, though unlike Barb, he chose the baked potato over the mashed ones. The waitress wrote the order down and walked off to the kitchen.

"So where are you boys headed?"

"North," D said.

"Yeah, just looking for some work. I have a friend who said he knows of something," Randy said. D was impressed at his quick reply and believable response.

"Uh huh."

"Yeah, just looking for work."

Barb looked around the restaurant. There were only a few other tables occupied, and the diners were either eating or had just finished. Barb shifted in her seat. D was content to text and Randy pulled out a copy of the dime paper from the little rack behind their booth. A few minutes later the waitress came back with a large tray and a tray stand. She kicked the tray stand open and put the tray on top of it. She distributed the food with a basket of rolls and looked around for refills. The uneasy silence of before was replaced with the easy silence of eating. Randy dug into his burger while Barb and D attacked their steaks.

"That was good."

"Yeah, I love steak. When I worked at Moto years ago we would grill steak on the weekends and have fun all the time, just me and my girlfriends and whoever we wanted. It was great, we were so young and good looking. I'm glad my kid is good looking, it helps! My daughter too, beautiful!"

"Let's get the bill and get out of here," D said. The waitress obliged a few moments later with the check. They collectively stood up and made their way towards the front. Randy paid the bill of $43.12 and joined D, who was leaning against the car, smoking a much-needed cigarette. Barb followed them to the front and disappeared into the ladies bathroom. Randy lit his cigarette from D's cigarette and waited for Barb to come out.

"She's crazy, she's gonna smoke and get crazier." D said shaking his head.

"Uh, I mean, I guess, sure, but we've been up for four days, you know? We need to smoke some weed and sleep."

D shifted on his legs. "I guess you're right."

"Let's see what happens."

"Okay, okay."

Barb appeared and D drove them back to the motel via a liquor store along the street for one of her "fruity beers," cigarettes, and cheap vodka. The trio landed back at the hotel room. Barb put ashtrays out and they all lit cigarettes and started casually smoking. D and Randy sat on the floor, and after a few minutes of sitting on the bed with her beer, Barb joined them on the floor in a small circle buttressed by the dresser and the two beds. D pulled out the cheap vodka and took a long drink right from the bottle and then handed it to Randy.

"Brad told me you had something for me."

"Lay it on her, Randy."

Randy took out one of the few bags they had left and a pipe and filled the pipe with the crystals and heated them so they melted. Randy passed the pipe to Barb, who inhaled the white smoke deeply. D took his share next and held his breath while he pulled out a grinder full of weed and loaded up the glass pipe. D passed it to Randy and then to Barb.

"This is what life is about! Good friends and good times! You boys are great. I need your numbers so we can stay in touch."

"Yeah, sure," Randy said.

Barb reached up and turned on the TV and started flipping through channels. D and Randy each prepared the pieces and passed them around again. Randy liked this; it was easy, there were no expectations, and after the intensity of the past few days, he loved the release, the way his body felt, the quietness of his mind and being close to D. Maybe he really did love him, maybe it was okay to love a man, maybe he could be in love with D and right now he didn't care. He enjoyed the feeling like a good sweater or hot water in the shower. It made him feel good. He hadn't felt in a while, and while he did not consciously understand it or acknowledge it, the feeling was welcome, it was new and fresh, something his life lacked.

The pipes made one last round. Barb crawled up into one of the beds. D and Randy lay on the other one. After several minutes, the hotel phone blinked red, and Barb picked it up. The caller was screaming, "I'm getting complaints about a strange smell from your room! What are you doin'? I can evict you and leave you on the street or you can find another hotel, do you hear me? Do you hear me? Clean whatever it is up! Now! Or I'll call the police!" The phone clicked, ending the call. Barb put the phone down and got up and opened the window, releasing the tainted smoke and air into the whole motel parking lot.

"Shut that shit!" D shouted.

"The whole place will smell like we're doing drugs up here," Randy said.

"But what about the smell? The owner? This blows…" Barb teared up a little.

"Randy, grab your shit, they're sure to call the cops now. Quick," D said, gathering his own items. Randy was confused, his body was not responding as it normally would. He fumbled around things. Zippers and such confused him. He felt fogged, almost like he was working through a mist or trying to control someone else's body. D waited for him and they walked down the steps. D opened the doors and they both put their backpacks in the back of the car. D flew into the front seat and pulled out of the parking lot. He didn't start out of town right away. He drove around the hotel and through some side streets and finally started towards the edge of the small town. Distantly, D could hear sirens and the faint blink of the police car lights. D raced out of town, and on the open road started to pick up speed and a few more hits of marijuana while they made their way west.

"I could have a decent night's sleep, I think. It's time for you to learn how to drive."

"Uh, right now?"

"Yeah, you ever drove anything?"

"ATVs a couple times and our little tractor."

"Good, it's the same idea."

D pulled over to the side of the road. D switched seats with him, and explained the pedals and what some of the switches did. D guided him onto the road and safely up to 55 miles an hour. D showed him how much to move the wheel around curves and turns.

"Perfect, you got it. I'm passing out, you keep going and just follow the route I told you. Wake me up if you need anything."

Randy nervously guided the car through the night towards home. A few hours later, D woke up and gave Randy a few more pointers on driving and enjoyed not being in control for a little while. The sun rose up on the hazy morning, and from the leaves on the trees to the temperature in the air you could tell that fall was well in place all around them. The men were about 45 minutes from the house when D fell asleep again. The sun fell gently across his face, neck and chest. Randy glanced over every chance he could just to admire, and to gaze at D, the man he was about to allow himself to be in love with despite everything in his body from his knees to his head telling him no. Randy wanted him and he wanted the love, the care, the affection and the camaraderie they had developed on the drive. Randy careful guided the car into the driveway and into the usual spot and let it rest. He shut off the motor and shook D awake.

"We're here, man. We're home." D stirred and looked around.

"Good job man, we didn't die." D sat up and rubbed his eyes. He looked around the yard and fell back into the reclined seat.

"Yeah, we didn't die." Randy leaned over across the center of the car and kissed D on the lips.

"That was sweet, Randy. Let's go see who's here." D opened the door and folded himself out onto the grass. They retrieved their backpacks and walked up to the front door. D tried the handle, but found it locked, so he knocked loudly. A moment later, Josh opened the door.

"You're home! Sorry about the door, Bob's paranoid! I'm so happy you're home!"

"Did you get my text?"

"No, I was sleeping."

"Whatever then, we got jacked for most of the end of our product but they didn't get a lot. Randy saved the money, though. Where's Bob?"

"Out back where he always is. Tell me all about it. Who jacked you?"

"I'll tell you in a little bit, I'm gonna go talk to Bob." Randy watched D walk out to the trailer. Randy rooted through his backpack for a cigarette and walked outside to smoke. Randy stood near the trailer. One of the windows was lifted and Randy could hear the conversation inside. Randy stayed still and silent as he listened.

"I wish it weren't like this." D said.

"Your momma died, your papa almost shot you until you got took away and sent to that bastard that abused you. That's how. You need your cocktail son, it's just so expensive."

Randy wondered what they were talking about but kept quiet.

D sighed. "Thanks for the recap, Bob. Now shut up." Bob shrugged his tank top covered his shoulders.

"I just tell it like it is. My brother is an asshole, that's all there is to it."

D exhaled towards the door and looked down at his feet. "Fuck him."

Randy walked around the end of the trailer and stood in another part of the yard and looked at D. D walked over to Randy, "He's got food inside, don't tell the others," D cautioned. Bob stood on the small porch of the trailer and waved the boys over. They joined him and he motioned for them to come inside. Bob closed the sliding door behind them.

"You got breakfast?" D asked.

"Yep. Bacon?" Bob said, pointing at a thin pan.

"Got eggs?"

"Scrambled."

"I'll have some," D said, looking for a clean plate in the small cabinets.

Randy sat on a chair near the door.

"Have you been taking your meds?"

D shot Bob a look and then looked at Randy. Bob held up his hands. "Sorry, sorry."

"I ran out about ten days ago, don't worry about it."

D pulled out two plates and put food on it. He handed a plate to Randy and produced a fork. The trio began eating.

"What meds are you on?" Randy asked.

"I'll tell you later." D said.

Randy was trying to process all the words he had heard. He didn't think D knew about him lurking outside the trailer. Was D sick? What was wrong with him and why was the medicine so expensive? Randy kept pondering this information as they finished eating. Randy wiped his eyes as they finished the food.

"You tired?" D asked.

"Yeah, just everything that happened is catching up to me."

"You have trouble out on the road?" Bob asked putting the dishes in the small sink.

"We had some problems but Randy acted real good and got us through it. We got through it together," D said shaking is head. Randy smiled at the complement. Randy couldn't remember the last time someone said something that positive about him or things he had done. D stood up and stretched out his body.

"Bob, I'm going to go crash out for awhile. Try not to fuckin' wake me."

Bob nodded his head and D walked out of the trailer and into the yard. Randy followed him, "Thanks for the food." Bob smiled at him. Randy and D crossed the yard and back into the house. Randy followed D to his room. D stopped him at the door.

"Go sleep down there bud."

"Huh?"

"I need to sleep alone. It's been a long few days, you know how it is."

"Uh, right, sure, I'll go sleep down there."

"Yeah bud, see you later," D walked into his room behind the white door and closed it behind him sharply. Randy stood in the hall for a moment. Loneliness and emptyness filled his chest and he took a deep breath. Randy shuffled down to the room he had started out in and looked inside for anyone. The room was empty as it was before. He fell into the bed and lay on his back looking at the ceiling. The events of the last weeks pouring through his mind. He didn't understand what he was doing but he was surviving. It was better than being on the streets. D gave him a warm feeling he had rarely known and he wanted that feeling to stay forever. Randy's eyes fluttered to sleep trying to take in all that happened and just as he fell asleep a fleeting thought about his life until passed over his mind.

It had been a long time since he was in highschool and on the basketball team and his biggest worry was talking to girls and winning his next fight meet. Now he was just making his own way and doing whatever it was he was doing here. Did he like it? Could he like it? Was it just the drugs or was it something different altogether. His mind couldn't conjure up a better answer other than to let him drift off to sleep.

Chapter 30

Randy's eyes popped open from sleep. His eye sight and mind began to clear away sleep and he oriented himself to his surroundings. Randy took a few moments to remember where he was but he couldn't remember what day it was, even the month was a little fuzzy. The room was hot so it must be summer he reasoned. Randy stood up and changed out of his clothes. He grabbed his towel and looked outside in the hall to see if anyone was near the bathroom. He walked down the hall and found the shower open and he washed his body under the warm water. He shaved again so his skin was smooth. He changed into clean clothes and went looking for D. He knocked on the door of D's room but received no answer. Randy stood outside hoping D would wake up and answer him but he was disappointed. Randy's stomach growled as he gave up and walked downstairs.

Randy searched the kitchen for something to eat. He felt so hungry. As usual, the cabinets were bare. There was a lone beer in the fridge and he popped it open. A young man, about 15, came down the stairs in only boxers and a head of brown hair that curled up at the ends. His body was flat and undefined except for protruding nipples.

"Hey," his effeminate voice squeaked out.

"Hi," Randy said.

"I'm Ben."

"Randy."

"Nice to meet you, handsome. What brings you here?"

"I just got back here, I stay here."

"Oh cool, they said some guys would be coming. I didn't know if that was you or not."

"I'm fucking starving; I need something to eat. Got any money?" Randy said.

"Just a few dollars. Mostly change. You?"

"Yeah, I got a few dollars. I think I need to go get on food stamps or something. There is never anything good in this house." Ben closed the fridge. Randy noticed how bare the cabinets were. There used to be food and a variety of things but now everything was bare. Ben closed the fridge.

"Why don't we got out and get something to eat and I'll take care of you after," Ben said rubbing Randy's arm.

Randy's gut was repulsed but he was hungry. Randy felt the weight of the key in his pocket.

"We can go to town and get some good somewhere," Randy offered.

"Okay, good! That's great, I just need clothes I guess!" Ben shimmied his shoulders. Ben ran up the stairs and returned in a thin shirt and jeans, carrying another pair of jeans, this one torn. Ben followed Randy out to the car and they both got in. Randy started up the car and slowly pulled out onto the road. Ben looked out the windows towards the open fields and stands of trees.

"How'd you come here?"

"That's a long story," Randy said as he deftly pulled into the parking lot of a local cafe.

"Always is. No one grows up dreaming to do this or be in this life."

"They sure don't, especially if they're straight," Ben said.

"I guess that's true, but if you're straight, how'd you fall into this life, I mean if you don't like boys. There's a lot of ass fucking going on."

"That's another long story."

"Yeah, I get it, life can be a real bitch sometimes. Let's grub."

The pair ate breakfast and then paid with their combination of change and bills. Randy walked back out to the car and Ben followed. Ben sat down in the passenger seat.

"This your car?"

"Nah, it's D's car, I hope he don't mind."

"He's usually cool."

Randy pulled back into the driveway and brought the car to a stop. D burst through the door and out into the driveway in bare feet. "What the actual fuck? Where were you two fuckers?"

Randy looked at the ground. "We were just hungry, I thought we could eat and I still had the keys, so I figured we could go eat."

"You stole my fucking car?" D said. He raised his hand to punch Randy but Ben ran around the front of the car and hugged D from behind. "It's my fault, I thought of it. It was my plan. We didn't mean anything. I'm sorry, I'm really sorry." Ben rubbed D's bare chest. "Please don't be mad D. Randy was just being a good person. I was really hungry. Please don't be mad."

D relaxed his arms. He hugged Ben around the shoulders.

"Yeah, sure. All right, just fucking tell someone next time before I freak the fuck out."

Randy nodded and held out the keys to the car. D took them from him and put them back in his pocket. "Thank you."

Ben smiled at D.

"That's better."

D turned back towards the house. Randy followed the pair. "You're going to be a good boy for me this weekend aren't you?" D asked Ben.

"Of course. I'm always good. That's my thing."

"Good, we have a party coming this weekend. Help Randy, he's only done a few parties. He needs help."

D took Ben by the shoulders and led him inside. Randy felt a shock of what he could only describe as jealousy. He recognized that shoulder hug. It was the same way D acted when Randy first arrived. Randy craved that kind of attention from D, the way Ben was getting it.

Ben shot a look over his shoulder at Randy. Randy breathed a sigh of relief that D wasn't more mad at him than he had been for taking his car. D took Ben and Randy downstairs to smoke.

D took out some drugs and put them on the workbench, "Ben you in the mood for some smoke?"

"Sure," Ben replied, "Always."

D loaded up the pipe. Randy stood against the wall and looked on. D stood close to Ben as they smoked. Ben inhaled a good amount of the white smoke and passed it back to D who waved Randy over.

"Come smoke man."

Randy walked over and took the pipe and felt the high begin but it wasn't the same as the last time. Ben cuddled on D and D smiled at the young man and his attention. The trio sat down in the basement to continue partying. Randy looked on at Ben getting D's attention and in so many of the same ways D was used to pay attention to him. Randy looked down between his legs at the floor.

"What's wrong? You need to smoke more?" D asked.

"Yeah, pass the smoke," Randy said holding his hand out.

"That's my good boys. I always take good care of my boys," D's smile almost seemed to beam as he said it. Randy shifted his body toward D so he could feel his touch, the special touch he had grown used to feeling with him. It was a strange craving but he craved it.

D broke the silence, "I have a special job for you boys."

"What's that?" Ben squeaked.

"I need you to do something really special for me at the party this weekend."

"I need you to gather some stuff for me from the guys that come here. I think I have a new way for us all to make some money and come out ahead for once," D said putting the pipe down. He drummed his fingers against each other, "If you guys can help me gather some items we'll be in it," D assured them both, "You guys can help me out right?"

Ben nodded, "Sure D, whatever you need hun."

Randy assented, "Always, yeah."

D looked at them both, "Cool. I know I can trust you guys."

Chapter 31

Randy was ready for the party. He was prepared, ready to make some money, and ready to have fun. He stood in the upstairs bathroom with the door shut, looking at the mirror, and just hated himself for this, for not leaving and not being able to leave because he loved D too much. He loved the high; every time, it was a new, exhilarating feeling. Was he willing to trade gay sex for a high? A really powerful, mind shattering high? Did it matter that he hated himself over time? Did it matter that D was the only person to give a fuck if he lived or died? Did it matter that he felt dirty and like a worthless faggot? Someone hit the door. A single tear rolled down his cheek.

"I gotta piss!"

It didn't matter right now. Someone had to take a piss. Randy opened the door into the hallway. Another guy in a white T-shirt stood in the hall. He looked young, with a pronounced Adam's apple, thick pink lips and dark skin.

"Who the fuck are you?"

"Evan."

"Pete. Everyone has the same fuckin' name here."

"Whatever, man. I didn't know we let niggers in here."

"Fuck you, man!" Pete tried to punch Randy, and missed him as Randy dodged, and his dark fist went through the wall. A few moments later, footsteps dashed up the stairs.

"The fuck is going on!" D shouted.

"This piece of shit white fuck called me a nigga!" Pete's baritone voice forced out the words.

"Randy, keep your little mouth shut. We got shit to do. Get your shit together, we can't have any fuck ups tonight." D marched downstairs. "And no more punching the fucking walls!" he shouted over his shoulder. Randy slipped past Pete and walked downstairs. D walked out to the porch and lit a cigarette and inhaled. Randy slipped out the door, letting the screen door slam against the frame, and started to smoke next to Randy.

"Thanks for saving me."

"You're welcome."

"Are you ready?"

"Not really."

"That's okay."

"I've never really stole before."

"It's easy, we just need their checkbooks or a check, any information, really. Once we have that then we'll be able to get started. It's really important. I mean, you do want to help me, don't you?"

"Okay."

"I know you can help me, it's easy. You're just so amazing. You'll like the money, too. I mean, you want to get out of here, don't you?"

The air filled in the house with smoke as all the boys paired off with the men who came for them. Randy noticed how some of them regressed and acted like boys when they hung around the house. The smell of cigarettes, drugs, and sex made the air stiff to breathe. By the end of the night, the boys were shirtless, sitting outside in the crisp air of a fall Missouri night. Randy was drunk in his mind, high in his body and exhausted from sex. His head was swimming. At some level he liked this and he never wanted it to stop. But then he saw the childlike innocence of Chris, Ben and Josh. Had they ever grown up? Had they ever tried to be men or just fuck boys? Randy didn't even know what it meant. He had never known what it was like to have that swagger, respect, or the friends or even a real girlfriend who loved him. He hung his head as these thoughts popped in and out of it. If only he hadn't killed David with that pan. Where did it even come from? It was just in his hand. "It was just there." The prosecuting attorney asked him over and over again.

"Yes, I just seemed to have it, and then..."

"And then what did you do?" His suit didn't fit well and he turned around on his heel towards the courtroom.

"I struck David." Randy never looked up despite his lawyers' advice to make eye contact with the jury.

"How many times did you strike him on the head?"

"I don't know."

"Were you in a rage?"

"Yes."

"All because of his actions towards your sister Kelly?"

"Yes."

"Did it occur to you to stop him some other way?"

"No, sir." Randy shifted on the uncomfortable wooden chair in the austere wood-paneled court room. Randy looked over at the judge in a kind of helpless pallor. The judge's mind didn't seem present at the proceedings. Randy turned back towards the lawyer. Every time he looked out over the courtroom, fear gripped his lungs and he couldn't breathe. He kept his shoes in sight so he could feel safe; as safe as he could in the vulnerable seat in which he now found himself, on trial for a murder he had no idea he was going to commit.

"Did you like David?"

"No, sir."

"Why was that?"

"He was fucking my sister."

"Why not tell your mother or call the police?"

"I didn't know what to say or do. I'm 15, no one would believe me."

"Are you sure?"

"Yes."

"Do you feel remorseful about your actions?"

"I'm sorry he died."

"Are you? Is that all?"

"Yessir."

D shook Randy on the shoulder. "Randy, Randy? Are you okay?" Randy was jolted from the courtroom back to the concrete patio behind the house. His face was wet and his hand flew up to his cheek to wipe away the tears.

"I think I just drifted."

"Let's go cuddle in my bed."

D offered Randy an arm and in a few minutes they were cuddled up in bed together upstairs. The two men slowly drowsed themselves away into sleep. Randy felt safe and secure. There was just one flaw that plagued his sleep-drunk brain: he could not let this define his life. He wasn't gay, he was a "real man", and he was going to prove it.

The frost on the yard was clear yet white. Randy stood outside in a hoodie and jeans, barefoot, smoking a cigarette looking at the diffusion of his breath with every exhalation. D joined him and flicked open his heavy lighter.

"I'm proud of you."

"What?"

"Crying."

"You saw that?"

"Yeah, you were sitting there, eyes closed, just crying."

"Oh."

"It's good."

"I'm weak, just a faggot."

"I don't think so."

"Whatever."

"Listen, I need your help. There are a couple of boys in the basement, in that room. Find some clothes that fit them and get them out here and in the car. We need to drop them off at a motel a couple towns over," D said in a low voice. He looked out into the yard and spoke with precision. Randy flicked his cigarette into the yard. There was a hiss as it hit the frost. Randy walked down the concrete steps and past the esoteric bottles and tubes on the workbench and around a corner. Behind the door, in what was once a bathroom, were the two boys. Randy opened the door and the faint light from the basement drove out the blackness. The boys were sitting on the floor. They could not have more than 14 or 15, from what Randy could judge. They were naked except for underwear.

"Time to wake up, boys," Randy stated.

They stirred and shielded their eyes with their hands. Randy left the door open. The smell was putrid. He presumed one or both of them had soiled himself. They both, on thin legs, stood up in the main basement. Their eyes were dark and their lips were chapped.

"Come on, let's get you washed up and dressed." Randy marched the dirty waifs upstairs to the bathroom and put them in the shower. Randy rooted around one of the bedrooms for some clothes. He found some clothes that were clean enough and folded them up. He found a couple pairs of shoes he presumed were theirs and took those with him. He went back into the bathroom and placed them in a neat pile on the commode lid, along with a large towel. Randy waited in the hall. A few minutes later, the boys appeared, hair still wet and looking a little cold. Randy walked downstairs and pointed outside. The boys walked outside, where D was already standing next to the car.

"Where are you taking us?" the smaller boy asked.

"To a motel, we're going to drop you off. Someone will be there."

"Okay," the larger one said.

Randy and D passed cigarettes and marijuana around the car as they drove into a small town 45 minutes north of the house. No one seemed to talk and D turned up the radio. D pulled into the two-story motel and up to a door. D slammed on the door. A neatly-dressed large man with a pot belly and thinning hair opened the door.

"You got the package?"

"In the car."

"Okay, bring 'em in here." D signaled to Randy. Randy and the boys walked the short distance to the motel door. The pot-bellied man stepped back into the motel room. Another man, thinner and good-looking sat on the chair watching the TV. The beds were still made. No one was staying there long.

"Do you guys want to smoke?"

D stood there and looked at him for a moment. "Yeah, sure. Randy, get the stuff."

Randy opened the door again and went out to the car and retrieved a backpack from the trunk. He passed through the door again. D put out the paraphernalia and started to distribute it. One of the men was already rubbing on one of the boys.

"You like to party, don't you?"

"Yeah, I like to party, you know, whatever."

"Good," he said.

The room filled with smoke of different varieties, and as soon as a few rounds of the group had completed themselves, the men undressed the boys. The larger boy immediately started to pleasure the men. The smaller boy was more resistant and even tried to struggle. The men thought he was being playful at first, but soon became forceful. The pot-bellied man held the boy on the bed.

"You want in on this?"

"Yeah," D said. After a few moments of pleasure, D looked at Randy over his shoulder. "Randy, get in here, I know you want to."

Randy was in the corner, enjoying his high, enjoying the head buzz, the body buzz. After what he remembered last night, the memory was gone, at least temporarily, and he stood up and forgot that the scene made him sick, how sick this was, how terrible and obscene this was and that he was there and it was happening. That all was gone in this moment. All Randy could do was speak a few words.

"Yeah, sure."

He walked over to the bed and began rubbing the boys' smooth feminine skin. He closed his eyes and dreamed. It felt like true desire. The men distributed the boys like a game amongst themselves, and Randy was a full participant. By the time D and Randy collapsed on the floor, night had fallen. D collected his clothes and the backpack and threw Randy his clothes. D checked to make sure he had the money, and then stumbled outside into the night. He found his key and started the car. Randy tumbled in, and they took off, sex drunk, high, and out of their corporeal minds into the night towards home.

Chapter 32

The sun beat down on the parking lot, but the day was not particularly warm. D hung his arm out of the car, letting the cigarette give off smoke. The skin under his eyes was dark. He looked tired, even though he had slept calmly next to Randy for ten hours. His skin looked pallid, and some of his arm hair had come off. He felt sick to his stomach, like someone was dancing with knives in his gut. He struggled through despite the pain, using his drugs, because there was work to do. Magic crystals to get going and weed to mask the pain and make him forget. It was a combination he had become dependent on. But there was a new member of the mix, and that was the man sitting next to him, about to go do his bidding because Randy trusted him. D knew Randy was in love with him. If he had to exploit that to get this done then so be it. No one could truly love him. At least, so he reasoned in the late nights when a man is alone with his thoughts. D dropped Ben off first and walked him through the process.

"When you get the money just wait in the area and we'll come back to pick you up."

"Okay D," Ben said climbing out of the car.

"

"You got ID?"

"Yeah."

"All you do is go in with the check to cash it. You say that you did some work for him and you need to cash the check."

"Okay, cool."

"Just like we rehearsed."

"Yeah."

Randy walked confidently into the small building with its sloped roof and arched windows. The carpet was old, and the glass in front of the old woman at the window was thick above the small metal pass through.

"Hi, how can I help you?"

"I'm here to cash this."

Randy showed her the check and his ID.

"Have you cashed with us before?"

"No, ma'am."

"Okay, great. There will be a $5 one-time charge to join and I'll need some information from you."

A few minutes later, after collecting the data and a nervous phone call to the issuing bank, Randy had the cash. He stuffed the bills she counted out into his wallet and walked out the door. He sat back down in the car and D flicked his cigarette butt away.

"You got it?"

"$285.42."

"Awesome. Now just three more places, then I'll go get Josh and Chris."

D and Randy ran around the town, going to every check cashing place, repeating the process. In between check cashing places, D would put his hand on Randy's knee and run it up and down his jeans in a stroking motion. Randy didn't know why, but for some reason that meant the world to him. D and Randy arrived back and the house in the early evening. Randy and D walked through the house out the back trailer. Josh and Chris were perched on the couch and merely waved hello, so as not to interrupt Josh's movie. D made his way across the yard back to the trailer. The door was open. Randy and D walked in on Bob sitting watching TV.

"Good news, Bob, I got $800 for you," D said pulling out a wad of cash.

"Really? Thank you, I appreciate it."

"Did you get your meds?" Bob asked, while putting his beer down on top of some papers that were held up by a cheap pressboard coffee table.

"No, not yet. I have go to the doctor for all that. It might take a little bit."

"When you going?" Bob asked, walking over to the fridge and pulling out a glass battle of MGD.

"Probably tomorrow. I'll drop the boys off and quietly go see if I can get my meds." D took the offered bottle and deftly opened it with his belt buckle. Randy stood near the door and listened to the conversation. He lit his own cigarette and smoked it but slowly.

"You don't look good, how are you feeling?" Bob said as he sat back down and turned down the flickering TV.

"Not that great." D coughed.

"You need these meds, boy. Take the money tomorrow, get your damn meds. You'll be better and I don't need you dying on me right now."

D coughed again. "I'm not dead yet. Uh, Randy, why don't you head inside, I need to talk to Bob for a bit OK? I'll come smoke with you in 15 minutes."

Randy nodded and walked outside but he didn't walk all the way into the house. He walked around and kept listening at the window. Randy knew something was up with what they were doing. It was wrong and he knew that but for D he would do anything but he needed to know what he had gotten himself into now.

"Good, he don't need to hear this and you keep it that way. Alive that is, just keep it that way."

"How are we on taxes?" D said as he took a slow drink of beer. The tingle made his throat feel better.

"Getting better. I had some things to pay but we're almost there. Getting there."

"Good. It's hard to keep up this for long when people start calling the bank about those checks. Things will get hot around here." D leaned against the faux-wood panel wall.

"You got better ideas?" Bob said, shrugging his shoulders and looking at the TV.

"It's not us going to jail."

"When do you want to get out of town?" Bob said.

"I'll let you know."

"Okay, let me know." D looked at the TV and instantly solved the game show puzzle. A few seconds later, he turned out to be right. Bob smiled at him. Silence fell over the trailer and Randy stepped quietly across the yard and into the house. He dropped his backpack in his room and waited in the basement for D to come down. What did they mean by go to jail? It must have to do with those checks they were cashing or something. Randy didn't really understand what was going on but he knew how that information had come around and he knew that D was using it to get money. Randy rubbed his pocket where his share still sat. Randy fingered the bills. Randy wanted to bolt but not without D, not without at least one more night or one more day. One more time smoking with him and laughing with him. As much as Randy wanted to leave, he could not get up the courage to simply stand up and walk out the front door. Randy didn't feel like he could leave D like that, never like that.

That night, when D crawled in bed next to Randy, he curled his arms around Randy's body. Randy loved that touch, there it was again. He coud feel D's skin against his body. D pressed his pelvis against Randy's butt and Randy moaned a little. D ran his hand through Randy's dusty light brown hair a few times. Randy responded to his touch. Randy nodded his head down and allowed himself the privilege of crying.

Chapter 33

D walked downstairs into the front room and sat down on the couch next to Josh who munched on some chips. Randy sat down next to Josh and D flanked him on the other side. Chris moved over so they could all sit. D's bare foot curled up a bit. He was in a little bit of pain and his stomach felt like it was eating itself. He looked at the TV for a moment.

"Josh, I got a deal for you."

"What's that?"

"A deal. Listen, I got this guy I know, he owned me some money and I got him to write me a check. I have some money out at the check cashing places and I had him make it out to you so that I can get the money. I figured if you cashed it we could split the money."

"Okay, D, I mean, sure, no problem. Can I get a ride to town then?" Josh laughed.

"It's easy," Randy added.

"Yeah, it's easy money," D repeated.

D turned around to Chris and smiled at him.

"Alright, alright," Chris said, "Don't even ask, I'll do it, you know I'm always down."

D picked up his phone and did some texting. Randy looked over at him texting and wondered what else he was planning. Now Chris and Josh were involved in this too and Randy had helped. Randy put the thoughts of his mind. D put his phone in his pocket.

"Randy, let's go outside and smoke," D said standing up. When they were alone outside, D gripped Randy around the shoulders, "Two other boys agreed to the deal, so we're good."

"Okay, cool."

"Let's get moving."

D and Randy put on shoes and neat clothes. D collected Chris and Josh and after an hour of cajoling D finally got them ready to go. D loaded up the car with Randy in the front seat and started to drive to town.

The sky was more cloudy than the sun-drenched day before. D sat in the car in the parking lot of a big-box store, his arm hanging out of the window. Chris and Josh sat in the backseat. Randy sat up front, his eyes squinting.

"Okay guys, you know the drill, I know you can do this. I mean, it's an easy way to get paid, right? You all have your lunch money?" They boys nodded in assent and poured themselves out of the car.

D had parked in easy walking distance of a few check cashing spots. They all started to walk off. D put the car in gear and took a deep breath. Randy stayed behind with D.

"Alright, I need to run a little errand, can I leave you with in the car?"

"Sure, no problem man," Randy said shrugging his shoulders.

"Good, it won't take long, just stay in the car."

D drove the car over to a bland building of medical offices. The are was a boring surburban office park with large, square buildings and expansive parking lots. Occupied buildings were obvious, the cars were only parked in front of those. Empty buildings had no cars in front. There were no markers outside the building to indicate what was inside. The parking lot was dotted with cars. He parked in the car in the lot on the side of the medical building.

"Alright, I'll be back in a little bit. Don't run off on me," D cautioned.

"I won't, you can trust me," Randy replied.

"I know, I can."

D left Randy in the car and started towards the building. Randy watched him disappear inside. D walked up the stairs to the 3rd floor and through the wooden door. The clinic realized that it was embarrassing for some of the men they served, so they kept things nondescript. The lady at the front desk recognized him.

"Good to see you, Daniel. I was really worried about you."

The exam room was austere and harsh. He sat on the table. He waited nervously until a nurse walked in.

"Any symptoms?" she asked as she checked his eyes, nose, and throat, looking for the familiar lesions.

"Nothing much?"

"You look tired, how are you feeling?"

"My stomach hurts sometimes. I guess I don't look that great."

"How long since you took your meds?"

"It's been a few weeks. That's what I'm here for."

"Very good. Sheila will be in momentarily," she said, smiling at him. A few moments later, the physician's assistant came in. She examined him.

"You're still very symptomatic, from what I can tell and from what my nurse wrote down. But I can see we have a working group of medications. How long since you took them last?"

"It's been a few weeks. I'm trying to get that taken care of today."

"Your lymph nodes are very swollen. You're down 15 pounds from the last time I saw you. You need to take better care of yourself. Are you using a condom when you have sex?"

"Yes, of course."

"I will refill your meds if you promise to come in more often. We all worry about you."

"I promise."

"I mean it. Go for your blood test down the hall. Your prescriptions will be at the front desk."

D hopped down from the table and waited at the desk for his blood test. The phlebotomist was able to draw the vials of blood on the first try, and D soon made his way down the stairs towards his car. D started to text the others and soon started to collecting his boys.

"Randy, load a bowl." Randy took out the glass pipe and a small bag from the glove box and passed the pipe around. The car filled with smoke between the weed and the cigarettes as D kept driving around town, not really going anywhere in particular, and looking down at his phone in his knee.

"Bob says that the house is crowded. I guess some guys dropped off some boys or something and things are pretty full up."

Chris and Josh looked at each other. Randy saw them in the rear view mirror, looking at each other in wordless communication.

"I think I'll just drop you guys off at a motel for a few days, until we can get some room," D said.

"Can we go by and get some stuff?"

"I don't see why not," D said, smiling.

D finally started out for the farm. He pulled into the driveway. Chris and Josh were the first out. The two boys with them casually stayed in the car; they looked around the yard, but did not otherwise move. They were almost running into the house. When Randy walked into the front room, Chris and Josh were stuffing their backpacks with Josh's DVD case and a few other things around. Randy walked up to D's room and collected his few belongings. If Chris and Josh were grabbing stuff important to them, then he had better do the same. His backpack barely zipped with the clothes he was taking with him, but he zipped it and walked back downstairs and straight out to the porch to have a cigarette. His stomach was tight and his heart was beating rapidly. Chris and Josh walked out and stood by the car. Randy followed them, and a few minutes later D walked out and casually lit a cigarette and looked out into the yard. The boys had gotten brave and had gone over to a stand of trees to urinate and were walking back to the car. D walked down the short porch steps and towards the car. He opened the trunk and they stuffed it with what they could. The rest ended up on laps inside the car. D drove back to town with his charges in tow and found an aging motel in a blue and white color scheme on the north edge of the town. D walked in, paid for three days, and then unlocked the door for the boys. They crowded into the room with their backpacks and sat on the beds.

"Okay, guys, I'll be back tomorrow. We're going to drive up north and see what we can do. Do you guys mind if I send some guys over here?"

Chris and Josh looked at the floor, but Randy was the first to speak. "Sure," he volunteered.

"You guys are awesome. I'll see you in the morning." D opened the door. Randy followed him out.

"What do you mean?"

"I need you to keep an eye on things here."

"I gotta go too?"

"Yeah, just for now."

"Fuck that."

"Come on, I need you now, more than ever."

"What about things here?"

"Keep an eye on things. You have the stuff. Get high, have some fun, there might be some guys coming by. I'll pick you up soon. A couple of these guys are moving on soon anyway."

"Okay, okay, whatever, I'll miss you."

"Don't do that shit."

"What shit?"

"Missing me shit."

"All this don't mean shit to you?"

"We all got problems, man." D walked over to the car and, without saying another word, drove off. Randy tracked the car with his eyes until he couldn't see it anymore. He stood there fuming. He was stupid to trust D, stupid to think he cared or even loved him. He was just so stupid. He kept beating himself into the night. Randy spent most of the evening leaning against the wall, smoking cigarette after cigarette, going through his meager stash. He looked for his worn journal. He opened his journal and started to write for the first time in months. But now he needed to get the anger out that was rising in his belly.

"I made the mistake of being a faggot and the mistake of falling in love with an asshole. I want my mom, I want Kelly to be alive and tell me that everything is going to be okay. I just want my life back," he scrawled across the page. He closed his eyes and could still see her, full of life. He could also see the scene of her death, and the blood spattered all over his body, the floor and the refrigerator. He thought about the closed casket funeral and the limp lifeless body inside that was just gone too soon. They were all ripped, all trying to escape the perilous situation they found themselves in. Chris and Josh huddled together on a bed. The two other boys piled together. Randy didn't even know their names. He didn't care, either. Randy found the phone that D had left him in his pocket. He tried texting him, but didn't get an answer. How could he let this happen? Why didn't he fight back? What was he feeling? The more he smoked, the more he couldn't really tell anymore. He welcomed the numbness, and he wanted it more than he had ever wanted anything. He inhaled deeper. The room was quiet. No one wanted to admit what was going on and no one wanted to talk about it. If they didn't talk about it, maybe it would go away. In the middle of the night, there were a few knocks at the door. Randy was the one designated to stand up and answer the door. Peering through the peep hole, he would let the men in. Randy didn't stop any of what transpired. He lay on his belly as the men took him from behind. Whatever they wanted, he gave them. The best, the worst, the pain, the beauty, the disease, the life, or the youth. For those men, at that moment, Randy was on full raw display. The motel room became a cornucopia of sex, drugs, and pure life-party. When the exhibition ended and the last of the men were gone, Randy lay on the floor naked between the double bed and the wall, writing in his journal. His body was sore all over and he needed a shower. His hair was wet with sweat and his stench settled around him like a thin fog.

"If I'm a man, I need to get out. I have to make it stop," he jotted neatly.

The sun rose up the next day, and Randy woke up to a light knock at the door. It was D. He was there to take the boys up north. They repeated the process. He handed his money over to D and D counted out his share. That was the only thing that made D smile; the god of money. Randy didn't say much to D as the sun moved across the sky. By the time it was lowering itself at the horizon, D smiled at Randy and put his hand on Randy's leg.

"I have a special surprise for you."

"Okay."

"We're going to drop off the boys here at a motel, and then you and I are going to spend the night together in a room of our own. Just us."

Randy looked out the window. "Okay, sounds cool."

D bought the motel room and dropped the boys off. The motel was run down and the carpet in the room had obvious wear and tear. The sheets were old and a few of the lamps just did not work. D left the room behind and drove down the road to a slightly nicer motel. He checked in the two of them and led Randy to their room on the third floor, facing a courtyard of scrubby plants and gravel.

Randy dropped his backpack and sat down on the bed. D picked up the plastic local food guide and ordered a pizza. He gave Randy the pipe full of marijuana.

"Greens?" he asked with a smile.

"Sure, dude." Randy took the lighter and had his share of the first inhalations. The pizza arrived just as the hunger was setting in. They ate in near silence.

"I know you're mad at me," D said, opening a box.

"Whatever, I don't wanna talk about it."

"I have one more surprise for you."

"What's that?"

D ate his fourth and final slice of pizza. He stood up and in seconds stripped naked. He stood in front of Randy. Randy sat on the floor and looked at D's waist.

"Wanna fuck?"

"Why?" Randy asked mid-bite.

"I need a top," D said, and held his arms out.

Randy looked up at him and his eyes turned black. He dropped his pizza back in the box and tore off his clothes. He shoved D violently on the bed, and in a few moments started grunting primally as he took D from behind. Randy raged. He couldn't hear if D liked it or not. He didn't care how well he could perform. This was about anger and his chance to let his wild beast free. Everything could be let go and nothing held back. Several minutes later, the pair collapsed on the bed in a pile of sticky, sweaty male flesh. Randy's chest rose and collapsed, and the blackness of sleep washed over him. He was jolted back to consciousness with a rap at the door. A four-second assessment showed that D had already gone. Randy was alone, and the rapping was more insistent.

"Randall, police, open up."

He stomach seized with fear. He crept over to the door and opened it. The cops forced their way in and in less than a minute had him arrested. They helped him get dressed and collected his belongings and led him out to one of the two waiting squad cars. Processing was invasive but not unfamiliar.

During the booking process he found out that the charges were check fraud, possession of controlled substances and prostitution. Randy sat in the metal chair quietly. His spirit was broken and his mind was a scramble. The police station was bland and white. Randy didn't even notice the details around him. He stared at the ground. He didn't feel anything. He didn't know where he was or what he was even doing. He heard one of the policewomen say he seemed slow. They asked him if he had a mental illness; he said no, but was otherwise not responsive.

The experience was unlike anything he knew before. Randy was taken into an interrogation room. The room seemed different from when he was in one last. He was shackled this time and that was different. He answered the cops' questions one by one. When asked if he was working alone or with anyone else, his answer was simple.

"I don't know, I was just working for some people. I didn't know I was doing anything wrong."

"Who were the people?"

"I don't really know them. There was a guy named Bob, I think. I mostly talked to the other one. I think it was his son or something."

"Remember his name?"

"I think he went by Josh," Randy lied about D and the entire plot.

"If you can identify these men, you could help us out," The policeman asked him. Randy shook his head. He refused to give D up.

"Sorry, I don't really know anyone else and I don't know where they are I just met them or whatever."

The policeman folded the manila folder shut and shook his head.

"You're only hurting yourself kid, they don't care about you."

Randy didn't reply to the policeman.

He shuffled in the baggy jumpsuit to the holding cell where they kept him. He shuffled back and forth a few more times. He was already missing D and the boys. He was missing the house and his mind was cloudy. Randy sat in the holding tank until they took him to be arraigned. Randy heard the charges again and they shuffled him back to holding cell where they then transported him to jail. Randy easily fell back into the routine of incarceration.

The days ahead in the unknown county jail were miserable. The county jail was louder and more rowdy than the juvenile school. People came and went at all times and there were people screaming, talking, and guards shouting at almost all hours. Randy kept to himself at first but he soon fell ill from the withdrawl of the drugs. As the drugs left his system, he rediscovered his real mind and his real body. He noticed how limp his hair had become, how ground down his back teeth were, and some of the sores and scrapes on his arms and legs. His joints hurt in ways he didn't know they could hurt.

His condition was noticed by the guards. The guard sent him down to the infirmary, where he spent most of his time trying to not hurt, throw up or defecate on himself. His body would convulse at times and Randy would simply black out.

The public defender visited him in the infirmary and explained the situation. The lawyer dressed in a cheap suit and carried a briefcase overflowing with files. Randy was led into a small area. Randy sat up in the plastic chair and looked across to the lawyer with dark circles under his eyes and matted hair on his head.

"You're Randall Carruth?"

"Yeah."

"Okay, let me find your file," he dug around for a minute.

"That's a nice list of crimes," he said upon opening the folder, "You want to avoid another trial and it looks they've already made an offer."

Randy opted to avoid another trail. The public defender put the offer in front of him. The state wanted 18 months of prison for the charges involved since the offense was non-violent.

"The prosecution's case is weak if we go to trial. Take the deal, you won't do any better for being a repeat offender."

Randy picked up the pen and signed on the line. "You made the right decision, Mr. Carruth."

Randy was transferred to another facility for his confinement. Randy wasn't well enough to travel but managed the transfer and slowly began to get well again. The uniform was green and white this time, with the familiar rubber sandals. Once inside, he was allowed his journals to write in. This time, Randy worked in the laundry. He made a modest amount of money. When he wasn't working he walked the yard and stayed out of fights. He played basketball sometimes. He kept to himself and his bunk in the cell of three men. He was still hurting, but he would survive. Randy looked up at the concrete ceiling and smiled for the first time in a year. He had survived, and he was free; much like the familiar caged bird, confinement had brought him a song.

Part 4

Chapter 34

Randy stood at the window at the end of the long beige hallway. The official behind the glass counted out his belongings:
1 shirt
1 pair of jeans
1 wallet
$425
1 pair of shoes
1 cellphone and charger
1 backpack
3 notebooks
2 pens
1 glass pipe
1 razor
3 condoms
1 key

The man guided him to a room to change. Randy quickly changed from the green and white uniform back into street clothes. He had gained a little weight between constant workouts and the terrible food, and the clothes were tight but manageable. His air had changed, marked by a bow legged walk, head held high and his chest out. He had found it, what he had always wanted. He found his maleness and his masculinity. He ran his own life and no one would hurt him ever again.

"Randy!" a woman's voice shouted the second he was in the open air and moving between the residual fences towards freedom. He had his belongings in a backpack with an empty paper bag. The officers nodded to him as he walked from point to point.

"Randy!"

The officers opened the final gate, and Randy's mother ran towards her son. She was still wearing her uniform from work, a pair of khaki pants and black polo shirt. She threw her arms around his body, still thin but filled out more. She held his face. "I've missed you every day, I'm so happy I found you!"

"Hi, mom."

Eileen pointed to her car. "Over here," she said, motioning.

Randy sat down in the front seat when she unlocked the modest sedan. Eileen pulled out of the parking lot and onto the highway leading back to her town. Randy noticed suddenly how much she had aged since the last time he saw her, in court, six years ago. The lines on her face that at once had been delicate had begun to get heavier and she had gained some weight, mostly around her waist and hips; he estimated about 15 pounds. The skin on her arm had started to slacken and she wore too much makeup, trying to hide her age, but to her credit, the effect was desirable. It was a stark contrast to the young vibrant woman that he knew before. This woman looked worn down, like someone had been grinding on her for years.

"I never thought this day would come!"

"I wrote to you about my release date after you wrote me."

"I know, I was just so excited to get you back and to see you!"

"Yeah, I guess."

"What are you going to do now?"

"I don't know yet."

"Okay. I'm just so happy you're home!"

"I'm glad you're happy."

Two hours, a stop at Eileen's cellphone store, and a gas stop later, they arrived at a small house. Eileen parked the car and stepped out.

"Welcome home!" she said with glee. "I'm so glad to have you home! I'm just so glad!" A tear rolled down her cheek.

"It's great I guess."

"I have a room for you and everything. We can get some stuff later, but I made the bed."

Eileen walked him upstairs in the split-level and showed him the small room. Randy walked in and looked around. It was clean, neat and a good place to get back into real life, the real world. Eileen stood in the doorway.

"I know it's not much, but what do you think?"

"It's good. Thank you for the place to stay."

Eileen smiled. "I'm going to go change. Maybe we can get pizza."

"Okay."

Randy sat down on the edge of the bed and put down his backpack. His foot bumped against something under the bed. He laid down on the floor and reached underneath and pulled out some flat plastic bins. He opened them up and saw the physical history of his life. All his uniforms, trophies, school books, one yearbook, and other childhood paraphernalia had all been dutifully packed up. He picked through the bin for a few minutes, looking at his lost life.

"I saved it all."

Eileen stood in the open doorway, looking down at Randy.

"Thanks, that means a lot to me."

"Let's order some pizza. What's your favorite now? Still pepperoni and mushrooms?"

"That sounds fine."

Eileen pulled out her phone and dialed a number. She ordered the pizza and walked out of the room. Randy sat on the bed for a moment and reflected on his surroundings. He laid back onto the bed for a moment and just looked at the ceiling.

"Do you want to come down and watch some TV while we wait?" Eileen shouted up the short stair case. Randy walked out of the room and down stairs.

The TV flickered in the simple living room furnished with an old couch, pressboard furniture, and an old rug. The coffee table was covered in papers. They sat together in silence, watching the programs on the selected channel. The doorbell rang, breaking the silence. Eileen pointed at the money on the coffee table. Randy stood up, pulled at his pants, picked up the money, and walked over to the door. He paid $22.50 for the two boxes of pizza and brought the boxes into the living room. They ate quietly for a few moments.

"You haven't told me much about what happened after you got out the first time."

"Nope, it sucked."

"What did you do?"

"I worked with some people, traveled around a little bit doing odd jobs."

"Oh, okay. Did you date?"

"No."

"Have any kids?" Eileen asked.

"Nope, I was good about that."

"That's good then. What are you going to do tomorrow?"

"Look for work."

"I can get you on at the restaurant, washing dishes, bussing."

"That sounds good. It'll be a start."

Eating and TV dominated the rest of the evening. The hour drew late and Eileen stretched out her body and started towards bed. Randy stayed up a little later before following her example.

Randy lay in bed that night on old sheets, rough with wear, staring at the ceiling. His first free night. His first night not being a threat or being threatened. He didn't have to defend himself. He was safe, and that was true freedom. His sleep was fitful and he woke at the slightest sound that broke the quiet of the house. There was no shouting, no moving of inmates and no one screaming.

The next morning Eileen and Randy drove down to the restaurant. The short, squat building sold mostly American food in a typical diner style with thick plastic menus. The decor was simple, with laminate tables and red vinyl booths. Eileen walked in early and talked to her manager about his need for a job. He waited in the car until she waved him in. The polo shirt he was wearing was small, and the belt barely held up his pants, but he was presentable for his first real job of his life. The portly manager in a white oxford short took him into the back office and spoke with him. The room was filled with papers, files, and a few old boxes. He sat on a plastic chair in the small office and answered his questions.

"You'll need a pair of black pants and good shoes. You can start on Friday, 2 P.M."

"Yes sir, thank you sir."

"That's good, I'll see you then." Randy stood up quickly and extended his hand and shook hands on the job. The manager showed him out to the main part of the restaurant. Eileen was already working. She poured coffee beans into the coffee maker as Randy passed by. She started the coffee and turned around toward him.

"Did you get the job?"

"Yeah, I start on Friday."

"That's fantastic," Eileen said. "I have a few hours left, do you want to walk around and meet me back here?"

"That sounds fine."

Eileen smiled. "I'm proud of you!"

Randy walked out of the diner into the wide street. It was only moderately busy, and the gas station on the corner was blaring music at it its one patron. The rest of the block was quiet. Randy walked down the street towards the pharmacy. He bought a small notebook and found the town library. Randy sat down at one of the tables and looked at the world passing by, and passively wrote some poetry. He went over to one of the computers and looked at getting a driver's license. He printed off some information and stuffed it in his pocket. He left the library for a sunny bench outside, facing a quad. This was the start, finally the beginning of life. He was free of being a deviant, free of the drugs and finally free of the torture of the withdrawals that racked his body in those early days of prison that made it more of a living hell than prison already presented itself to be. For the first time, he took a really free breath. This was his chance to discover who he was, to write more, and to take control of his life. The new job was just the start. At 21 he was finally able to start his life.

His heart was steeled against a man ever touching him ever again. When he remembered, his stomach felt hot and his fists clenched. It wouldn't be him. He wasn't going to do that ever again, and he didn't have to now. He hated himself for doing it. But he wasn't a bad man, he reasoned. He was a man who was caught and taken advantage of. He hated the guys that did that. He hated D, Bob, and every man he knew from that life. Nice, polite family men by day while they were fucking boys like him by night. He looked up just in time to see a girl looking around.

"Are you lost?" Randy asked.

She walked closer to him. "Oh no, I'm waiting for my friend." Her straight blonde hair rested on a simple T-shirt that hugged her faint curves and stretched over her generous chest. A metallic belt and some hip-hugging jeans with a short cloth purse completed the outfit.

"What is your friend doing?"

"She's applying for a job with this place."

"Oh cool, want to sit down?"

"Sure."

"I'm Randy, by the way."

"I'm Brandi."

"Randy and Brandi. It rhymes."

"You're funny."

"I've had time to refine my sense of humor."

"You're dressed up, court?"

"Nah, I just got a job, bussing tables around the corner."

"That sounds like a good job."

"It's okay, reliable work and shit."

"That's good, jobs can be hard to find."

"Yeah, it's good. What do you do?"

"I dance at Jiggy's outside town."

"Stripper, eh?"

"I prefer pleasure professional."

"That's funny."

Randy slipped his arm around her back. They kept talking and traded numbers.

"Come out to Jiggy's tonight. I'll get you in free. I'll be working or whatever, but you'll have a good time."

"Okay, sounds cool."

She got up and smoothed her T-shirt and slid her small purse over her shoulder.

"That's my friend, actually. I'll see you tonight?"

"For sure."

"Bye, Randy Carruth."

"Bye, Brandi Lynn Sumner."

He watched her find her friend and get into her late model car and drive away from the area. Her warm pressure left him with a warm feeling of closeness, acceptance, and hope.

That night, Randy dressed up in a plaid button down shirt over a white T-shirt. His black plain work pants and white shoes completed the working class look. He pulled out the bike he found in Eileen's garage. He had pumped up the tires and they held air. He liked to bike, the wind and the freedom.

He started his journey to Jiggy's. The building was short, and looked like its exterior had seen better days, but the sign was in good shape and made it quite obvious what was on display. A curvy woman with obviously large breasts covered with a wooden sign that lit up the letters J-I-G-G-Y'S.

Cars, trucks, and motorcycles were parked out front. Randy checked his short haircut. Ready for anything, he strode into the club, and presented his old ID after waiting in a short line. He mentioned her name and the large doorman dutifully directed him without cover towards the bar and the elevated dance floors. A lady at a small counter offered drinks. Randy ordered a beer in a bottle and made his way towards the floors. He looked around to see if she was on a stage yet or if he had to wait. He tried to look like he had been in a strip club before. Through the poor lighting and smoky-grey air, he saw Brandi. She was dancing in large clear heels around a metal pole to his left on a small stage.

Most of the girls offered dances and a show to the over-hyped club music blaring from the DJ booth going through the motions almost mechanically for each man that placed a line of dollar bills on the vinyl rests that lined the stages. Randy noticed right away how Brandi actually felt the music and it made her dances intoxicating and magical. Led by this magical topless woman, Randy sat down at the stage. He saw two other men who were watching. They had each put out five $1 bills.

Randy followed their lead and kept up with how much beer they drank. She pulled herself up to the top of the pole and let herself down slowly. In that moment he was sold on her and on getting her to be his. It was a symbol of his new life and what he should have had all along. He waited patiently as she attended each man in turn. He noticed how she revealed herself and got so close as to let the sweat and body heat waft into their senses but never touched them and they never touched back.

By the time Brandi gyrated over to him, he felt like he was ready. She moved her body like a river and he just stared in awe. He drank his beer until she had collected all of the dollar bills and moved back to the pole. Randy's body felt warm, and he stayed until she was called off the stage and into the back. Randy took her time away to walk around the rest of the club and looked at the other girls. He noticed the other blondes, brunettes, and the one black girl in a tight purple leotard. He enjoyed a few more beers and waited for his girl to come back out. About 30 minutes or two beers later, she reappeared to be watched from afar as she worked. An independent woman is a thing of its own beauty, and Randy appreciated that. Around midnight, she went backstage for the final time. Randy started in on his last beer, and when he had finished it, he decided to wait outside next to his bike for her to come out. 30 minutes later she walked out with a large bag.

"Hi there."

"Hey, how are you?"

"Tired, but I'm ready to spend some time with my new favorite guy."

"Okay, do you want to get out of here?"

"Yeah, how did you get here?"

"I rode my bike."

"Do you want to leave it here? We can come back and get it tomorrow. Let me tell the guys." She walked over to the large men in suits with badges marked "Security."

She walked back towards him and pointed to her car. Randy opened her door. She put her gear in the back and sat down. Randy climbed in the passenger side. She started to drive towards her apartment building. Randy put his hand on her thigh and reached ever higher. She reached over and started to rub him. Randy squirmed.

"What's wrong?"

"Nothing, it's just been a while."

"You aren't a virgin are you?"

"No, I'm 21, that would be a problem."

"Let me help you." She pulled up to the apartment building, and when she parked, she turned to him and reached over for the first kiss.

"Did you like that?"

"Yes."

"Let's keep going." She opened the door and led him up three flights of stairs to her apartment. It was sparse but neat. They climbed into bed together and began to explore each other's bodies. He enjoyed the softness of her breasts, the length of her legs and the heat of her womanhood. She became intoxicated with his attentiveness and his lithe body.

Brandi wrapped her body in a sweatshirt and some shorts. The stood on her small balcony, smoking a cigarette and a bowl of fruity-tasting cannabis. Randy was barefoot, clad only in his jeans. The cool night air struck his skin, but he did not mind the cold.

"Thank you."

"For what?"

"Understanding."

"You're a good man, Mr. Carruth."

"I'm just trying to get my life on track."

"You will. I'll help you."

"Yeah, maybe. What I need is a good woman in my life."

"We can do that together."

"Let's see where it all goes."

Brandi smiled at Randy and laid her head on his chest. The pair returned to bed for an intertwined sleep session into the late morning. She drove back to the club to dance the afternoon shift. Randy found his bike and pulled it out of its small spot and rolled into the parking lot. She slung her bag over her shoulder and kissed him right before she walked into the back entrance. Randy let the feeling stay for as long as it could before he straddled the bike and began his own ride to work. He pedaled back towards the restaurant and changed in the bathroom. Clearing tables and washing dishes didn't require much training, and soon he was scrubbing away in the small kitchen. The space was perfect for one or two people, with a dishwasher and sanitizer for plates and flatware and another for glasses on one wall, plus a row of three large metal sinks with two sprayers above them for faster washing, and all kitchenware. Stacks of bins were gathered under the sink for the bussing cart. Randy completed his first eight-hour shift and rode his bike home for a shower and to get some more sleep.

Chapter 35

The cart was full of dirty dishes when his pocket vibrated for the fourth time. He pushed the bins of dishes towards the kitchen behind the counter and down a short hallway that lead to the back of the restaurant. He picked the grey food service bins off of the cart and set one into the sink and the other on the floor under the sink, and put the cart back into the hallway with two clean bins for bussing.

"Can I head out for a smoke before I put those in?"

Randy's boss was a surly fellow of 54 who looked like an aging David Hasselhoff, complete with the "you owe me" attitude.

"Go ahead, we're not busy. But I want those cleaned double time."

Randy nodded and walked through the double doors, through the loading and freezer area, and out the back of the metal safety door. He lit a cigarette and took out his phone to notice the four text message notifications from Brandi.

He texted back, "At work."

"I know, I need to see you tonight."

"I'm off at 1."

"I'm working after hours. I'll see you at 4."

"I'll stay up."

"K."

Randy finished his cigarette and flicked it into the parking lot. Those dishes weren't going to load themselves into the dishwasher and sanitizer. Randy dug into the pile of dishes and loaded the plastic bins into the machines. He picked up the short order pans and passed them from wash to rinse to sanitize to get them back to the kitchen. Even though he was on aching feet and his back and shoulder were hurting, he was happy to have some honest work and a good woman in his life. His pocket kept buzzing from time to time. He ignored it and kept washing, letting his problems and cares go into the soap. If he could make this relationship work, redemption might be possible. Randy didn't have many needs like fame or fortune, but if he could make up the sins of the past and redeem his actions, he could be free. He pulled down the sprayer to start to rinse out the sinks.

"Are you going to her house tonight?" Eileen asked Randy.

"Yeah, she's working late so I'll hang out there and probably sleep over."

"Okay." Eileen wiped her hands on her apron. She looked down. Randy looked over and looked at how sad she looked.

"Something wrong?"

"No, no, I know you need to do your own thing. It's just…I miss you. I don't want to lose you again so soon."

"You're not losing me, I'm just dating this girl."

"I know, I know. Don't forget about your driving test tomorrow. Just wake me up, okay?"

Randy stuffed his things in his pack. He opened the metal safety door and slung his backpack over his shoulder and rolled his bike out to the curb and then rode to her apartment. He took out the key she gave him and opened the door. He turned the TV on. There was a late-night re-run of a sports commentary show on. He flopped his body down on her low futon couch and passed the time alternating between the TV and quick glances at his phone, waiting for 4 P.M. to come around. He didn't bother all the clutter in her apartment. Magazines were strewn around and a couple dry houseplants stood in one corner.

"Hey, are you on your way?"

"Yeah, I'm just tipping out."

"Okay."

Randy watched the small clock as the hour passed by. Randy wondered what was taking so long. But he decided to leave her alone. The clock read 5 when Randy heard the door unlock and saw her large gym bag of clothes and makeup shoved through the door.

"Hi babe."

"Hi Brandi."

Randy stood up clumsily and kissed her. "How was work?" she asked.

"Wet."

She laughed as she dropped her bag. He could always make her laugh. "I'm sure it was, you wash dishes."

"Yeah."

"Are you ready to smoke that blunt?" she asked.

"Yeah. But I have a game."

"What's that?"

"You have to find it."

She walked over and folded herself down on the carpeted floor next to his bag, and started rooting through. She searched for several moments, but found nothing.

"Okay, I give up."

"It's in my secret weed pocket."

Randy took her hand and showed her an elongated zippered compartment in the sidelining of the backpack. The perfect place no one would suspect or know to look.

Randy lit the brown flavor-wrapped blunt and inhaled deeply. They passed it back and forth, making the air in the room more and more hazy.

Randy exhaled a particularly long stream of opaque smoke, and at the end let the words "I love you" fall smoothly out of his mouth.

"What did you say?"

"I think I'm in love with you."

Brandi looked down at the floor like a chastened child. "I'm a stripper."

"I know, I fell in love with a stripper, like the song."

"I don't know what to say, I just don't know." She pulled her hair away and looked away from him.

"We're great together, we have fun, we have great sex, we smoke, and you make me feel like a man again. I haven't felt like that in a long time." Randy rubbed her shoulder as he passed the bowl.

"I like being with you too! I look forward to coming home to you every night, and I've enjoyed this time. I know you've been through a lot, and I care about you, but I just don't think I feel the same right now with you. I've been through shit too, and love is hard, it complicates things."

"What? Why?"

"I care about you, I care about you a lot, I do, I really do, but I don't love you, Randy Carruth."

"What?"

"I'm not in love with you."

The wave of emotion flooded his brain like a tsunami of chemicals, rage, and pain. His mind spun with thoughts he couldn't keep or hang onto. Not being able to control his emotions or his body was an unfamiliar feeling. His body seemed to go into some wild contortions as he picked up his stuff, threw his key on the floor and escaped the confines of her apartment. He carried his bike downstairs and rode. He just kept riding. He didn't know where he was, but he kept going anyway. The tears flowed freely down his cheeks and struck the unforgiving earth. He had been strong for too long and now all he could do was fail. The emotional dam had been broken and everything bottled up was going to come out until the pressure in his chest had been released. Questions moved through his brains like cockroaches leaving the light.

Why did he do what he did?

Why did he allow himself to be degraded?

Was there any redemption?

Where was he going to go or do?

He finally opened the quiet door of his mother's duplex. He walked back to his bedroom and flopped down on his bed. The room was still plain, with little on the walls. He stared blankly at the ceiling until sunlight started to peek into the small window. Slept finally swept him under its dark wave until a gentle shaking tore him back to reality.

"Randy, Randy, wake up, it's time."

His eyes flickered open and his mother came into focus.

"We got 20 minutes until your test appointment."

Randy swung his body onto the floor and stood up. His needed to relieve himself. He hadn't shaved and there was no time now. He washed his face and followed his mom out to her car as she drove him to the office. The young man was close to Randy in age and was friendly. The test was simple and Randy executed all the driving movements asked of him and passed. The lady in the big glasses snapped his picture and gave him the temporary print out for his license. She informed him the real thing would arrive at his address in two weeks. By the time everything was concluded, it was time for both mother and son to go to work.

"Why don't you drive us, newly licensed driver!" Eileen said with a smile as she handed Randy the keys to her car. Randy took them and piloted the car to the diner and parked on a side street. They walked back to the diner and into the back safety door. Eileen tied on her apron and put her purse in her little cabinet. Randy put his backpack on the floor and put on his long rubber apron.

"How are you tonight, Eileen?"

"I'm all right, how about you, Vince?"

The young black man rubbed some lotion on his hands. "I'm doing all right. Just getting ready for tonight."

"Randy got his driver's license today!" Eileen said, smiling over her shoulder towards her son.

"Good job man, now you just got to save up for a car."

Randy didn't smile or say anything. He just walked down the short hall and into the kitchen.

"What's wrong?"

"I don't know. I'll have to talk to him later," Eileen said, and she walked out towards the dining area.

Randy could hear his mother greeting some customers with a pleasant "Welcome to Charlie's!" as he worked on some dishes for the kitchen and loaded the machines with bins that hadn't yet been cleared. He steeled his mind and focused on his job. By 9:30, Randy was sitting outside, cigarette in hand, waiting for his mom to come out so they could go. He had flicked his last cigarette into the parking lot when the door moved and Eileen came out, to go boxes in hand. Randy stood up on aching feet and knees and started walking towards the car.

"Are you going to Brandi's?"

"Nope."

"Why not? Did something happen?"

"Don't want to talk about it."

"Oh, okay."

Randy stood by the car. Eileen handed him the keys. Randy slipped into the driver's seat and drove to the small duplex. They sat and ate their dinner in silence, TV flickering. Randy didn't dare think. His mind had become a dangerous minefield where he felt powerless and could not predict his actions. His phone buzzed in his pocket. He pulled out the small device and saw who it was. He deleted the message without reading it.

"Is that Brandi?"

"Yeah."

"You're not going to talk to her?"

"Nope." Randy took a big bite of his chicken fried steak.

"Whatever it is, you guys should be able to work it out. You're a cute couple."

"Leave me the fuck alone!" Randy looked right at her with a angry gaze.

"I'm sorry Randy, please don't get mad, please!" Eileen let the matter go and focused on eating.

Chapter 36

Randy hadn't seen Brandi for almost a month. He had not returned her many text messages and was ready to have her number blocked. He didn't even ride by the club or go in. He just didn't bother to think about it and put himself through the pain. His mother had grown distant since the incident. They didn't even ride to work together anymore. Eileen drove her car; Randy usually took his bike.

Randy saw them come into the diner and sit down. Randy looked at a group of men walk into the diner. Randy counted a crew of seven guys. The truck said "All Night Harvesters." Randy took extra time to clear tables and clean up the diner while they ate. He listened to their conversation. They needed a few more guys. That was Randy's ticket out of this place. As the tall man in the green overalls walked out to their truck, Randy walked out after them.

"I heard you need some help?"

"Yeah, are you interested?"

"Yes, very interested." Randy had to crane his neck to look the man in the eyes.

"Ever operated farm equipment before?"

"No, but I learn quick and I drive a stick."

The man reached in his breast pocket for a business card. He offered it to Randy.

"Call me tomorrow and we'll see what we can do."

The next morning, Randy called the number on the card, hoping the phone would ring. There was no answer and he left a short message. Just as he was getting ready to give up hope and get ready for a short shift, his phone rang its little pert ring.

"Hello?"

"Hey Randy, sorry I missed you, we were out working. Listen, I got work for you. Can we talk?"

"Yeah, I'm about to go to work, if you come by there."

"No problem, no problem. I can come by there."

"Thanks."

Randy flipped the phone shut and started the trek to work on his bike. Later that evening, the man did come by, and Randy put in his notice that he was moving on. He was excited for the solid pay and work, at least for the summer and fall season. Randy fulfilled his two weeks' notice, by day working for Gary in nearby fields, learning the machines and how to run them, and by night working at the restaurant. He counted the days until he was free.

"How are you, Randy?" Vince said one night, as Randy was getting ready to take on the pile of dishes waiting for him.

"I'm good. Last night, Vince."

"You'll be missed for sure."

"Thanks Vince."

Randy worked his shift into the early morning hours, putting the last dish back at 2:30. Eileen had started to work early mornings to avoid seeing Randy there. But tonight was his last night, and she was waiting outside to take her son home before he left her again. Randy slid into the car and put his backpack onto the floor. She pulled out of the parking lot and onto the main road through the town. Randy looked out the window.

"What took you so long?"

"Took me so long to what?"

"Find me?"

"After David and Kelly, died I could barely function. Seeing you on trial and reading what the newspapers had to say just broke me. Once they locked you up, I started drinking more, like David did right before he died. I kept drinking for awhile. I sold the house, and there wasn't much money left over after thing was said and done, so I started living with this guy I knew, George I guess. He came from some rich family out west. He was weird. He liked to drink and so did I. He was kind at first, and then he started to get violent and mean. Finally I left. He took what little money I had, and so I was homeless with nowhere to go. But I was lucky. I walked into a church run by a woman named Doris. I was looking for food and maybe a place to stay. Doris was kind and helped me get back on my feet, got me into AA. Doris found me a lawyer who sued George for all the money he stole from me. I only got some, but I got enough to put down on the house I have now. Then once I was settled, Doris asked me about you, and I said I didn't really know anything. She decided that she was going to find you, and that is how I found you and wrote to you."

Randy looked out the open window and let the smoke from his cigarette curl around and be whisked away by the wind.

"That sucks," he pronounced.

"You would have never found me without that charge on check fraud."

"No, probably not, especially how you said you were living."

"Yeah, I guess I was lucky." Randy let silence fall. "Did you miss me?" he said.

"Every day until I came home, especially in AA."

"That's good."

"I know you're hurting. But you don't have to leave."

Randy shrugged his shoulders.

"Why not?"

"We're just getting to know each other again."

"We ain't going to make up that time."

"I know, but I'd like to have some time." She grabbed the top of the wheel from below to make a U-turn.

"Maybe you should have thought about that when you married David. You knew he was raping Kelly. You didn't do shit, mom. You just kept your mouth shut." Randy raised his voice.

Eileen was quiet and tears began to flow.

"I had two kids to raise, on little money and a lot of love. When David came into my life, I felt like a woman, Randy. I felt like a woman." Randy turned towards her. She held onto the steering wheel even thought she had brought the car to a stop in the driveway.

"He molested your daughter."

"I know, what was I going to do? Maybe Kelly needed to learn the ways of the world. Sometimes we women have to make sacrifices. If a little pussy solves the problem, that can be the difference of life or death sometimes. I know it's harsh, but it's true."

Randy tapped his fingers on the door moulding.

"You would sacrifice your own daughter just so you can have a nice fucking house, a nice fucking car, and a nice fucking life?" Randy shouted.

Eileen broke down, wailing.

"What do you want, Randy! What? Yes! Yes! Yes! I would! I wanted a decent life, and as long as he had Kelly, I got what I wanted. Am I a bad person?" she sobbed.

Randy waited several moments before he answered, "No mom, that doesn't make you a bad person, just a really fucked up person."

She looked up at him with red eyes and a blanched face. Her drug store makeup was running down her face. "Can you ever forgive me?"

"We'll see."

Randy opened the door and lit a cigarette. The smoke and cold air hit his lungs at the same moment. He inhaled deeply in quiet reflection of what he had just heard. Was he happy? He always knew she was culpable, and now it had been said out loud for god to hear. Eileen was broken from where she lived in the justification of her own mind down to the pit of her stomach. Several minutes and two cigarettes passed before Eileen finally opened the door and stepped out onto the concrete pad. She slung her purse over her shoulder and held her apron in one hand.

"Please forgive me, Randy, please."

"Let's go in, mom."

Mother and son opened the door into the side of the duplex and sat in the living room. Eileen wiped the tears off her face, removing almost all of her makeup. Randy saw her real face for the first time since they had lived together. He watched her count the night's tips.

"Was it a good night?"

"Yeah, $125, good night."

"Good."

"I wanted a good life for you kids, I really did. I tried so hard. I need a fucking drink."

Eileen got up and walked into the small kitchen. She reached into the back of a cabinet. There was a bottle of Tullamore Dew. She grasped the bottle and started to shakily pour a drink into a nearby coffee cup. The golden liquid had not reached the bottom of the cup when Randy put his hand over hers. He looked her right in the eyes.

"Please don't."

"Just to calm my nerves."

"Don't crawl into the bottle again."

"Why not? What does it matter?"

"Because I forgive you."

"Really?"

"Really, mom. I forgive you. I miss Kelly every day and I wish I could talk to her, hear her voice. I wish my last memory of her wasn't on the floor covered in blood and mayonnaise. Maybe you did the best, maybe you didn't, but you did what you did, and for that, I forgive you."

Eileen dropped the bottle on the linoleum floor and it shattered. She threw her arms around Randy's shoulders. The love and the whiskey pooled around their feet.

The sun was coming up as Randy pulled his clothes on to leave for his new job. He stuffed his backpack and a small bag with a few belongings. Gary was already outside in the truck. The sun was peaking over the tree tops in the cool of a humid Missouri morning. The air was crisp as Randy climbed up into the truck. When they stopped for breakfast, the coffee tasted good, for the first time in his life. The food was substantive. His sight was sharper and the world was real again.

This was life after horror and trauma. Even though redemption was not available to him, he had the next best thing. Randy had sweet, beautiful, flawed, hard, impossible, good, life. He could love again and be again in that moment, a 22-year-old man with the bright hope of a 15-year-old-innocence that had been taken from him. The murder, prison, and mistakes no longer mattered. It all fell away as Gary piloted the truck towards their next job. It felt good to breathe, to be on the earth, in the earth and apart of it. He was rich in life that morning. That was what mattered now. To live and to live life to his utmost. The second chance comes to those brave enough to reach out and take it.

Cast Iron

Epilogue

Randy worked as a travel farm crewman for three seasons throughout the south and midwest. Every chance he had to go to bed with a woman, he took it. He was surrounded with men, real men that he could understand and emulate. He felt safe in that environment, the structure and the consistency. The expectations were clear and there was no one who needed him to do terrible things or compromise his newfound manhood. He spent the winters with his mom in Missouri and when spring turned he was back on the road with his crew. Like a collective fatherhood, they raised up young Randall Carruth.

He had heard about Greeley from one of the crew. He decided to make his way up there. He took a bus to St. Louis and then a train to Denver and arrived in Greeley on the big bus on the east side of town at 7th Ave and 23rd Street. The bus to Greeley was filled mostly with quiet migrant workers looking for jobs or visiting family. He stepped off the bus and looked for a motel. A small squat building a few blocks west served the purpose.

When I first saw Randy he was dressed simple in the fairly common uniform of the proletariat. Work pants, white T-shirt, plaid over shirt. He was to help me cater these events at the small BBQ establishment that employed both of us. He was friendly and focused. He had no car, just a bike that he had managed to get by some means. Randy was good at getting things. He biked everywhere. The boss said that he was flighty, but I managed to work with him well, and he always showed up for me. One night after an event, he asked if I wanted to hang out and smoke some grass. I decided free weed was better than no weed, and I drove him and his bike in my van to his house. He was living in a small basement apartment on 5th Street north of town. Some people called it Taco Flats because of the large hispanic population that had been living there since the 1920s. He rolled a blunt and stated talking. It was one of the most fascinating conversations of my then 19-year-old life. I had never heard such a tale before, and I had yet to experience his side of life, which was far more vulnerable than my cloistered college life. I was sitting on an old couch in a basement apartment with a man who hated black people and gay people. I was both. I sat there transfixed as he spoke about his life. I was scared and spellbound, unable to fully understand what I was hearing, but I kept listening anyway. As his tale curled together like the smoke rings of tobacco and marijuana into the air, I felt forever changed. The last thing he told me was that he wanted his story to be told. Sometimes healing can only occur in the bright light of day.

"I guess what I learned was that there isn't redemption except what you give yourself."

"Why do you say that?"

"Because no amount of sex or work can fix this." Randy pointed to his chest.

"I'm a bit surprised."

"At what?"

"That you don't like black people."

"Black people only caused me problems, man, I just don't like them."

"But I'm black."

"But not that kind of black."

"What kind is that?"

"The nigger kind that causes problems." He puffed on the blunt, and silence held space. "I guess I'm sorry, there ain't no happy ending."

"No it's alright."

"But I got a place and my fighting stuff."

Randy pointed to a white Jiu Jitsu robe hanging on a wall in full display.

"Are you seeing anyone?"

"No, I still can't get over Brandi."

"She never loved you."

"I don't believe her. I think she was scared."

"What about Kelly?"

"I miss her every day, man, I still have the same picture."

amcontent.com/pod-product-compliance
Source LLC
urg PA
38250626
00001B/235